Speaking of Summer

SPEAKING

OF

SUMMER

A Novel

KALISHA BUCKHANON

Counterpoint
Berkeley, California

Portions of the novel appear previously in the following publications
under the following titles: "Speaking of Summer," *Intellectual Refuge*,
Volume 8 (June–August 2015); "Speaking of Summer," excerpt, *Cat
on a Leash Review*, Volume I, Issue I (Fall 2016); "Night Wind," *NYU
Black Renaissance Noire*, Volume 17, Issue 1 (Winter 2017).

Library of Congress Cataloging-in-Publication Data
Names: Buckhanon, Kalisha, 1977– author.
Title: Speaking of summer : a novel / Kalisha Buckhanon.
Description: First hardcover edition. | Berkeley, California :
    Counterpoint, 2019.
Identifiers: LCCN 2018052245 | ISBN 9781640091917 (hardcover)
Subjects: LCSH: Sisters—Fiction. | Missing persons—Fiction. |
    Bereavement.
Classification: LCC PS3602.U264 S74 2019 | DDC 813/.6—dc23
LC record available at https://lccn.loc.gov/2018052245

Jacket design by Jaya Miceli
Book design by Wah-Ming Chang

COUNTERPOINT
2560 Ninth Street, Suite 318
Berkeley, CA 94710
www.counterpointpress.com

Printed in the United States of America
Distributed by Publishers Group West

10 9 8 7 6 5 4 3 2 1

For M.C.

To live life as a woman is to live life on the defense.

—Brie Larson

A man's face is his autobiography. A woman's face
is her work of fiction.

—Oscar Wilde

Speaking of Summer

PROLOGUE

I was the nice-looking, well-dressed woman running down 151st Street in Harlem after school and before evening rush hour on a bright day at the end of August in 2015.

If you saw me with my purse half-open and my balance tested more than once, you were wrong to laugh and right to be alarmed.

If you saw me trip and bust my lip, you were right; it really did hurt. If you thought I was being chased and you failed to call the police, I thank you for your apathy. We are cityfolk: hard to shock and minding our own business. I get it. I've been you before.

If you were the person who crashed into me on the obstacle course of bodies and bags we wriggle through every day, I didn't want your apology. I didn't let you pick me up on purpose. I didn't appreciate your concern. I didn't care you cared. I didn't trust your help. I didn't believe you were safe.

If you were the driver of a car that almost clipped me, I wouldn't have let you call me an ambulance if it had been worse. The last place I wanted to see was a hospital. I had enough of those in the past few years. I would have blocked out the pain, pushed past the limp your shiny bumper gave. Maybe you broke my stride, but I kept on.

If you had been someone who knew me, I wouldn't have answered to my name. I wanted to forget it. That's why I was running.

If you had been one of those block meddlers or self-appointed neighborhood-watch folks who just have to investigate, you wouldn't have caught up with me. I knew where I was going. Harlem is my home. I know its corners, curves, and crevices like a palm reader gazing down on it, marking its history and predicting its future.

If you got high on my perfume floating in the uptown air, you could have never named the scent. It was a combination of high street, fight, flight, and period coming down on a woman made by another woman who ate heartland dirt while I formed in her stomach.

If you were one of the men who saw me like that, but mostly you drooled over my tits flopping and my ass hopping, I was running from you along with everything else.

If you were a woman who saw me like that, but you were busy running too, please know I was running for us all.

If you thought about me later and shopped for my face on the internet or the news to see what happened to me, you were disappointed. I was under the radar, off the grid, insignificant and all alone. I would not have made the news unless I was murdered, and I suspect my headline would have faded quickly, if the fact was even newsworthy at all. Then, you would have forgotten me once your curiosity was satisfied to know "Whatever happened to the nice-looking, well-dressed woman running down 151st Street on a bright day at the end of August in 2015, with her eyes glazed over and her whole truth paused?"

Nobody was any of these people. That is why I'm telling all this now.

FOR YOU, MY LITTLE STORY would have started that day. But for me, it started in my old house back in Illinois, where me and my twin sister Summer and my mama and my grandma lived in a peace I only appreciated after it was gone. A man came along and, suddenly, me and Summer had to shine our faces and be quiet and act "normal," as Grandma put it. We had to sit upstairs in our bedroom with dolls and storybooks and a fairy tale 45 on the toy record player. We had to wear good shoes and bobby socks with no holes, and keep them on so the bottom of our feet didn't get dirty. We had to "Act like you got some sense," and "Don't you embarrass us now, you hear me?" We had to "Ma'am" and "Sir" and "Please" and "May I?" We had to keep our elbows off the table and not stuff our mouths. We had to not kick each other by play accident, or mock anyone's speech, or slurp our juice. We had to eat our vegetables and pick at little pieces of dessert. We had to shunt our personalities into forms less disorienting to men.

"Murphy's a good man," Grandma said. "That's all your mama needs. Soon as she get a good man, she'll quit being so hung up on your daddy. Things'll turn around in here. You mark my word."

She meant no more pottery smashed to a cement floor in our shed out back. No more neighbors knocking to peer in and whisper: "You guys okay?" No more feasts one week and famines the next. No more hitching familiar passersby for a ride to the bus stop, since our mother was a crumple of bedhead on the couch, and her tart morning breath slurred, "Have a nice day, girls." No more retrievals way too early from our Catholic school classrooms. No more no-shows to pick us up after school when the others were all gone, so that we must color quietly in the chapel as the confessors straggle in after dark.

Mr. Murphy first drove up to our house on Trummel Lane in his gleaming black Cadillac, with a hard briefcase and warm referral from a woman my mother swam with at the Y. He was a salesman. Insurance: life, medical, homeowner's. He even sold end-of-life care and premature burial planning, at early-bird discounts. Cole Murphy—blue suit, yellow tie, gold clip, white handkerchief, bald head, centipede-long moustache. Everybody knew his face from the State Farm sign at the big barbershop on Court Street, where he arranged an office through a side door. And I also knew his face from the phone book, and on the billboard over the junction tracks past the dog food plant we passed to get to the one mall in town. He first rang our house one Sunday after church. I answered the bell.

He stayed talking and laughing for a long time. We couldn't take off our tights, so I hated him for the itch. Mama didn't buy a thing from him. Me and Summer and Grandma watched him walk out to his car. He waved before he opened his door. His engine started softly, with no struggle. Grandma sucked her teeth and called him "Slick." She stuck his beige business card on the refrigerator, pinned under a green *M* alphabet magnet. I remember she laughed and said, "Murphy go good with money."

Grandma gave him store German chocolate cake with heavy cream in his coffee that first time—and the next time. Mama still bought nothing from him. So he stopped coming by in the day with a hard briefcase. He showed up at night with flowers shivering in crunchy green paper. Mama left with him in the clothes she wore to church, usually beige leather pumps to match this one camel suede purse. She and this man would be gone for time she normally hung in with us, watching BET videos or Lifetime movies with a Virginia Slims in her hand and rollers in her hair. I missed her pot of Lipton's tea with a full, clear bottle next to it. I didn't know what was in the bottle back then.

On those nights she left us, Summer and me whined for permission to eat in front of the TV. Once Grandma was snoring, we turned off the lights and pretended to sleep. We were really making silly jokes and impersonations of people we knew under the covers, giggling until we had to go pee or sneak milk. We started waiting later and later to hear Mama's heels slide up the steps, the screen door pull back, and the front porch wind chimes sound.

In the September me and Summer turned ten, Grandma crocheted us a maroon blanket, a birthday present. And we were all set to go to Pizza Hut like Mama promised. But a tornado warning whisked through our central Illinois plain. Soon, as we all got on our galoshes and raincoats, the sirens sounded across the charcoal sky. So, that was it. Summer stomped up the stairs to our bedroom. I sulked on the porch on the swing. Grandma finally fussed at me to come inside. Lightning scared her.

I ignored her warnings: "You're gonna get struck and turn to salt!"

I saw the Moynihans and Calhouns and Davises dash away in bigger, shinier cars. The families who parked trailers near the bridge or at the river headed out behind them. They raced past our winding lane in Jeeps and pickups, quivering tarp stretched over the beds as tires whisked up gravel. With hindquarters up, Mr. Johnson's German shepherds howled in his yard across the street. Then came Mr. Murphy's Cadillac onto our leafy block, down rural roads landmarked only by a few silos and windmills. He met me on the porch.

"Heard there was supposed to be a little birthday party today," he said. Mama swooshed him inside, hugged him tight, and gave one last peek out to the coming storm. The worry on her face slacked down.

I saw two bags he carried: Carson Pirie Scott and Kroger. A checkered derby covered his head. Sprinkles dotted his tan trench coat. His umbrella was taller than me. It was our birthdays, so me and Summer already had on good shoes and socks. Our faces and knees were oiled. By now, it was automatic to flaunt our best manners and forward our best faces for Mr. Murphy's stops. We were maturing, and we wanted to.

Turned out Mr. Murphy had not noticed we were maturing. But at least the wild-haired, brown doll in a long cream box came with a certificate, not a little orange sticker like everything Mama gave us. I helped my sister pull out the doll. It stood up to our knees. The tiny feet stuck to a round display base with glitter on the edge. We touched her handmade taffeta and chiffon dress, ivory barrettes, and real pearls in her ears. Her sudden place in the china cabinet brought out chipped dishes, to be put away in the attic.

That night, a few shots were left on a roll of film in my mother's camera she loved. The first snap became the doll we could only look at, never play with. The last became me and Summer over a Kroger sheet cake. Grandma had found candles in the junk drawer. In the picture, we are blowing out the candle. Beside us, Mama blows up a balloon. Grandma looks off-camera, like she hears somebody walk through our door without knocking first. Mr. Murphy took the picture.

The tornadoes hit Ohio, not Illinois. But even when it was no lavender-gray sky or weather horns or panicked birds, Mr. Murphy set his hat down on the table until the next morning. He soon bought a new coffeemaker, more boxes and bags for us, a pottery wheel for my mother, a Hoveround for my grandmother, and more booze for the china cabinet.

With Mama calmed, me and Summer started to talk about separate paths, beyond ideas from the amused faces encircling us to marvel at our resemblance. Everybody took it upon themselves to point out their plans for our presumed matching futures: actresses, Alvin Ailey dancers, doctors, models. On TV, we saw other girl jobs we felt better for us—Oprah, Silkwood, G.I. Jane, Julia Child, Christa McAuliffe, Sally Jessy, and Anita Hill. We made books about our bigger, older selves. I drew the pictures. My sister wrote the stories.

Slowly but surely, the comparisons between us started to die off along with Mama's attention and Grandma's energy.

After that doll and blanket, we never shared birthday presents again.

A lot happened in the years after Mr. Murphy and his hat on our table and tornadoes and balloons.

My last view of the story is a disquieting but quiet reel. The reel makes no sound besides the tick of a film projector, home movie–style: an early morning a few hours ahead of daybreak in winter, a curvy woman's body in a slip, wind talk to her hair, a bowing hem at her knees, black tar shapes of her feet carving footsteps in shallow snow on a rooftop. A south-facing Harlem brownstone and Manhattan's skyline meet a vanishing point. The movie's film scrambles, then stills on a close-up: little French-pedicured toes at the tip of the very top, curled around a cornice.

My sister is gone, hardly forgotten. Whatever came for her is coming for me, too.

Winter

ONE

Unforgiving cold couldn't deter me from reaching the nearest precinct on 151st Street. Normally my eyes filtered out all the trash stuck to the uptown curbs, lapping at my ankles. I was used to it. Litter was the only shawl for a dead gray cat along my way. Its odor cut my breath off. It was March but looked like June. Sunlight warmed the corpse over days I spent mostly inside now. I would have called the city to complain, about indignity to the animal and us good hardworking people of Harlem. I would have used a stick to move it to rest in peace. But I ran late, again. When I stepped to cross Lenox, a man crept up beside me. He donned a blue afro and green python around his neck, gathered down to his waist. When he noticed me look, he winked. Then he licked his lips. That made just seven minutes outside my door before a man reminded me he was a man. And it wasn't even a record.

Property owners and the city did not bother to salt the streets yet and the old snowfall was juicy now. I almost slipped on my way inside. Thank God for Uggs' strength and dependability. I needed steadiness on this latest trip. I hoped for some real news finally.

Still, three months after my report, "Summer Spencer" was not listed in New York State's online Missing Persons Clearinghouse. There, I saw haunting photos of hundreds of men and women, all ages and walks of life. They listed disappearances as recently as last month. My sister's absence from them wasn't a mistake. It was a disgrace.

My quest to find out what happened to Summer was a noisy, gobbling goal I couldn't quiet. I wasn't aiming for a sticker, trophy, degree, paycheck, or title at the end. I was losing my security, stability, and mind along the way. Friends listened to me say I wanted answers. If distant family heard my questions, I guessed they pretended not to hear. Neighbors treated my sister like someone who never lived in our brownstone with us. They carried on with a dark pause in their minds, forgetting that woman who went up to our rooftop and seemed to vanish into icy air. But my body moved in her ideas and habits like a sepulcher she remained alive within. Deep inside me, she remembered. She thought. She planned. She felt. I knew if I listened hard and fought and tuned into her spirit strong enough, she would show up again.

Three months ago. Last year, actually. An early December morning. Or late December night, depending on the viewpoint. I climbed a frigid stairwell. I saw our rooftop door open and footprints in the rooftop snow. I called 911. Cops came, then turned to the other misfortunes that would hit Harlem before dawn. I never again saw the night-beat cops I reported this strange scene to. Days passed. I did not sleep for them. Summer never came through our apartment door. A week passed. My dealings with the law upgraded to a long wait, a statement, an interview about Summer's habits and crew. That was it.

I could get further on attention with an online petition or crowdfunding page and social media–friendly headline: "Nobody Gives a Fuck My Sister Is Missing." Then, tens of thousands of anonymous names and email addresses and credit card numbers would mean more than my lone voice and Summer's single human life. But I predicted it to become a distraction. If Summer joined legions of other Black women trying to eek out concern for our lives and became a hashtag, then I would become open to scrutiny and intrusion my fragility couldn't withstand. I was mourning. I needed to do it outside of any spotlight.

However, I could bear to hassle police until I became a familiar to the day officers at the precinct desk. Two women officers, Black and Latina, always greeted me with warmth. They liked me, I felt. Their kindnesses served as their condolences.

"Good afternoon," I smiled. "I'm here to speak with Montgomery. I'm a little late."

They looked at me, then whispered to each other. I fidgeted with my scarf.

"Montgomery's out to lunch, I think," Officer Torres explained.

Officer Jackson looked up from papers on a desk, and nodded, "He is."

"Well, when is he back?" I asked. "I've come all the way here in the cold."

They had their duties. I had mine. I hadn't been there since February. I became exhausted of shouting out my tiny voice. I was a Midwest transplant to New York City. I scrambled for attention with twelve million other people. I was Black. I wasn't rich. I was a freelancer, not a company head. If I didn't make myself known to the powers that be, I wouldn't even get my order taken at a decent bar let alone help a missing person be found.

I focused on the station bulletin board. A notice for a missing girl or woman stuck out. From so far away, I could not tell her age and ethnicity, or see her name. All I could decipher was "MISSING." I envisioned all the flyers of Summer's face I taped on trees and building gates, laundromat and bodega doors, in subway stations and parks. They yielded one call. It was a Korean woman who owned a nail salon down by a Brooklyn friend's way. I did not change out of clothes I'd worn in there the day before and fallen asleep in at home. I hustled back at breakneck speed. She laughed when I appeared again, desperate and manic. She said the flyer just reminded her of a customer she'd just seen: me.

And, for all my time and effort and printing costs, that was it. It was karma. I'd often had a choice to zoom in on similar flyers rolled around streetlight and station posts. Instead I chose to stare down choked streets for a headsign, or into dark passages for a train light. I now needed people to stop, notice, care, and recall. But I saw we people were all just alike.

More than thirty minutes later, Detective Noel Montgomery waved me past the public corridor into his tight side office. It was always so neat and perfect for an NYPD space, like a television show set. His water cooler was full, as usual. He offered me a tray of herbal teas atop it. He had the audacity to display polished rocks with positive words painted on: LOVE, HEALTH, HAPPINESS. He kept a sandy wooden hourglass within reach.

He shut the door and I didn't wait. I got right to it. My soliloquy was long.

"Miss Spencer," Detective Montgomery said when I finished, "I'm not sure what goes on with that clearinghouse or what the criminal justice division's posting criteria are. I can check on it for you. How you doin' overall? Is your rooftop door still locked?"

Over the doorway to the stairs up to our rooftop, the landlords tacked a sheet with a peace sign emblem. Back in the day, they had promised us a rooftop garden. But none of us tenants climbed up there more than a few times. And, never at night. That door was always just a possible intruder entrance or exit. I had requested the landlords seal it off. The gaudy sheet covered a thick slat to the outside door, adjacent to my apartment door and up a few steps. A padlock looped between chain links through the deadbolt. Hooks attached to keep robbers out.

"I'm not worried about anybody coming in there now," I told Detective Montgomery. "The landlords have us locked up now like we're on Devil's Island. I'm more worried about who came through before."

"I see," Detective Montgomery said. "There's never been break-ins at the brownstone. The precinct confirmed no criminal reports for that address. Not even noise complaints. So anybody who gets to your roof either lives there or let someone in to do so."

"I wonder if Summer's pegged low priority, and not a real missing person, because she's Black," I told the detective, a still and poised man with glasses.

"That has nothing to do with it, Miss Spencer," he answered. "Trust me. I'm Black. I get what you're saying. That's why I'm here doing this. But if she just ran off and—"

"Summer always had an aloof side," I interrupted. "Well, I told you that. She was moody. I don't think she was the best judge of people always. But that girl is strong. When our mother died, Summer held up well. She broke at the very end, like that did something to her, snapped her out of her mind. But we both picked up our load and carried on."

"I agree it sounds atypical for someone like her to up and run away," he said. "And I have the same concerns you do about foul play. I don't think investigators took time to interview as many people as they could have. Yes, deprioritizing most Black people's cases is a fault of the system. Did you bring any mail that could help us?"

"Her mail stopped." I thought. "None since the New Year now.

Christmas greetings from a few distant relatives, but that's always addressed to both of us. If she was abducted, or worse, wouldn't the perpetrator see her name on IDs, stop mail on purpose?"

"Hmmm," he sighed, "there'd have to be motive to be that elaborate and thorough. Which brings us back to who lives there or who she knows, someone who would plan, not a random incident. I'll push a police check on formal mail stops and a forwarding address."

Of course. A forwarding address. She could be out there somewhere, with a new address I didn't know, maybe under a new name, for reasons she would apologize for.

"Look," Montgomery said, "you say you two hid nothing from each other. Look through her things again. Maybe you were still in shock at the time, so you could have missed something. This might be a woman who is upset or mad about something, and ran."

He was used to people's theories of mourning: intended to rewind time back to whatever could have been prevented if only one had known, or to exact revenge if it was to be had . . . *Someone has to know the truth. What about this guy or that one? Can you take another look? Are you sure this was really the case? But, I just talked to him or her. They were fine. You missed that bitch. Can you question her again? Gimme the file. I said gimme the file. Son of a bitch motherfucker . . .*

Detective Montgomery took a sip from his plastic Popeye's large drink. I was robbing him of a peaceful two-piece spicy lunch.

"The cell number you gave is disconnected," he continued. "No recent text messages or calls. And, according to you, she was anti–social media and whatever. So, her online footprint is scant and no help. Did she meet a man?"

"I would've known. Did you call every single number in the phone?" I demanded. "I did. But I'm no authority. People don't have to answer me."

"Even you said you recognized the names of all the contacts, so there are no strangers in your lives. Responding officers processed your roof. No signs of struggle, Autumn. No blood. A clean path to the edge. Just one set of footprints in the snow . . ."

It snowed that night. By the time cops took their time to respond, other footprints could have filled in. I paced around, calling for her. I could have shuffled snow atop them.

"Autumn, Autumn?" I heard. "You got any friends?"

"Any what?"

"Friends," he repeated. "You know, people to go out with, talk to sometimes?"

A detective, of all people, shouldn't expect a woman with a close missing relative to be the world's greatest conversationalist. My tunnel vision was explicable and excusable. It was even above average. I could be tearing files off his desk with my bared teeth, or thrown from the lobby amid a piercing tirade on discrimination.

"I'm quite fine, Mr. Montgomery," I replied. "And I have many friends, thank you very much. But partying is not my biggest concern right now."

"You ain't gotta party," he said. "But just go out a little bit. Have some fun. Take your mind off Summer for a while."

"What makes you think I don't?"

"Miss Spencer—"

"Autumn is fine."

"Autumn, I'm not trying to get in your business. But, I go through this kind of stuff with people. You're hurt. You're shocked. You feel helpless. The only way to feel better at a time like this is to try to keep living life. You have a bright future."

"So I'm unreasonable just because I want to know where my closest living relative is? Now, not later? Because I expect some answers and accountability for how a healthy young woman can just up and disappear?"

"No. It means I've done all I can do until new leads and information turn up. It doesn't mean I don't care. It just means I'm telling you that."

"I'm her sister. Twin, born with her. I can't go on. Part of me is missing, too. My head is split on her all the time. My heart is broken in half. What about that?"

He pointed his hands together on his chin. He walked to a low file cabinet to jam his hands between what I imagined was too much work. He handed me a bright, shiny brochure.

"What's this?" I asked.

"This is a group for people getting over lost loved ones and other catastrophic events. They have firsthand experience with what we normally just read about in the news or see in movies. Loved ones murdered, suicides. Losses no one prepares for. Kind of like if a sibling just up and disappeared, with no answers for it yet. Thankfully, only a small group would know what that really feels like."

The brochure, to "We Go On" or something like that, was his parting gift/final say/hint. So I could leave. So he could return to other human beings—dead and alive.

So he can brush us off, I heard her say.

It was Summer's voice, clear as a wrong note in a well-known song. I didn't actually hear a voice. I wasn't a nutcase, after all. She was just my inner wisdom. A megaphone for my own thoughts perhaps, but continuous in message: *Don't let them shut you up. Not now, not ever, not just about me. Forever, and for everything.*

I knew my time was up. I would roar back in next week, more brazen and energetic than ever. Montgomery at least checked on what I suggested he should and shared his own ideas. He pushed it further than I could go banging on doors, hanging up flyers, and seeking out information all by myself. I had to keep him around for all he was worth.

"I want to be your hero here," he said. "I really do."

"Well, no matter where she is now and when she's coming back, she'll always be my hero. She's the best sister anyone could ever hope for. That's a fact."

"I'm sure she is," Detective Montgomery agreed.

I HAD LEFT SUMMER'S FINGERPRINTS on her dressing mirror. I joyfully borrowed her clothes. If I breached her journals or notes or emails, I heard her voice saying her old words and I felt better. I washed her scent from her pillowcases, sheets, and comforter. I switched her bedding and moved in to her room, to feel she was still here. My bedroom, the smaller one facing the brick gangway, never invited the breeze. Now it was just my dressing closet, in need of a good sweeping and dusting. The comforter crumpled and twisted at the foot of my Ikea bed. I finally threw out a rank coffee cup with spoiled cream and a saucer of pizza crusts on the nightstand. One day, I stomped from Summer's bed to smash down my digital alarm clock, automatically set to go at 7 a.m. I arose around noon now, later in rain.

Her absence clogged my head with memories of our life together, now separated. I just wanted to know she was okay, alive, because without that assurance my mind produced a steady carousel of conjecture. Each stop was dark, terrifying, and sad. I drifted from most so-called friends. None of them knew what to say. Sadly, I suspected some suspected me. I failed to return calls from back home, not that I received many. I felt betrayed, and guilty. I wanted to know what I had done, or what someone else did. I didn't want to intrude on her new life, if she wanted to start over so fresh I was unwanted. We had, after all, estranged from our history and nearly our own mother, before the inevitable. Our last parent's dying left us no choice but to repair the breaches. With our whole history and origins dwindled, it was possible one more lost person might not add up to much.

Two

I walked home slower this time, my body loaded with some regret. I had wanted to tell the detective all I could to help us, but I was cautious with my trust. Strangers preferred to discredit one another than expand to new people to sacrifice their time to.

At home I checked the mail, in hopes Summer sent a carrier pigeon. She did not. A big check was too much to expect, though a few enterprises owed me small ones for work on their websites and steadily unnecessary paper marketing. I was a Big Apple "slasher" with a grab bag of media and communications talents in a gig economy, beat up by computerized resume readers and even video auditions to interview for some real jobs, now a find as preposterous as a pot at the end of a rainbow. In the best of times, it was a feat to stay disciplined and entrepreneurial. In the last year, with Mama's care and then her death, followed by my sister's vanishing act, I lost spunk to promote myself online and network to new clients cutting out full-time employees.

I left behind the only things in the box: bills and junk with my name on it. I ran my fingers along my mailing label, and scratched the space where now only my name was listed. Autumn Spencer: the last living trace of my parents, Grace and Ricky Spencer.

I felt my father as sporadic warmth and tightness inside my chest. The most I know about him is he loved doing tricks on motorcycles. This killed him right before I carried a metal My Little Pony lunchbox and Rainbow Brite umbrella off to busy, sunny classrooms for the first time. Mama died in my Harlem apartment, after Valentine's Day, in 2014. A whole year now. She passed in a fog of gentle panic and mental slippage the painkillers toned down. She came to live her last days with us. I was the daughter who insisted on it. Now I know I should have let it be, kept the moment distant and remote.

Before we could even mark the one-year anniversary of our mother's passing, Summer apparently went to our brownstone's rooftop and I had not seen her since.

I am thirty-four years old. No children. No nieces or nephews.

I exhausted my IRA. Mama's life insurance policy paid half its $100,000 after the medical bills and taxes. My "double income" was my sister.

Who will take care of me when I'm old?

I climbed to my hallway, pausing at the few colorful abstracts Summer gifted our environment. I walked up two little steps to the very top of the building. I pulled back the peace-signed sheet across the rooftop doorway. I never liked that door, wood-paneled like a prop of seventies television. I put my palm to it. It was cold. A padlock and chains, screwed in separately from its original construction, were warm. The landlords' gesture came after Summer stopped letting herself in, stopped greeting them in the foyer, stopped dousing our brownstone in her scents.

Why hadn't it been there before?

Detective Montgomery brought up an interesting point. I grew up as a twin girl in a house of four women. I learned to leave other women's shit alone. Women detect disturbance and changes too easily. As Mama hid the severity of her cancer from us, I joined her old maid of honor and her sister to go through the majority of our house on Trummel Lane. Mama was not terminal then; she called it "paring down." I carted out toys, one too many little rocking horses, nice sweater bundles—all finally passed on to others' children. I became more disillusioned about her that week than I had in my whole life. I never had any idea she made as many good paintings and as much decent pottery as she did. I felt ashamed I had dismissed how much anonymous creation meant to her, as if it were a tendency she passed on only to Summer. So even in normal times, we live around people and their things but don't see who those people truly are. It was certainly possible I'd missed a lot while looking through Summer's things, one eye fixed on the door she could walk through.

I plowed through stockpiled industrial wine and foraged through Summer's sketchbooks and unpolished artworks. She was enviably neat. My bookshelves strangled the hallways, since I turned out to be the bookish one. Summer's small contribution was a few heavy books about art and artists whose names I could never pronounce, to spite my education in words. *Caravaggio, Frankenthaler, Modigliani, Klimt.* The biographies and retrospectives mixed with fine arts and foundation books on color theory, life drawing, and portraiture, so much heavier and more demanding than my grammar manuals, paperback novels, and self-improvement guides. Her notebooks held more doodles than notes. I was the freelance wordsmith she asked to check over the tiniest writings, like her Dear John letters to needy booty calls and her resignation emails to odd jobs. Summer drew versions of herself all her life, leading family and friends to call her recuperative self-portraits "art." What else were we supposed to say to visions of noose necklaces and self-inflicted stab wounds? Later I helped her submit this stuff to contests and editors who always declined.

The Black and women artists' catalogs she collected had much to do with the number of times she was tardy with her part of the electric and cable bills. I was fine to tag along to the Bronx Museum, Studio Museum, and tiny eclectic galleries as a spectator; Summer needed to bring the experiences home. Sometimes the books accompanying these shows cost nearly $100, just to sit untouched and tight together like artworks themselves. *Basquiat, Ligon, Ringgold, Bearden.* It comforted Summer to know people of color broke through the ceilings, wooed patronage, and achieved name status. I flipped down a Kehinde Wiley catalogue. I joined Summer at one of his first shows at Studio Museum, when I'd arrived to New York to escape a certain future writing corporate copy in Chicago.

Summer pasted the book's receipt on the inside cover of promising portraits that foreshadowed Wiley's eventual ascension. The pages gave way in the middle and a piece of paper floated to my feet. I leaned down to pick up a Xerox of newsprint, with thick block borders and letters time had deformed into unreadability.

It was an archived feature from *The Hedgewood Sentinel*, our local paper back home. I was a paper girl for it once, drawn to an entrepreneurial fate and life of words by the time I was in middle school. Then, I got high on the lemony scent of a stack of fresh newspapers. Later, I held off conversion to online news as long as I could.

This article, however, was before my time as a paper girl in Hedgewood. It was also before our family expanded to include Mama's local star boyfriend, Cole Murphy. Summer cared to dig up in online archives that Mr. Murphy's resigned from the local NAACP leadership, as the article's headline and brief story informed me he did. One look at his businessman headshot cornered my memories to childhood, switched from disadvantage to privilege due to money our real father left for a nice house and money a surrogate father brought into that house. I put the article on the pile of filing I needed to finish. It was destined for a manila folder of similar *Hedgewood Sentinel* keepsakes: our honor roll and graduation listings, annual events we attended, my parents' obituaries.

It felt spooky to dip my hands into thatched dark bamboo cubes where Summer kept odds and ends in her living room workspace. I remembered her in there, on stained beige sheets, curled cross-legged in the corner or on her stomach. Our candles and incense mostly covered the smells of her pastime: not just paint, but the enamel and glues. I kept her unfinished statement in that space. She shredded fashion brand names and labels she cut from stacks of magazines. She glued them to canvas and spray painted them in light metallic tones. She was just half done on the side where she managed to rubber-cement scraps into texture and grade. It was part of her efforts to join the natural and "meaningful" art crowd, to be more politically and less personally focused, to go the direction the art blogs and dark bar small talk told her to if she wanted notice. I didn't get it. I liked her less flashy work with faces, as damned and disgruntled as she intended them to be.

"Nobody cares about Black angst anymore, Autumn," she said about them.

For that acerbic take, I helped her wrap and stack her oil and chalk portraits of imaginary friends. Together, we buried them down in our cellar storage space. It gave me something to do to retrieve them again. She rarely framed. It was too expensive. So I carried the light canvases up a few flights, at night, all by myself. The neighbor boy, from the floor beneath us, helped me once. I was fine alone. But he insisted. He reminded me when young adulthood smelled like red candy, grass, and Vaseline. And not because those were his scents. It was because they were not. Nowadays young people smelled like sour candy, smoke, and electric current. His efforts, and Summer's laziest paintings, gave me occasion to talk fondly about where I came from.

These makings were nostalgic, juvenile even, as she took subjects like our old backyard shed, and titled it *Summer*: A fringe of pastel dots along the shed's bottom border was supposed to be the petunias, marigolds, and geraniums sprouting every year. *Autumn* could have been mistaken as saturated honey wands bundled together. It was the little-girl view from our bedroom window down onto the front yard every fall, before the gilded boughs of oak trees detassled. Another picture was Grandma's rocking chair. I recalled it towering to the height of my chest, proud for a mere piece of furniture. Summer rendered it squat and flabby. She painted a mock family portrait of stray cats we used to feed, though I did not recall them in the dull colors she portrayed. So much of her work on our old house was hasty and incorrect, as if she rushed to document the nest before Mama sold it.

Her other artworks were the same unrevealing things, mostly peddled online and at little fairs and to Harlem shop owners, because she couldn't figure out the people and places and games to leap into real galleries. I gave up on her stuff to go to my photo albums she hated—the cheap sticky plastic-sheet kind. I thumbed through pig-tailed school pictures, shots of frilly dresses at dances. They weren't fancy art, but I know Summer pulled the albums off my shelf often. She always put them back crooked or out of order. A few really old ones were upside down. I savored those most, because they were filled with my father and his family.

Over the years, we girls became Spencers in name only. Birthday and Christmas presents stopped from my father's side of the family. They missed our graduations. If Mama didn't make efforts to take us to see them, we didn't see them. Summer and I talked often about forcing a relationship with Daddy's people, all the aunts and uncles and cousins we used to see at the funerals until we stopped flying back home to even see Mama. The money dried up. Our tries at dream jobs demanded us. Time, we thought, was tight. Now, I had regrets. I wanted more heritage in my future.

I went to my desktop to check the train schedules back to my hometown. Fairly straight shots from Penn Station to Chicago's Union Station, then one short layover until a route would drop me off in back of Hedgewood's main post office. The ticket price was not high. Perhaps Mama's death pushed Summer into regret about distance from the Spencers. For all I knew, she was back home. The Big Mamas were feeding her well. She was looking at our baby pictures in their photo albums. She was hearing what our father was like as a child. She was closing that past wound, finding that part of herself, reclaiming a legacy. She was driving past our old house on Trummel Lane, to relive blissful times when the biggest thing we had to manage was time: to rake all the leaves, to dodge every earthworm after a rainstorm, to chase down our school bus filled with pink and yellow faces we never fully fit with.

"But why not do all that with me?" I asked out loud.

The Hedgewood Police Department was little to no help. Summer was not a formal resident there for almost twenty years. We left for college and never looked back for more than holiday visits. We became expatriates and rebels relatives eventually forgot.

House lights, streetlights, and headlights from Harlem's dense population appeared like iridescent algae through my front windows. I dreamt of the journey, adventure, and escape Summer found. Even when I should have, I never considered leaving New York. Now blocks of darkened houses, low rooftops, and spread-out silence seemed a solution worth fleeing for. I would reach out to family again soon.

By the end of the night, I proved Montgomery and myself wrong. Not one earmarked page of Summer's books indicated anything but her observations on color, shading, angle, and lines.

The occasional biographical tidbit she found interesting, but little more. My sole discovery was a detached eyelash.

Useless memories and thoughts took over too many moments. I could never complete a thing without them. They were my water cooler breaks from hoping, wishing, waiting, and listening for Summer's key to turn the front door lock. I could not get through a night without believing I heard that sound.

I grabbed a pen to write on my necessary "To Do" list waiting, always, on the kitchen counter. I crossed off the first thing.

1. Look through Summer's things again.
2. Respond to emails from the precious few clients who are not abandoning me for tardiness, slow response, and my typos in their content.
3. Renew subscriptions to Entertainment Weekly and Writer's Digest.
4. Go out for toilet paper.
5. Skip the wine tonight.
6. Eat.

I procrastinated on numbers two through six. They weren't as important as braving to peek more inside Summer beyond what her work showed me, and indeed all of us, for quite a while. We were the ones who chose to think hauntings and disorder were just her chosen "style," all about art, with no truth in the bones.

THREE

At night, the heat in my top-floor apartment was punishing. Practically speaking, the building's old boiler did what it was supposed to. Theoretically, the temperature could have easily arisen from Mama and Grandma's spirits boiling over. Their lecture would start off like this: *We raised you so much better than this.*

I couldn't deny it. *You did*, I'd respond.

They would be referring to how I let my grief, immaturity, and needs cloud my judgment to give in to a man who was not really mine. A man who still cried about Summer sometimes, and I let him. The confusion and stress he and I both felt, me more than him, had driven him away for weeks. Tonight was his first back with me again.

I planned, in time, to tell Detective Montgomery, and anyone else who could help, that I had indiscretions with my sister's man and I know she sensed it, in an intuitive mist where all women know what that odd call or perfume scent means.

I limited it. He respected that. We never spoke of it. She never confronted us. Life went on. I exhaled. I thought she'd never know. Now, I had to consider she did.

At first, Chase Armstrong was just one of the constants I could depend on as Mama was passing away. He was always there, whenever we needed him. He belonged to Summer, but I knew he was there for me, too. Summer was no real help with Mama's affairs, doctor's appointments, prescriptions. Damn the "sensitive artiste" in her. If not for Chase, and Mama's hospice nun Penny, I would have been on my own. I suspected Summer sensed Chase could be attracted to me, not because she and I had exact looks or personalities. We weren't those kinds of twins no one could tell apart in a glance or two, and we were no more alike than any other siblings who grow up together.

I can only hope depression from Mama's death encouraged me to cross the line. He claimed intimacy at a time like that was a mere mistake. I told no soul, not even Detective Montgomery, about us. If he and anyone else knew Summer had real motive to get away from us, and better yet to punish me for betraying her, they would not help me search for her.

But it still did not account for why she'd punish herself in freezing cold on our rooftop. Footprints only. No shoes. Door wide open. No notes. Never seen again.

At first, it was just one time with Chase. That one time was one too many, but I took solace it happened when Summer had put him on "off" in their off-and-on thing. We stopped, completely. I ended our friendly chats when I was just to take a message over the phone. I stopped asking about his job. I played dead in my room if he came over. I pointed to my desk if Summer invited me to a movie or party with them.

It went this way until several days after I called 911 to report I thought something happened to Summer. Chase finally returned my call, and she wasn't with him. Our calls and meetings at bars were all about her. Then, when our hysterics that Summer hadn't come home reached boiling points, we fell into bed as we were just supposed to be looking through her things. Or, maybe we were just calling around looking for her. Maybe we were just sitting around talking about how this could have happened to her. To us. I can't recall what I was thinking, but I know sex wasn't my drive. I'd never even thought Chase was especially attractive. Now, I saw beauty in his valor to emigrate from the West Indies alone to make something of himself, and his honesty and commitment to me, while I knew it was also betrayal.

"I'll lose you both when she returns, because I can't play that game," he'd told me. I just put my head in his palm in admission we were only a matter of tainted time.

And he said—no, promised—it was not about sex for him either. Did it matter? No matter what happened or how it happened, it was happening.

We had left the TV on. The Roots were signing off the Jimmy Fallon repeat.

Chase thought I loved spooning tight, with my spine sunk into his ribs and his hairy thigh over my hip. But his affection smothered me. Summer was my sister, after all. I couldn't flaunt it, no matter how much security and serenity I felt when I was in bed with him again. I sat up in Summer's four-poster canopy bed, its grand posts and headboard out of character for me. Summer and I dismantled and hauled the bed so many times it felt like an old friend. "What about ice cream?" I asked aloud, as if I half expected Chase to leap out of bed and get it for me. Specifically, I wanted Häagen-Dazs Vanilla Swiss Almond.

Neapolitan was my flavor back when Mama coughed herself to final sleep. There was something organizing about moving my spoon across the carton from white to pink or brown to white or pink to brown, depending on the brand. With Summer gone, the new flavor was much simpler and less fattening. It took so long to suck the chocolate off the nuts stuck in the ice cream, I ate less of it. I thought to walk to the bodega alone in ChapStick and bedhead,

to buy it through a bulletproof window slit. Maybe one of the bodega cats would be out. The regular ones all came to me by now.

When Mama came to visit her big girls, "alllll grown up in
the big city now," she cringed to see us leave out after midnight
to buy orange juice and milk and eggs. "Why can't you wait until the morning?" she always asked. She never understood every
need in life wasn't clouds and mileposts and winding roads away.
She regarded the black plastic bodega sacks we brought back with
suspicion, like they held babies kidnapped from Harlem Hospital
down the road. She listed a cascade of farfetched outcomes to cap
our biographies: men in black come through our screenless open
windows, insane cabbies to be the deaths of us, baby-faced gang
rapists in train cars before morning rush hours. It was part of the
"wild imagination" Summer inherited from her, their eccentric
personalities the relatives called it, their *You just don't understand
her* gossip shields. Now I knew all the evidence of those outlandish
warnings from Mama were based in true stories. I may not have
been alive then but she was, and she had never forgotten the tales,
and the daily news reports I was too busy living life to the fullest
to pay much attention to, and the implausible possibilities more
years on Earth show everybody. Like Mama did for us, one day I
would tell girls they would disappear if they were not careful.

I untangled from the maroon crochet blanket I was sad to
have all to myself, finally. Summer and I both watched Grandma
put the blanket's final knot into place, right at the corner edge of
a slight rouge border one must squint to see. Summer curled up
in the blanket without asking me if I wanted to toast with her.
Later that night, the feathers in my down comforter may as well
have been gossamer. I kicked it off out of spite, so stayed with a
cold that winter, the stinking and barking kind. Then, Summer
took the maroon blanket to camp. She didn't need it. It was hot.
She dragged it to sleepovers with the friends I was not invited to

know. Finally, she took it to college. Now, it lies between me and her past lover.

When I slipped Chase's arm from around me he growled, stretched, and sucked his tongue before going motionless again. He never snored. His farts were unalarming, almost banjo twangs. He made Godiva coffee in mornings and decaffeinated tea at night. He had yet to leave the toilet seat up or lose the toothpaste cap. He loved to cook. He actually could cook. This did not stop him from ordering in, and tipping well. Besides the spoons after sex, he kept to his side of the bed and never hogged the covers.

At the edge of the kitchen, with my eyes on the microwave's time—3:21—I realized I glided down the hall naked. Not even a robe, in March. I was still hot. I remembered no footsteps. When I turned, I saw another memory of Summer to join the many others twisting around my mind these days. Ever the artist, she had made her own black-and-white copy of the photo of our first birthday with Mr. Murphy in our lives. It hung inside a cream mat and copper-colored pewter frame. I knew the balloons were pink because I remembered the day, the moment, the tendrils of lightning before clouds shattered and Mr. Murphy set his hat down to stay the whole night. I saw the rocking chair in the background, and considered Summer's viewpoint could be more accurate than my memory of it. The back of the chair no longer looked as tall as I had thought it was.

"Hey, baby."

By the time I knew Chase was out of bed, he had his hands on my shoulders and his chest against my back.

"You all right?" Chase asked.

He turned me back to bed, to lie naked next to him. Soon he was asleep again.

I was far from promiscuous; I once aimed to keep lovers at five, before I grew old with one. Chase made it eight. I still hadn't figured out how to use it to marry up, no matter where the number went. Chase made money, but he made it for New York rent and more student loans than I had defaulted on. He owned nothing but career advancement, to send stories of the American dream back to his Caribbean homeland. Summer and I had the only suitable love nest. It wasn't even soundproof.

My downstairs neighbor, Belinda, clued me into that. Her three kids and no man were her Section 8 guarantee she did not have to pay the raised rent we did. She hinted diplomatically: "Well, you know, my kids' windows face the back, uh . . . just like your bedroom." It was a thorny noise complaint to make, unlike our tolerance to never report her for her old Phyllis Hyman and her kids' new rap music.

Though we weren't exactly friends, I felt bad my sex was too loud. I learned to muffle myself and pat Chase out of his own moments, the worst of which sounded like movers in the middle of the night. I picked up a cheap mini-carpet. We moved the monstrous bed to place the carpet under it for some soundproofing. The comfort and escape our lovemaking gave us graduated to tough: bite marks, hickeys on brown skin, and fingernail dents. We tried, but could not, wrestle out of this nefarious blossoming in the shadows of my sister and her bed we slept in now.

"It's a record," he said, his eyes half-open. He wasn't asleep after all.

"What, how long we managed this time?" I giggled.

"No," he groaned. "How long it took you to wake back up after I put you to sleep. Three hours. Up from two and a half."

"You're counting?"

"I'll try harder next time."

He passed back into sleep, with my unspoken permission to replace me with Summer in his dreams. I deserved nothing more. I certainly had no shortage of men around me, but I never trusted men like Summer could. A few serious boyfriends proposed to her. Some paid her bills between taking her on trips. Meanwhile, what should have been my robust bachelorette life eroded into a serious relationship with my computer. I only found a few brief hookups from online dating.

I asked Chase if he felt sorry for me. He laughed I would think such.

"I don't know why I can't leave you alone," he'd said. "I'm mixed up right now, too."

As the weeks and then months passed, he tamed his compulsion to fixate on the predicament while mine became more disobedient. We drifted to two opposite poles. Like me, he started off zealous and pushy for answers. Then, he just paused. His face adopted a stoic gauze. His eyes became a simplified film. It could have been men and women's different natures. I felt more like that mother who'd wait by the door or phone for decades to no end if her child went missing. He operated like that father who would dismantle the swing set and throw out the bike.

To doze off again, I zoned in on the repeat news broadcast. The face on the news looked like any one of them I passed on the street every day: light or dark brown, late teens or twenties, baby or senior dreadlocks, a half-triumphant and half-defeated face, brand-name tennis shoes, sagging pants and handcuffs. A White attorney's hand and his legal pad shielded this boy's face. I heard something about DNA. The somber male investigative reporter explained Jaylyn Stewart was arrested on suspicion of the rapes and murders of sixteen-year-old Dejanay Little and forty-two-year-old Shanice Johnson in Harlem.

The Black women's and girls' stories weren't repeated enough for me not to forget them. I had forgotten their names but remembered a little of their tragedies. Fragments of it all came rushing back: Dejanay went out to Crown for a box of chicken and never came back, the last trace of Shanice was her Metro-North ticket after work. In weeks apart last fall, a garbage man and church janitor found their bodies in nearby dumpsters.

I could tell Chase was back asleep; I left him for my other lover: my desktop.

PayPal declined my digital *New York Times* subscription charge once and I forgot to renew it manually, so I hit the paper's paywall. I had to settle for a Google search. I did see its headline on a Harlem killer. Every other Jaylyn Stewart headline was connected to Dejanay or Shanice. *The Daily News*, *New York Post*, *NJ.com*, *Star-Ledger*. Before the birds started to chirp, I mined enough headlines to learn Jaylyn was twenty-six, born in the Bronx but raised in Harlem, and the first child of a forty-year-old mother. His father was unknown or unmentioned, and he and five younger siblings were once wards of the state after incidents of questionable care, including one sister's hospitalization because an uncle raped her.

I wandered to the Murderpedia vortex of mass murderers, rapists, and serial killers. I had my fill of snapshots of depositions, police reports, and biographies of society's deplorables. Then I watched two twenty-two-minute *Forensic Files* episodes on YouTube. The killings were in small towns, not big cities, but still relevant. The stories were about women's murders. I learned resistance, not rape, hurt female victims most. Their attackers wanted power, and defensive wounds proved these women wouldn't give it easily. Summer was that kind of woman. Pride and will could override her fear anytime.

I revisited the Black and Missing website (I bookmarked it at the New Year). In 2014, almost sixty-five thousand Black women and girls were missing. Where was uproar, outrage, *20/20* segments, sniffer dogs, two-hundred-volunteer search teams, TV specials, addresses from the White House? Still, in the Missing

Persons Clearinghouse, I could not find even one of the many pictures of Summer I gave to police.

I noticed daybreak only when I heard the shower. Chase awoke without an alarm right at 6:30 a.m. I wasn't the amateur barista he was, so I was happy to find a Café Bustelo bag on hand, which I measured with a shot glass for two instant cups.

"What're you doing up all night?" he smiled. "You're gonna make yourself sick."

"Relax, I had a deadline," I told him. "I scared up a speech-writing gig."

"Get it done?" he asked.

"Almost."

I warmed up toast and cut up a cantaloupe going soft.

Then he showed me three dents curved around his left shoulder, in the middle a small slit of broken skin my teeth made.

I was not ready, yet, to tell him how much I wondered if Jaylyn Stewart had more victims than anyone realized. That morning, again, Summer remained our unmentionable, both the reason we should not be together and the reason we could not bear to be apart.

FOUR

My other downstairs neighbor preferred to get intimacy from her customers. Asha Goddess claimed this connectedness as a "claim to fame" in her combination detox-healing-bodywork services. A few weeks after Summer seemed to slip off not just our roof but the face of the Earth, Asha slipped in Jill Scott or Jewel when she knew I was on my way down. My favorites. Just for me. I appreciated her efforts to lift my spirits and provide a retreat. Technically, I wasn't a customer. I was just her neighbor, the sister who moved in to subsidize Summer Spencer's mock Manhattan penthouse her many odd jobs and few art sales could barely afford. But I gave Asha much credit for her effort to halt this crisis from getting the best of me.

"Okay, from the looks of your posture your chakras are imbalanced. And, your sitting bones too elevated. That's 'cause you're a desk potato. My meditation partner is a proofreader at a law firm. She threatened to sue the partners if they didn't bring in stationary bikes for the proof girls. Fifteen minutes of movement for every forty-five minutes of sitting. Run in place, jumping jacks, pace. Anything to get blood circulating and stop bones from atrophying. And, the ass from spreading. You know your crown is balding? Well, it is. Sorry to bear bad news. 'Bout the size of a pencil head, from what I can see. Every day you need Jamaican castor oil for your scalp. Then a tablespoon of molasses. It's an acquired taste. Hmmm, your eyes are nice. Color of a pile of rice. So, that's good. Long life. Heard your knee crack. Pick up cod liver oil too. I can see from your tongue you need cold foods: cucumber, celery, lettuce, apple, pear, cabbage salads. Nothing hot now. Stay away from the meat. No peppers. Dump the cinnamon and ginger. None of that nutmeg you gave me my last birthday. And I feel a fever. Not much. But still, it—"

"Sorry to interrupt, but can I sit up now?"

Asha had tried and failed to jigsaw me into happy baby pose. To open my sacral chakra and push my aura to take up space. My butt was on the floor, my legs in the air and my arms stretched over the backs of my knees. I was light-headed.

"If you must," she answered.

My free "treatment" was barter for me to do her website she delayed buying a hosting service for.

Asha ran her odd business from the garden apartment. She found the cold body of its prior tenant—the eighty-year-old deaf and mute maid of the mansion—before the original owner's children broke the home up into rentals. Asha first met the old maid by helping her up from a crack in the sidewalk. After this, she stood in for the maid's distant New Jersey and Queens relatives. She daily delivered her lottery tickets, an ice cream sandwich, and large black coffee. The misfortune to find its maid dead handed Asha the fortune of our Hamilton Heights brownstone. It was an upgrade from her fifth-floor walkup in a nearby tenement. When Summer moved in at the top of the renovated apartments the mansion became, Asha told her the whole story. So Summer thought the maid haunted the place. She cited common proof I barely noticed.

Autumn, that little tapping didn't keep you up last night? No, it had not.

Autumn, why do these hallway lights twitch on and off or just go dark? I almost broke my neck dragging paint cans up here last night. We've got to complain to the landlords . . . For some reason, the hallway was always well lit for me.

Autumn, I saw snakes crawl from the garden up to the roof. Manhattan had snakes?

I've never lived anywhere in New York that had no pigeons on the sills—ever. Now, she had a point there.

As Mama became more fragile last year, Asha donated Reiki. She said it was a solution to the story our bloodshot eyes told. Asha proved purple curtains, nag champa incense, and Santeria-emblemed candlelight could lure enough business to pay Manhattan rent. What was I doing with a CV and master's degree aspirations? Asha showed all it took was potions, herb pots on sills and in hedged patches of a cement garden, a shelf of books in odd languages, a tincture cabinet, mats on the floor, tarot cards, and a cash box. She even had a crystal ball squished between a lava lamp, spider plant, and bong.

Asha hung a few small watercolors and what looked like facial composites on her walls because they were her "ancestors." She explained them as "they're my spirit guides." When Asha mentioned them, Mama became quite lively to show she had artistic tendencies, too. In contrast, her framed Chinese calligraphy and posters of new age quotes came from Marshalls and Target. The bathroom was in the back of her place, across a wall kitchen with a checkered tile floor, rare and dizzying and hypnotic.

"Lemongrass and licorice tea?" Asha asked.

"Yeah, sure. Thanks."

This was our ritual. I pressed to Asha's door rather than sit in my apartment alone waiting for a meeting or for Chase to show up at night, or thinking about Summer all day. Our building's owner was a woman named Fran. She and her husband, Gregory, appeared to be well into their sixties, with working tattoos and retired piercings. Nobody could pinpoint their professions beyond collecting rent from us and timeshare tenants in the Poconos. Including them with Chase and Asha, my urban tribe was whittled down to four people. I did not count those I had to commute for.

Asha walked to the kitchen and her black porcelain kettle. I lay on her futon and scratched my neck against a hemp throw. Boys cursed and laughed on the sidewalk outside her window. I wondered if any of them knew Jaylyn Stewart. I felt compelled to ask Asha if she was following the news, and if she had any prophecies on this enemy nearby. But the teakettle started screaming.

So I imagined snatching open the curtains to curse the boys out, to ask if they knew how their women neighbors felt to be washed down with *bitch* and *pussy* and *hoe* on such a lovely day. I had a Foxy Brown inside. She carried a rifle and cursed like a drill instructor with a fresh crop at boot camp. She never smiled. She punched the teeth out of any man who told her to "Smile, sexy." She left a dark cave in their filthy, boring, typical mouths. I bought a toy pistol in the dollar store. I would try it one day. I fantasized pulling it on all the men who hit on us without our permission. I bought Asha one, too. We had plenty of targets.

Past the window stood beautiful boys with ancient faces, the kinds I may have married without mitigating circumstances I could write a dissertation on. Instead of walking down the aisle with one, I cringed to walk past one on the street. I spotted a common familiar face, dented from acne, with yellow teeth marijuana smoke left. As usual, the boy stared at me but also looked past me. In my stare, I questioned him: *Was it you? Do you know? Where were you on a dark and cold night three months ago when all I knew changed?* Had one of these been obsessed with my sister—stalked her, hunted her, taken her away?

"I hate that shit too," Asha called out.

"Wha—?" I asked.

"Brothers can be so insensitive," she answered. "I should go throw cold water on 'em. That'll clean 'em up. The kids nowadays ain't got no home training. Or wait. Girl, those ain't kids. Those are grown Negroes. Jesus to the Lord have mercy . . ."

What I thought were my silent conversations were out in the open more and more these days.

In came Asha with a tray of two teacups slick with mist and a mason jar of molasses.

"You need the iron, my dear," she told me.

She squeezed in more molasses than I would have permitted had she asked. We sat at edge of her futon and sipped in silence.

Asha was a personality I could share quiet with. Silence was no awkward pause. She said all she wanted to say when she felt like it. She never diced off a syllable. She seemed to have no back of her mind, only a front. I could trust her. She rarely brought up Summer anymore, and this was a welcome courtesy At first she was more hysterical and disoriented than Chase and I were. She lived with Summer longer than I did, after all. Soon, probably because none of that got us anywhere, Asha resumed her wizened recommendations and pillared disposition.

"History is stubborn," was her last theory on my sister's vanishing. Then she probably sank into a bad memory where both a room and a sentence could include melting ice cream sandwiches, a silent TV on caption, and a nice old lady's body on the floor. Even if she could hunt down the poltergeist that jinxed all of us here, we couldn't afford to move.

Now, she gulped a molasses spoonful and said, "I remember when the boys were nice. Harmless. They just used to pull braids your mama chunked up in three parts, maybe four. You know: one at the top and in the back, and two on the sides?"

"I sure do," I told her. "My sister wouldn't go for it, though.

We always had our hair twisted round with ribbons to match our outfits. She was fancy like that."

"I wish I'd had a sister," Asha said. "May have changed things. I didn't grow up with a teammate to take a tomahawk to the boys, right in the middle of their pants, under the zipper. I was all by myself. Two brothers running me 'round Stankonia."

"Where?"

"Georgia. You know, where I'm from."

"You told me you were from Atlanta."

"Honey, that's cause don't nobody know where Lithonia, Georgia, is. What I look like running around Harlem saying 'I'm from Lithonia'? You hear what we gotta contend with outside this window. Georgia's bad enough."

"You make me feel like a hillbilly," I told her. "So should I stop telling people I'm from Hedgewood, Illinois?"

"You do what you want to do. I'm only telling you what works for me."

What worked for Asha was heavy cotton head wraps, tarnished ankh rings, painted moons and stars on her nails, clamoring bangles, bracelets stacked to her elbows, and Roy G. Biv eye shadow. She had a past she dropped almost unheard, like a morphine drip, as she treated her customers, answered to our problems, calmed our nerves, and gave us touch to tune our spirits. That past included a father who ran dogfights (he made her bandage the wounds after), a Morehouse boyfriend who slapped her onto the UGA dropout track, a girl crew who pushed weed and was too busy to bail her out before the weekend, a fire she started herself to collect renter's insurance, a bumpy Greyhound ride to Penn Station to try working in fashion rather than stand out so much where she was. The closest she got was folding jeans at Old Navy for a while.

Any time I left her place with complimentary treatment and

readings (as her prop and practice), I did feel better. Something squeezing at my temples stopped for a while. My eyesight sharpened. I tipped her for this: a train pass in the days after we paid rent, free time on my hi-speed Wi-Fi, my plunger, Drano. I once gave her a Donna Karan winter coat on my way to drop it at a consignment in Chelsea. January off the Hudson had proven her quilted parkas and handmade saris wrong.

It was Asha who first showed me the roof. We went out with coats but no shoes, to smoke some good weed Asha traded for administering a sitz bath. I was never much into intoxicants, yet I was culture-shocked when I first came to join Summer, and grateful for assistance in relaxing. My high came down as all that smart hip-hop Bad Boy and Def Jam once made barreled out of the radio Asha brought up with us. Our four-story brownstone kept us lower in the sky than the upscale Manhattan high-rises ascended their occupants. Yet still, the view of Uptown's expanse against the twilight dizzied me to all good things coming my way here. Asha paced the soft tar clearing to point out where the herb garden, vericomposting bin, and beehive should go when our landlords got their act together.

Harlem was still a neighborhood then, teeming with foot soldiers and African dress, and black and brown families pushing carts up its daring hills. The storefront paints were faded and the Spanish carried. The most striking folks strut from jobs downtown or their own ventures right in our community. The many brownstones widowed of their owners blended in eventually, boarded behind sidewalk edges of tall grass. Vagrants sawed the padlocks off fences of empty lots to create tents nobody complained about but the police dismantled anyway. Those who were born here could not understand the mass immigration or the fuss. And too many were accustomed to their White property owners, for they had always been.

Every day, more and more trucks arrived with men to carry sheetrock and piping into unboarded doors, aired-out windows, and swept great rooms selling for more now. More and more Whites fell out of moving trucks in two categories: the ones who smiled at everybody too much, and the ones who smiled at nobody at all. I put my trust in the latter. I heard the chitchat and banter from old men based on corner stools, the testy objections in their West Indian or born–New Yorker voices. The gracefully dictated bullshit of telltale liberals amused me: about how it was a good thing to mix cultures, elevate property values, bring in healthier stores, and give "natives" something to strive for and compete with. Still, the crumbs I saved from Mama's life insurance could not purchase a building like this one I rented a sliver of.

And the wonderland our rooftop was to become never transformed as such and was now off-limits, a site of strange circumstances none of us could explain.

But Asha had a dream to grow her business beyond rent money and hang-ups on bill collectors. She would own her own brownstone and healing place soon: community roundtable center, day spa, and famous dignitary rest spot all in one.

She had told me all this, over and over again. So we said nothing now.

FIVE

Even shadows are promising when someone you love is lost. Every face and body shaped the same, even a little bit, grabs your attention and hope. Then the lack of recognition, just a glimpse of familiarity, is a defeat you didn't ask for. This guaranteed failure made going out so hard for me. Or, maybe it was just my excuse to give up on wanting more out of the world. But I was determined withdrawal wouldn't equal laziness.

The New York City Office of Vital Records kept me on hold over ten minutes. I managed impatience with the day's *Daily News* and *Post*, neither reporting stories of any unidentified Black women's bodies I could call a hotline and demand to see. I reread another email from one of Hedgewood's two detectives (both past retirement age).

"Ms. Spencer: No trouble at all to check things for you again. All bodies in our town hospital and morgue are identified. And none have been found, knock on wood. I gave your description and photo to COs at the county and beat cops on the streets. If a woman fitting your sister turns up, I'll tell you. God bless you."

I believed it. The town was too small for travesties police couldn't unwind just by showing up at the right bars after witnesses had the right number of drinks in them. He did not rule out authorities searching for Summer in Hedgewood. And he did confirm she did not go home to wind up dead, knock on wood. When a veteran big-city government employee returned to our call, he was less absolute.

"I'm just not finding any death certificates with that name on it," he announced. "Whadya say it is again? Autumn Spence?"

"No," I insisted. "Autumn Spencer is *my* name. I'm alive and well. And I'm the one talking to you right now. The decedent's name would be Summer Spencer."

"Oh, yes," he chuckled. "Sorry, I had my note upside down. I did look up Summer, of that prior address. You live there, cause they would've come to—"

"I'm not here every second," I interrupted. "They could've missed me."

"What relation would you be to the decedent, ma'am? Only spouses and—"

"I'm her sibling," I interrupted. "According to your policies I'm authorized to obtain a certificate. She has no spouse or children. Our parents are dead. I'm legal next of kin. I'd have to notify what family we have left, tell her friends."

With a death certificate, I could rest well again. I could shut this gaping hole of not knowing, and get back to order. I could start on Summer's affairs: run an obituary, transfer money from her bank accounts, address any bills she left behind, and (most importantly) do what Mama would want most: I would purchase her magnificent headstone for our family plot that Mr. Murphy's business mind pressured her to pay for in advance, away from our father's Spencer family burial ground in another town cemetery.

"Okay, when was this again?" he asked.

"She's been missing since December 20. Or, maybe it was the nineteenth." I sighed. "Look, I don't know. I remember it was a frantic Christmas. But whether it was last year or last night, you'd have a death notice for a dead New York County resident."

"Well, it takes a while to generate. And wait, you say she's missing, or dead?"

"I'm saying I do not know, *sir*. No one does. But if by chance she has died, an accident or God knows what else in New York City, I am reporting as next of kin to see."

"So if it was that recent and if some ID was on the decedent, something should be in our system. You be surprised how many people nobody bothers with. They get welfare burials, belongings auctioned off. But I have looked in—"

"Jesus Christ, sir, is there a supervisor I can speak with?"

"Ma'am, maybe you can come down here to Worth Street and fill out—"

I hung up. It was the third time I had called. I had completed two tasks of the day: checking coroner's office procedures to look at unidentified black women for possible identification (I did not qualify for clearance) and pursuing a death certificate. Now I had to get down to Worth Street, and I would not make it before five o'clock.

I switched to finding more about Jaylyn Stewart, and more Black women I never heard of who were killed in Harlem. My top inbox was piled with stories that Google and my last days of a paid LexisNexis subscription helped me compile.

Regina Desormeaux was bludgeoned to death in her Morningside Drive garden apartment. The killer came through a sidewalk-level window that, in code violation, was missing its gate. Robbery was the apparent motive, with both jewelry and signs of sexual assault missing.

Graciela Alvarez was also killed at home, though technically not in Harlem but Washington Heights, past 159th Street. Her attacker was known: an ex-boyfriend. No rape.

Monique Salter was fourteen, and a fight with her grand-mother (over boys in the home) ended in her falling down the stairs of their Mount Morris walk-up. She broke her neck.

Twenty-two-year-old Kameika Williams was found in a 135th street SRO strangled to death. It was unclear if sex was forced or consensual. A little cash was on the nightstand.

An unnamed woman was pushed into a gangway, her purse and cell phone taken, and her face slashed. She was still alive. This one committed by a duo. They were still at large.

There was also a professor in her sixties, walking into her brownstone after a class. The university was unnamed, but given the crime's location it was probably City College. She was car-jacked of her and her city official husband's Lincoln Town Car, parked in a rare Manhattan driveway. She had not stereotyped the "Black male" who walked behind her for several blocks. He made his move quickly. She survived being thrown to the cement with only a broken hip. No arrests were made.

There seemed to be no boilerplate habit or way of being that could shield women from the unthinkable. It was possible I had heard of all of these lives and endings, from the news and online, but I blocked them out for fear of compressing my own vulnera-bility with too much possibility. And, compassion fatigue set in often.

I put the sad pile of tragedy down and walked to the bathroom. I used bleaching toothpaste against wine and coffee stains. Then I boiled water for instant coffee as I ate two cherry Jell-O cups. The water bubbled to sizzling drops on the stove, breaking me out of imagining all the Jaylyn Stewarts out there waiting on women like Summer (and me) to waltz down any street on any night.

WHEN MAMA CAME TO LIVE with us on Thanksgiving 2013, we sisters put our fears of unsafety at bay. So many long weekends

Summer and I alternated had added up: in plane fare and missed work. What a team we were, together. When I could not get away, Summer went alone to mitigate my guilt and I gladly did the same for her. Mama's brother was never around to help. One of her sisters was dead. The sister left behind, my Aunt Mae, had her hands full. My in-town cousins were lazy. Other nieces and nephews were distant. The Illinois winters were aggressive. The house was too big. The money was too tight. The days were too numbered. The Trummel Lane home sale was worth its weight in health insurance deductibles.

So Mama and her Medicare finally came to New York. Her first visit was her last.

By the time we departed our Amtrak sleeper cars, too exhausted for a restaurant dinner to mark the occasion, Mama was answering to her oldest daughter, far above Summer and me. Her name was Virginia Slims. But only we were there to manage the combination stomach and lung cancer their lifelong bond brought. By Christmas, it came out of her every few hours as a light green stream. Penny, her hospice helper, was a modern nun. Penny gathered the pan for us to measure the output. Sometimes Summer and I helped Penny hold the measuring stick. Always, we expected the sturdier and better-funded New York City doctors to phone, their lab results a reversal of fortune.

That call never came. But Chase phoned Summer, all of us, often. His ticket to live decently in New York was SWAG Marketing: his college buddy's multicultural branding firm. He was the token Golden Negro there. So his excuse to bail on our ordeal many nights was convenient, but true. We all struggled to manage. Summer was interrupted in painting and making things, stuck home rather than at street festivals and tiny gallery openings. She lost money on postcards and print-on-demand T-shirts and totes she sold in online stores. I myself was delayed from heading back to graduate school. Or coding bootcamp, if only I could save up enough money for it. The value of my bachelor's had expired and I had to learn how to use a different language if I was going to make it in the world.

It was a nice time, more time than I had spent with Mama since I was a child.

IT WILL SOON BE SPRING.

Over three months past Summer's disappearance now . . .

An investigation is "ongoing."

No arrests have been made.

With no body, my sister's disappearance could not be ruled a homicide and thus graduated on to the manpower and attention we deserved, as we held no fame or prominence or money to command it otherwise.

So it is ruled something else: Women of color don't matter in America unless we are rich or famous.

Summer's detective is "doing all I can."

The mailbox broke my heart every day. Nothing ever came from Summer. I feared the ink-smudged cards from names, addresses, and signatures across my networks instead. They had hearts scribbled by the names or fancy insignias pasted on back of the envelopes' seals, making me have to do more work to open them. Address labels showed off the senders' donations to the Easterseals, Sierra Club, American Society for the Prevention of Cruelty to Animals. But I did not have to go out or move too much for the most wretched automatic habit of all: checking voicemail. Those who were privy to my cell phone number got a clue and finally kept their distance. They adapted to the reality—efforts to dial Autumn Spencer got them nowhere. A few left messages on the home phone, whose number I gave only to the most tolerable relatives and high-paying clients. Their spoken notes ranged from perfunctory to pathetically un-hilarious to disciplinarian, to plain shocked and confused . . .

"Hey. This is your cousin Sandy. I'm just giving you a call to see how you are. We put some fresh flowers on Mama's headstone just the other day. Love you!"

"Hey, baby. This your Auntie Mae. I need to know what's going on."

"Autumn . . . Oh my goodness. I ran into Jonathan Parks at the NAJMBAX conference in Houston about a week or two ago. And, well, we weren't at all gossiping, but your name came up, since it's been way too long since we've gotten together for drinks or anything like that and . . . Well, I won't repeat it here. Just gimme a call, girlie."

"Autumn, this is the *second time* I've left you a message this week. I know all that's going on, but I can't believe you won't call me back. Call me back. *Please.*"

The most promising were the upbeat ones recking of avoidance.

"Sooo . . . I was Uptown the other day. Just wanted to go to that one great vegan spot over there by your place, to stock up on their version of crab cakes and gluten-free muffins. My son loves those! Anyway, I wound up on 1-2-5 spending all my money on clothes for the new baby. My goodness, when that bill hits. Well, anyway, enough about me. I hope you're well. Just thinking about you."

I figured this must be my college buddy Cathy. Messages like these were left by the people most likely to succeed a relational breach preceded by tragedy, extreme life change, or estrangement for a prolonged time. Such largely anecdotal communications and nonjudgmental, non-assignment-oriented messages revealed characters who yearn for connection with the individuals they seek, but who also display comfort with rejection or relational impossibility until the offending and triggering separator dissolves. Such successful overcomers of life's relational ebbs and flows are characterized by the rich variety of their friendships, social activities, spiritual practices, and superior physical health levels. Such personalities are most likely to forgive a self-separated or alienating individual.

Or so it said in a book I happened upon at the Strand, when I went searching for a classic I had yet to read. Instead I bought a manual about bouncing back from grief.

"Autumn, it's Noel Montgomery returning your call. I'll be away from the desk all afternoon, but you can contact me in the morning."

Now this was a message I could use.

He was brief, unrevealing, and undetailed. He didn't just check off the task to return my call. He told me where he would be, and when I should call him next. He had to have something new to tell me. Messages stacked up so high I did not know where he belonged in the queue. Should I have called him yesterday or today? Or should I call him tomorrow? Was I prepared for whatever he had to tell me?

I couldn't figure out if an accident or a murder was more palatable than an unsolvable disappearance. The first one was consolation that something was fated or meant to be, no matter what. It was more proper to bring up in normal conversation, a better interlude to reminisce about the good times, a normal event to give sympathy to. The second option would silence me for life. Nobody would want to hear it. This fact of my sister's life would always have the pall of controversy and violence, a repellant to any mind outside of a movie. But an unsolvable disappearance was unspeakable. All loved ones are blamed and viewed as apathetic assholes. I could never cry enough tears to convince anybody I really cared for her, advocated for her safety, and didn't let her slip away.

I dialed Montgomery's direct line. He did not answer. I hung up, not knowing what to say or how I would wait to call him again.

My "no wine before dark" rule lapsed into just a little wine before noon. The tinkling downpour into a glass ignited me like caffeine. I returned to bed, the only place I sensed a semblance of naïveté to staple to my soul. I froze under Summer's duvet, feeling her beside me. I manipulated the remote to put Virginia Rodrigues on surround sound, so at least I would not understand the Afro-samba beyond its joyous drums and up-tempo. I settled in to read the arrest affidavit and search warrants made public from Jaylyn Stewart's case today.

Most women have imagined waking up to a dark block covering what they would normally see in their bedrooms. The closet, door, and window dressings are still there as usual. But something is in front that was not there before we closed our eyes. After sweat and lightning-fast heartbeats sprint forward to leave us immobile for an eternity, we will determine the block is a person. The person is a man. The man wants to do things to us and the things will feel excruciating, and we are already at a disadvantage called shock. So, we will just close our eyes to pretend it is all a dream. And as we are waiting to reawaken, we will repeat blame on ourselves: for leaving the door unlocked, the window open, both eyes shut.

The looming block in my bedroom had hands the size of rosebushes. I smelled Hedgewood, aroma of fresh cut grass wafting from nearby yards. I saw scarecrows we kids made in those yards. This was the dream I fell into as the block did more than cut up my space, but come toward me. I blamed myself for not moving the hell out of a building my sister already proved was unsafe.

THE SHOWER REFRESHED ME AND just the smell of coffee made me more alert. I wrapped a towel around and came into the bedroom. Chase dabbed a wet sponge at soft magenta stains from the bougainvillea leaves fallen to the light comforter and carpet. He had cleaned up the ruined plant's potted soil. Then he gathered

and neatened all my research, notes, and news printouts I meant
to examine before I passed out. He skimmed a few pages, shook
his head, and sighed.

"Autumn, you really need to stop looking at all this stuff. No
wonder you acted like I came in here to kill you. This ain't healthy."

I kissed him to distract from taking my notes out of his hand.

"I'll do that," I told him. "It's my fault things are a mess."

"No, you get dressed," he said. "I'll do it. And I'm sorry. I'll call
next time."

But of course, I also should not have been dead to the world
at 6 p.m., when Chase was that guy every girl wants. He remembers
even the mistress is a lady. He remembers to celebrate milestones
and make reservations. He picks up flowers with significance, not
just roses in a hurry. I adjusted to his surprise eventually. My terri-
fied response to him using his key to let himself inside was a knot
on his forehead and scratch on his cheek.

I chose a red shirtdress for the evening we had planned weeks
ago, but work kept us too busy. We missed the steakhouse reservation and had to settle for walking in like the younger crowd. It was
our anniversary of sorts. In Chase's telling, it was "A night to let
the drama go for a while and remember what brought us together."

My sister brought us together, technically. Chase was her man
first, off and on. In retrospect, only our mother's deterioration
pushed him *on* more often for her.

Perfumed and put together in killer heels, I hugged Chase
in the back of our cab to Lower Manhattan, the night air more
even-tempered and cool. His gesture forced us out of my apartment where Summer's absence made her an ongoing presence. Yet,
I marked our "anniversary" in secret thoughts of my argument
with Summer that led me into this affair. She and I never resolved
the last time we had Mama with us, alive.

I was single. Caring for my ill mother provided my excuse to bail out of a six-month egomaniac ordeal. But Summer had the nerve to refuse Chase's invitation to accompany him on a business trip to his homeland, Grenada. We had spoken in hushed tones away from her bedroom, the one Mama took over, the larger one capable of holding her rolling carts of medicines, pain packs, and drawing stuff.

"Most guys just want to drag us to the Poconos or Atlantic City for a change of sex venue, Summer," I told her. "He wants to take you to Grenada."

"He's not taking me," she snapped back. "His job is."

Chase's bright marketing idea was a story and photo shoot on a ninetysomething Grenadan author named Gabriel Johns. Chase dreamed of launching a Grenadan author as a Wolcott or García Márquez in the world. The win-win was a smarter, patrician image for a men's luxury brand seeking more than pretty boys who couldn't drink yet to sell their goods to the kind of men who drank only the best. Out of everybody he could have brought along, Chase invited Summer. She found his offer rude, in light of Mama's care needs.

I continued to scold her: "Most guys wanna jiggle us out of meeting their mothers. He wants to take you thousands of miles away for it. Maybe he'll propose."

"And what about Mama?" Summer wanted to know.

"It's only five days," I had argued. "Somebody's gotta break out of this tomb."

"Fine, you break out." She walked back to answer our mother's latest moan.

The fact "somebody" wound up being me was the reason for "anniversary" now.

Chase wriggled us into a South Street Seaport restaurant with a river view. He ordered us a Chianti. We waited for his steak and my whole snapper. I spoke of celebrity gossip, avoided my own.

He was especially happy for his work updates. I appeared to enjoy him. I celebrated us as friends, above everything else, always
without question, even if Summer waltzed in tomorrow, to tumble
our house of cards. The prospect always loomed in both hope and
paranoia, undergirded in deceit.

But the dinner table's candlelight drew me in like Summer's
greedy and mocking eyes. They'd been so different from Mama's
proud ones, vicariously living through my sweepstakes trip with
the nice young man who came around. Summer's eyes had dis-
turbed me when I set out that morning for the getaway she pushed
me to accept in her place. For the favor, she didn't even help me
to the taxi with my bags. She just crossed her arms at the top of
our hallway staircase, her dramatic "Bon voyage!" in the tenor of a
child who seized the last cookie in the jar, or a victor wearing the
cape our grandmother crocheted for both of us, or the icebreaker
with a party joke at her sister's expense. Mama just said, "Go, go,
go!" As our mother weakened, she relaxed her hold, encouraged
us into adventures, women of a different time she may have caught
up with had she been granted more than sixty years on the planet.
I was the underdog in a joust I never picked up my sword for, hurt
by the eyes of my sister who purposely got rid of me via her boyfriend, just so she could be the only scared little girl our weakened
mother was to coddle for a while.

It was February 2014 when Summer dispatched me so Chase's
special guest didn't become another woman, and I sunk down a
notch in my commitment to Mama, which Summer was certainly
flaunting now. With one gesture, she'd played us both.

Six

We left reeling in the news that Philip Seymour Hoffman had overdosed down in West Village. I trusted technology to obstruct total alienation from Mama—in good spirits—and the godsend that was our hospice helper Penny, now on my mother full time, to assist Summer as I traveled.

We flew business class from JFK to San Juan. Then we transferred to land at Maurice Bishop International Airport in the capital of Grenada, Saint George's. Door-to-door, it took an entire day of travel to get to the bed-and-breakfast on Gabriel Johns's nutmeg tree estate. When we touched down, our limo was outside with its driver holding a sign with Chase's name. Well, our limo was actually a sandy Jeep, very necessary to roll through steep hills and sharp turns on to Saint Andrew Parish. Our driver explained the history I had researched beyond *Wikipedia*. I took a moment from his spiel to discover the hidden cost of downgrading to a pay-as-you-go smartphone to save money. It had a full battery but no signal.

I took that as a warning not to call Mama every second. I returned to the spiel.

Gabriel Johns was nearly a king in his parts. He spent his days in a coach house back closer to where his trees grew. He was one of the first in on the burst of tourism after the United States' 1983 invasion to restore order, in our Congress's mind, to back-to-back violent coups of Grenadian Parliament heads. Maurice Bishop, the beloved former head of state for whom their airport was named, was executed by firing squad once a rebel military regime captured him. While casualties and battle on their soil created animosity between the small island nation and the States, our vindication of Bishop's death overrode natives' lingering hostility, to make us welcome allies in no time. We should rest; they love Americans.

"Not bad for where we come from," Chase laughed at the end of the driver's stories.

The atmosphere and panorama bewitched its strangers, as a history of mayhem and violence and disasters seemed utterly impossible given my view.

The estate manager greeted our Jeep at the gravel road where the driver pulled up. Chase stayed behind to tip the driver as I fluttered out into the sun. My water bottle drained, I was parched in just the two hours it took to go through customs, find our driver in the tiny airport, and drive there. But the manager, tagged OLIVIA, carried a tray: moist towels and cups of iced tea spiked with gutsy rum, as one sip told me. The laughter of the men behind me was dedicated to my figure, I guessed. It was the first time during the trek anyone saw Chase and me as a couple. Why wouldn't we be? I had seen the obvious pairs myself. They walked with matching luggage and bags in the same color family, in perfect step or leaning behind one another on the automated airport walkways, their intimacies such that they turned pages of books and magazines as near choreography. They even dozed in time.

In all this time, I did not notice a strange man watching me, or feel like I had to watch myself lest I do anything to encourage a strange man to watch me (though it didn't have to be much, as bending down or uncrossing my legs would do). Chase was a shield against the constant pressure of men's flaming tongues, lusty eyes, and foul mouths.

After I quenched my thirst, I introduced myself.

"I'm Autumn Spencer, just here to help the man in charge."

"And a handsome man he is," Olivia said. "You're lucky, my friend."

"No, we're friends," I corrected. "I'm just here for support, and a needed break."

"Oh," she smiled. "I beg your pardon."

"He still has good taste," I laughed. "He belongs to my sister. She couldn't make it."

"Well, tell him to find his brother for you, my friend." Then, she looked puzzled.

"Something wrong?" I asked

"No," she said. "It's just, I thought. I'll have to . . . well, never mind."

Chase walked into the warmth of our greeting.

"Chase Armstrong," he said to Olivia. "Pleased to make your acquaintance."

They hugged each other.

"Greetings, Mr. Armstrong," Olivia said. She put a small towel and slick glass in his free hand. I lugged a Fairway tote, Times Square suitcase, and Nike duffel bag. I felt so oddly American.

"I hear you're one of ours, yet your speech betrays us," Olivia said.

"I haven't lived here since I was a little boy," he told her. "Yankee talk took over some time ago, but my heart lives in my country. It's why I'm here."

"Well, we are happy to have you anytime. You may now call this your home, too. Our door is always open to you for your lovely work on Mr. Johns. Shall we?"

I thought she would never ask if we could get out of the sun.

Not all Black people love the sun. I was a Midwesterner, child of big oak tree shade and awnings and air conditioning four months out of the year. My overseas travel among the African diaspora was limited to a few Caribbean cruises. I was the color of copper, spared the undue humiliation of being called "black" and warnings to stay out of the sun. My desire to avoid a tan had nothing to do with self-hate or lack of pride, but the spoils of being an American.

Chase inserted the complication of a selfie in front of the estate landscape, an obligation to document every moment for SWAG's social media feeds.

"If you don't mind," he smiled. "I'll be sure to spell your name and title right."

"No, I'm used to it," Olivia said. "How funny your generation is. Everybody wants pictures here and pictures there, and with me—a total stranger except for a time. I've never been so popular."

"But I'm sure you've always been so photogenic," I said, as we squeezed in.

"You're too kind," she laughed.

Olivia guided us through a side door, straight to the kitchen. Two dark faces had bright teeth matching starched uniforms. They stood at a butcher's table and butler's pantry.

"Please use this entrance if you happen to come in and need a cold drink right away, or a stiff one," Olivia offered. "Meet Damian and Delbert."

The men appeared to re-polish surfaces absent of a fingerprint or smudge. They stopped to bow their heads to us with genuine sincerity and dutiful practice.

"They've been here with Mr. Johns for quite some time," Olivia said.

"Forty years," said the one called Damian. His face and voice seemed barely forty. "Since I was a fisher boy and Mr. Johns gave me coins for my catch."

"He's the boss," the other man laughed.

My guess was the daily morning walks of these communities, as well as the dearth of cigarettes and abundance of good marijuana, protected youthful appearances. I speculated how old Miss Olivia was, her hair tousled into a girl child's ponytail fastened only by her own hair. Her sundress fit for a woman just loosened from an athletic girlhood. She seemed completely comfortable with on-demand versatility.

A Keurig on the counter surprised me. I wondered how many Western products managed to invade the close knit island. Olivia caught my eyes on it.

"Would you like some coffee or tea, Miss Spencer?" Olivia asked me.

"It should be about that time for her," Chase chimed in.

"No," I said. "I was just wondering how much American influence there is on Grenadan consumerism now, after our unfriendly invasions here in the 1980s?"

"More than we would like," Olivia told me.

Behind her, out the back window, was an orchard of Gabriel Johns's famed nutmeg trees, the culprit behind my sudden taste for vanilla ice cream. It smelled heavenly all around.

"But I believe our Queen's head is probably bigger than your Statue of Liberty's," she continued. "We look to the British much more over here, but American interests and tourism are certainly not spurned."

"I'm really grateful Mr. Johns agreed to this. We market to Europe, some parts of South America. We're hoping to break Asia in a few years. So, this stay is nice of you."

"Well, your colleague arrived this morning. A White man?"

"Uh, yes," Chase stammered. "Is that a problem?"

"Oh, no, money has no color," Olivia said. "I was just making sure you two were together as he said you would be. Since it seems

I mixed some things up. I'm unsure if a proper room is prepared for both you and the lady."

"Oh?" Chase asked. "I said I was bringing someone."

"Yes, and I forgot this was business for you," Olivia said. "The lady's already clarified she'd prefer a private space."

Chase looked at me oddly. But he kept to his word we would not mention any sadness back in Harlem.

"Well, I understand if she wants her space now. That's hard to come by in New York City, so we'll take it how we can get it. Give her what you have prepared. Sleeping in a hammock between nutmeg trees is a long-held fantasy of mine, a beautiful woman with me of course. But, we can't have everything we want."

"Oh, no," Olivia laughed. "I will not have *that*. We have four rooms here, two on the upper floors, shared bath on each floor. The servants' quarters are through that door right there. There's no cellar, on account of the hurricanes and flood potential. I live in what used to be an unforgivable mess of an attic. If anything, I have relatives not far from here and you may have my separate apartment for your stay."

"I couldn't kick you out of your home . . ."

"No, no, Mr. Armstrong. I insist. It was unprofessional of me not to have asked for room preferences. Let me show you both to the room I have set and ready, so you can at least shower and freshen up. I'll look at the register to see when the next guests depart."

The first-floor open rooms had soft mauve walls with sea foam–green baseboards and entryways, what would be a design disaster in our stainless steel America. Chestnut and mahogany china cabinets lined the walls like exposed safes, for we were all friends there, it felt; nothing must be put away, hidden, unmentioned, or untouchable. It was like going down South for a funeral, as I did on a few occasions when young. The camaraderie between strangers was relaxing after my daily urban trances, spent constricted and braced in scarce, unmarked personal space. I saw our room was the size of half my apartment back in Harlem, and our view of the tops of trees stretched for what seemed like blocks. The room's lone rectangular table was decorated with a spray of overwhelming, gorgeous magenta and red flowers. They called me to them as Olivia fluffed the pillows of the king-size bed.

"Those are my gift," she said. "It's our national flower, the bougainvillea."

"I've never seen these before," I told her. "The fragrance is so powerful."

"It's expensive to export," she said. "But we get many orders for sure. I should leave you two to get settled. And Mr. Armstrong, I'll have a solution for you soon."

"Take your time," Chase said.

It took me two minutes after Olivia walked out to shift the mood.

"I wonder how Mama's doing?"

"I'm sure she's happy you're happy," Chase said. "We'll be back there in just five days. I'd take a lot of notes, do some interviews with locals if I were you. This could be part of a travel-writing package down the road. Those are trending now."

"You're right," I nodded. "I came this far. I'm not gonna turn around and mope about home. Who knows when I'll have another vacation again in life?"

I lay back on the bed, careful not to let my sundress come up high.

"Don't trouble yourself," Chase told me. "You sound like frozen-over winter and not a colorful autumn. If you think like that, then things won't be good."

"I'll try to do better, sir."

I felt a pang of more closeness to Chase for this peek into his background. I could contextualize him deeper than the prep-wear pretense and coffee-date banter of men like him in New York. I was eager to meet his family, as I imagined them in the simplicity of the life I had assessed in less than thirty miles of the country. The contrast to largely Black regions of America was inexplicable. Back home, the city spaces of color bound me into feeling trapped in what I should not want to escape. Even Chase's patience with Summer and gracious concern for Mama seemed rooted in a less harrowing cultural memory and much easier pride for it.

"Why don't you shower first?" he asked me. "I need to find the photographer and see what he's up to. He's probably out chasing tail."

I was sure he felt the need to be respectful, leave me privacy, create a clear line.

"You know how men are when they get to the Caribbean. I'm watching you . . ."

"Not necessary," Chase said. "Watch yourself, babe."

And we stared too long. I wondered what he was thinking, or what I thought for that matter. He broke our gaze first.

"Lemme get on to Johns," Chase said. "I should change clothes at least."

I noticed he held blue boxers in his hands along with his pants, fresh shirt, and Clarks sandals. I don't know why I noticed his apparel. I just did.

People laughed and talked in the hallway on the way to their room. I wondered if I would meet them, what they would ask, and what I would tell them. I tried to cut it off: "My mom has stage IV lung cancer and we didn't even find out until stage III. Imagine that. How can anything but a thief in the night be so sneaky?"

I'll try to do better, I thought.

My mere appearance at the group dinner would be an intrusion. People don't spend whole paychecks to go overseas to be forced to console strangers. It's awkward to scoot back from tragic reveals just because you're full at the dinner table or the wine bottles are empty or the closing lights signal you out of the club.

I heard streaming water and imagined what awaited. Real country hard water that scrubbed like no city water pressure could? A pedestal sink? A claw-foot tub?

I allowed Chase to text confirmation we arrived safely, to count for my promise to keep in touch, as I told Summer I would. I knew what she was up to. My grumpy distance served her right. I was in another part of the world, but my own world with all its cloggy dread and confusion and bittersweet snuck into my suitcase. I kept it shut. I was asleep by the time Chase finished in the bathroom. He left a note atop my suitcase, to tell me he wouldn't be back with me until much later that night.

I ate my first Grenadian dinner alone with strangers I would ordinarily remember in detail: where specifically their version of English originated from, what brought them to Grenada, what hobbies I could make small talk about later. But the meal was a blur.

After dinner, the other tourists hung out in the gazebo with cigarettes, rum, and a radio I heard from down below. I was alone on the floor, so I soaked in complimentary lavender bath wash and a few drops of clary sage oil. I figured the downstairs was too dark to burrow in the office to peck at a keyboard, like just another day in America, fretting over what opportunity would bring my next check. I went to bed alone as well. Only travel exhaustion made my mind slow down to sleep.

In middle of the night, Chase came into bed with me. Whatever we did gave me orgasms to awake to just as I reached over to see he was not really there.

SEVEN

"You, my child, are a lovely girl with too much going for you to trouble yourself so. So young. Smart. Far too pretty to be so sad. In all this life, God has a plan. All our days numbered from the moment we come out of the womb. Hell, I smoke a pipe all my life. I do still. Look at me: be ninety-two years old come this July. And I eat. Boy oh boy, do I eat. The women-folk detach the pig and chicken head for the menfolk to split them down the middle, take all the guts out. The Whites don't eat the innards. Well, why not? I do. Once the chitterlings clean it make the best broth. That is what you must do, child. Eat. I want Da-mian to cook for you, hear me? You, just you. Tell him what I say. Or bring him to me. I tell him myself. You like pineapple cake? He make a good one for you."

My privilege to have Chase introduce me to Mr. Johns in his study, at what was supposed to be a professional interview, went badly. I took one look at Mr. Johns and wanted my mother to be so ancient too: swathed in a soft gown and cottony slippers. I knew she wouldn't be. The bluish stardust in Mr. Johns's eyes, his coiled gray hair, his real natural teeth the color of light brown eggs, his trail of pinhead-size moles on his cheeks, his throaty deep laugh.

He reminded me of Grandma in her last days. He showed me what my father could have looked like if he had made it past his young days. Olivia, Damian, and Charles . . . all felt like surrogate relatives I missed.

"I'm sorry, Mr. Johns." I wiped my face with a handkerchief he gave me from his red housecoat's pocket. "I shouldn't have brought it up."

"No, no. no," he said. "All things in time and place. Why wouldn't you have? We are all friends here, are we not?"

"Yes, sir, we are," I said.

The man put out his hand. I held it for a long time as Chase tapped at his notepad. He was surprisingly rested after a night sleeping on Mr. Johns's couch. The other guests left that day, so he could have his own room. He and his subject were already old buddies by the time I came along after their breakfast together. I could have joined them. But a surprising green dot and flashing bar on my cell phone cleared me to call the States finally. I did so, a few times. I heard Summer's wordless orchestral greeting.

So I texted: "Everything's going well so far. Phone troubles, but you have the estate's number. Stay by the phone this evening. Give Mama my kisses. x."

In an hour, without one ring or ping, my digital egress closed back to a red dot and static. I presumed Summer was tied up with her campaign for Daughter of the Century. But of course the second-class daughter has not even called. I went down to ask Olivia to try to reboot the internet in her pre-Y2K haven, where the staff still did paper filing and expected guests to come to disconnect. With Summer's selfish nonresponse, the best I could do was send Penny an email and hope she checked it.

Her quick reply was the soundtrack for my mind that morning: "Mum is just fine my honey. Do not worry your pretty head.

We had no accidents at all today. She sleep all through last night. Now, she's reading one of your books. Enjoy, sweetheart. I wish you to have fun and come back safe and sound. All is well. God is good . . ."

I wiped my nose on a special dress I felt suitable to meet a notable man. It was a fresh pale yellow. I gave him the I Heart New York T-shirt I brought overseas for him.

"I'm not helping the interview . . . I should go," I said.

Mr. Johns held my hand tighter across the small round table where we sat.

"No, I like these kinds of interviews. I get to learn something too, for a change. I don't have too much to offer. My life very simple. I just wrote a lot of books."

"We can at least talk about your books rather than my problems," I said, becoming better. "I read *Night Wind*, about how you survived Hurricane Janet. I'm sorry. I wanted to get to more of them. But with caring for my mother and keeping up with work—"

"No, *Night Wind* is the one everybody want to talk about. I wrote twelve books before it and thirty after. About rebellion and growing up by the sea. Even love stories. One about my mother, too. But nobody knew my name. I struggle to find work. I go to the shore to get with the fishermen and they run me away. Too much competition. They say I have lady hands, and call me a sissy: 'Go back in de house n write de book like de ladies.' For long time I live with my sister and her husband and children. A shame, a disgrace for a grown man can't live on his own. But, after *Night Wind* . . ."

The novel was his masterpiece. It was one of the required readings thrown in my world literature college class. Chase was so impressed to see the book on one of my shelves: nearly five hundred pages to describe just three days in September in 1955, when Johns's whole house was swept into the Atlantic and his pregnant young wife went with it. The wife and child was something Johns's literary agent had already cautioned Chase not to bring up. It was essentially true fiction, a memoir puzzle, an account of life gone awry and masses left scattering to rebuild or reunite. So in some fortuitous way, I was the one to give Chase this whole big idea for SWAG Marketing to bring attention to Mr. Johns.

"This lady got me to read *Night Wind* again," Chase interrupted. "I tell people about you all the time. You got nominated for a lot of prizes for it. All around the world, the States and Britain and even India, it was published. I pulled up reviews online."

"On where?"

"Online," Chase said. "On . . . the internet?"

"Oh, yes, the computer thing," Mr. Johns chuckled. "Typing slowed me down. We write by the hand. Pencil. No pen, because you can't erase and it all gets messy. Then, if you lucky enough to have a pretty girl, she type it for you, with the carbon between the papers so you can send it to the publisher. In my times. Everything so easy today, it's bad. Instant rice? Why such a thing? Even love. Once you had to really, really *love*. You could not just pick up the phone or send the email. I hate the email. I don't type. Now, my hands hurt. I need Charles to listen to my words and record."

Chase recorded nothing. We would remember, for sure, everything Mr. Johns said. Mr. Johns's daughter wanted to review Chase's profile and sign off on it. Chase didn't expect to produce draft copy until he got back, but he couldn't refuse Mr. Johns's daughter. I would be on my own later in the night, again, while he worked.

Mr. Johns insisted we have lunch together in his study: breadfruit, callaloo, jamoon, and a noni fruit and avocado salad. More local rum. I was a big girl. I could hold my liquor. But the homegrown brew was nothing to play with. I stuck with guava juice.

Chase and Mr. Johns noticed, and laughed. He was full of stories and charm, perhaps grateful a photographer wanted more than that "native thing" for a portfolio spread. He never once mentioned his wife.

OLIVIA WAS GONE WHEN I came in to use the phone to call home, as technology kept me in a dead zone, now of all times. I accepted she could not live her whole life at her job, babying guests like me who appeared to escape harrowing realities back home. Only she and Mr. Johns's family had an office key, not Damian or Charles or a teenaged lady maid I met. I could not even check my email for an update. I asked the men to leave me a note when Olivia returned. I was being silly. I could not believe Summer would not pass along an update through Chase, or consolation of nothing to update. I knew her need to dominate and indeed I was accustomed to it. Peace numbed judgment. I forgave her new level of bitchiness and self-absorption.

Nothing was near the estate but modest tin-roof homes, a hop bar a half mile from them, and a few roadside fruit and drink stands. Without a train map or yellow cab or tour guide or bellman in sight, humdrum looked psychedelic. At dusk, I took my first excursion out alone in Grenada. I walked around the twenty acres of not only nutmeg trees, but cotton and almond trees. My hands luxuriated in the soft and hard grainy textures. I massaged my feet in the wild grass. So long had it been since I'd had an empty mind. I was thankful to the Caribbean skies for swallowing it for me whole, gently.

My first "faraway" trip had come courtesy of Mr. Murphy. My mother thought we'd take the train to Cedar Point in Ohio. Just two states over. But Mr. Murphy asked, "Do you know who I am? An hour on the plane, and a car takes us to O'Hare and picks us up when we land." Now, my sister and I could go back to school able to compete with what the other sixth graders said about their summer vacations. Cedar Point was a memorable otherworld, watery and humid and loud. We got right to it: boat rides on rolling waters through makeshift rapids. Summer laughed at my frozen hold on the raft's bar. She and I rounded the stony binge to go into the dark waiting tunnel. I looked at Summer and took a breath. A confederate in doom should it come, she reassured me. I looked back to wave at Mama, to show her my courage. But she was looking at Mr. Murphy and not her own daughters.

"Would you like some nutmegs to take back with you?"

Olivia had come up behind and pushed me out of my memory. I lurched from watery rapids back to the sunny grove.

"I didn't mean to startle you. We all need quiet time."

"Oh, no," I told her. "This place is almost too quiet. I was just, well. Thinking . . ."

I cut off "about my mother."

"Yes, the gentleman was wondering where you had gone. He went upstairs to work before dinner."

"Yeah, I wanted to give him and Mr. Johns some time alone."

If I was to learn to make conversation, without my mother healthy or even alive, I needed to start. I could not have another episode like the morning's. I could approach this like a new job, or essay, or deadline. I knew how to do those: research, patience, details, questions, answers, digressions.

"How do you cultivate the trees and harvest the nuts?" I asked. "I mean, how does all this turn into a profit?"

"With a lot more workers around here than you see now," Olivia said. "Peak harvest time is July. But, we call in boys from town to handpick what doesn't fall to the ground. They give me good price for their hands. Fingers throw out the bad ones before they make it into a batch. Machines cannot do that for you."

She sifted through a few fallen seedlings on the ground. In her fingertips, she held a round green ball encircled by what appeared to be a spider on fire. She stuck a fingernail between the tentacles and began to peel away the thick casing.

"This is the mace," she said. "Very powerful and hot."

"Wait, like pepper spray mace?" I asked.

"Exactly."

"We girls need this back home," I laugh. "We buy a little spray canister and attach it to our keychain. For the freaks that come out at night."

"The stories I hear from my people in your country," she said. "We hardly have prisons here, and yet you all sound like daily American life carries out in one. But I don't want to dwell on the negative. You are welcome back anytime to remind yourself it can be different. We let our guests handpick, too. It's great exercise."

"We'll definitely be back," I told her. "My sister would love to do that."

Success. I did not say "my mother." I had learned that quickly.

"All your friends will be jealous when you bring back a bushel of nutmeg to grate, nut by nut. The spice lasts better that way, whole. I can give you just enough so customs won't make a fuss."

"Thank you. It would cost an arm and a leg for me to get that in America."

"Not here. You bring it straight from the farm, for free. Well, I will leave you."

I wanted to tell her not to go, as she creased a fold between the moment and the worries. My mind would wander from the effortless glamour around me to the inelegance of illness. Or Chase. It was inconvenient not to be in love as Mama's life threatened to pass. The enormity of my inexperience in the situation forbid me from noticing the male body, let alone pleasing one. I'd always seen myself as the more prepared sister. Summer followed Mama to demonstrate that sometimes reliable men are the most preparation women can make.

I stayed out until the great trees around me sagged to giant faces with no expressions in the darkness, silent messages and secret stories in their towering personas. I was far inland, yet I felt my blood yearned to be drained of all of its vital elements, until only seawater remained. I would levitate as droplets of the rainy season, liquid more furious than fire and impenetrable than land, renewable as the wind. I would bring my mother along for the ride. Together, we'd join my father.

Those are the fonder memories of the time.

THE NEXT DAY, OLIVIA WAS hospitable enough to keep the office door closed but unlocked, so I could slip in to sit online. Life was too short to struggle with technology. Besides, the wide monitor gave a much better view than my small phone screen. Two Skype chats between me and Penny, afternoon and evening. Mama, however, was asleep each time I could connect. Summer sashayed in the screen's background. She stopped just long enough to order me to tell Chase to call her. She could have told him herself when he called from a *real* smartphone SWAG afforded him.

On the third day, a sensation of lift and ease settled in my gut and gait. Olivia left a basket of whole nutmegs outside my door. Chase had a full day alone with Mr. Johns, for more men talk. I walked headstrong to buy passion fruit and noni juice at the talkative vendors' stands. A child no more than ten swindled me to pay $5, plus tip, to pet his mona monkey. Once during my few hours of adventure, I was momentarily curious but ultimately undisturbed by a prevalence of small snakes entwining a sapodilla's trunk. At the side of sandy roads bound by devil trees and presumably wild ganja, I dropped off the bitter taste of Summer's beguiling. I forgave and understood. I planned some beguiling of my own. Chase was officially like a brother in the closeness and trust our journey demanded. My onslaught of date-night recommendations would be unyielding, for him to keep Summer occupied out of our house. Then I would enjoy my solitary time to elicit Mama's recipes, lores, and secrets.

But on the fourth day, two days before we were to be back in New York City, a clerk from the Grenada Tourism Authority sped onto the neat front lawn of Johns's estate. He had a strained request for "the Americans here." I would remember him as the loudest person I'd heard in Grenada. He yelled about the unanswered office phones.

And, an American nun called to send him to us.

The shared bathroom was too occupied earlier for either one of us fit in between a London couple and backpackers from Brazil. It was already ninety degrees by noon. Chase and I were hot, unshowered, sticky. The patient clerk was parental in his insistences. Olivia organized us, directed everyone to stay calm.

"Mr. Armstrong," the gentleman explained, "it's best for you both to come into the office to discuss a matter I don't want to bring up here in this setting."

I would be over 2,100 miles away from her side when I found out, in a small office fit for barely five people, Mama passed away.

I only grasped it when Chase repeated what the clerk repeated several times: "Grace Spencer, Autumn's mother, was pronounced dead in the home this morning."

The sentence tasted like silence.

The words went down like scorched soup scalding.

The shift absorbed all my blood energy to clamor for rebuttal.

Mere strangers heard my childhood and every fragment of it howl.

•

DAMIAN AND CHARLES SET DOWN a hot buffet early for us, before the general community dinner. The photographer understood. Chase would meet Mr. Johns in the morning for more interviewing and recording. My flight back to New York left right after that. Chase's would leave two mornings after mine. He charged my changes to his company American Express. They, too, understood. Mr. Johns heard. He wanted me to come to him, but I wasn't up to it.

I came so far and did not even see the wondrous land. Gone were the extra two days of pleasures we planned just for ourselves and social media friends: a local chocolate factory, the rum estate tour, the nature walk. All that remained was what Chase would never have left Grenada without: the twenty-five-minute ferry ride to the nearby archipelago and its fishing village where he was born, for a half day of garlic-laced fish, lobster, and lambie meals with his mother and other relatives he had not seen in two years.

The fact came up often between us now: I went to support him on his dream project, which gave him the side benefit of seeing his mother again after a few years away. His reunion with his mother led to me never saying good-bye to mine.

The other fact of the trip thorned our histories and possibly, if Summer discerned, our future.

Chase's room was above mine. A more humble one. Its construction was stunted by a padlocked storage closet that stored Mr. Johns's memories and papers until auctioneers took it all away to the highest bidder, most likely an American or British university after decades of not teaching his work. I wanted Chase to do what he felt he shouldn't: disturb me.

My brief call to Summer was productive. Gratefully, she was

the one in the States and so it was her burden to inform our relatives, who'd most certainly deliver maudlin performances in spite of their failures to visit. This task passed time I could not easily. So I walked up to a gold light stream from under Chase's door, carrying my tall glass of straight sweet rum in my hand. I was probably drunk. I heard cheerful voices from the room behind me. I whispered to him in between short, quick taps:

"Chase, it's me. Please open."

He did not answer for a moment. Then I heard his footsteps. He opened and we stared at each other. I had tried to moisturize my face and fix up my hair. I had not cried yet, so my eyes were not red, but maybe hooded. He let me in, hugged me close.

"Autumn, I am so sorry," he said. "I didn't think. I really didn't think . . ."

I did not talk. Not a sound, even when I dropped my glass and it broke. I let him hug me in the middle of the room until I—not him first but I—put our lips together. I held the back of his head until he kissed back. When we fell into bed I was on top, and I never answered when he asked me, "Are you sure?"

SUMMER HANDLED HER TASKS TO see Mama's body away and alert the family, then she washed her hands. I got off one plane just to board another one the next day, to fly with my mother's body back to Illinois alone. Summer's excuse for leaving me to my tasks?

"It's easier to look at the dead when they've been dead. And now we can tell them all to go to hell, for leaving us orphans another man had to take care of."

Summer never made efforts just to be polite. I didn't have time or mind to push her to be more grateful for all we'd had, even if it did not last as long as it could have. Nobody told us to go off and be so ambitious. Her discourtesy left me alone to negotiate the insurance matters and burial arrangements, done through Mr. Murphy's agency of course. He was still alive but in assisted living after a stroke. I busied on caskets, program orders, and flowers. I had obituary writing down pat.

I could not stay at the house on Trummel Lane. It sold, at a loss, vacated of anyone to nurse the piled-up renovations and repairs. Mama's sister Aunt Mae made room for me and funeral repast for family. When I could finally retreat to hang my black interview suit and veiled fascinator, to crash in my cousins' bunk bed, I understood the place where I was born no longer had a place for me in it.

EIGHT

One Hundred and Forty-Seventh Street was packed with many buildings like the five-story walk-up I looked for. Their units waited on new parquet floors, faux marble kitchen backsplashes, and doubled rents once the long-term tenants were evicted or dead. Across the street, boys scooted around concrete and banged a basketball against a netless hoop in a defunct school's yard. Apparent Rastas rolled fat blunts on the stoop, next to barbecue grills and foil pans on card tables alongside the building. Women sat in fold-up chairs next to the tables. Some glared at me, then went back to turning meat and picking bones. A CD player blasted dutty wine. Children danced. The men nodded at me as if I were a relative.

One month past his arrest, Jaylyn Stewart became an even bigger Black boogeyman. His dark face, dreadlocks, and arrest record replayed so often I barely had to look for them. I easily found an article that listed his seizure at a building address where I hoped to find his old door.

A month was long enough for any media stampede to have died down here. The small building crowd wasn't on guard. I always had the benefit to blend easily into Harlem, if not on that particular block but into the little city unto itself. I wore sunglasses

and a lime-green headwrap. I carried a faux Louis Vuitton tote
from Chinatown, standard, although I saw girls far younger than
me keep it official. The weather was broken. Uggs were now unnecessary. I slipped on sneakers. I hardly looked like a cop seeking
a Black boogeyman, or a reporter seeking a story, or a sister seeking her sister's kidnapper. Rapist. Maybe more.

I reached into my bag for a stack of FIND SUMMER SPENCER
flyers. I gave my best "How y'all doing?" in a country twang. The
accent got me further here than it ever could back home. After
slight acknowledgement and bare pleasantries, I got to the point.

"I just wanted to ask y'all a favor. I'm looking for someone,
and maybe one of you can help." I spared five flyers for the small
crowd.

A man took one of my notices. He blew smoke in my face, and
rubbed his bald crown framed by locks. He stated the obvious:
"Look kinda like you, ma."

The raucousness I found so charming in Harlemnites ensued,
to wash the moment of the solemnity I intended. But of course, it
could all seem like one big joke. I smiled.

"Yes, she's my twin sister. Some slight differences between us,
though."

"Well, now that we seen you, we know exactly what to be looking for," a senior lady theorized. She scratched at her scalp with a
cigarette in her hands, and out of practice she missed scraping her
bandana with the cherry. "Why you lookin' in Harlem?"

"We live here," I said. "Together. Well, until she disappeared
a few months past. I did the standard report. There's been some
investigating. But, not much."

They had the usual questions: "Word?" "Police ain't done shit?"
"Why we ain't heard nothin' bout this?" "You sure you know all
her people?" And they gave their own answers: "You know chick
gotta be rich in Harlem for these cops to care." "They'll wait till

she turn up dead 'fore we know anything about it." "You gotta watch who you let in yo house, ma."

"Summer Spencer," said the balding dready, whom I assumed to be the leader of the pack. "And you are?"

"Oh, forgive me for not introducing myself. I'm Autumn."

Their chuckles razed any legitimacy I had been going for. Not sure what to do, I simply laughed along. I must have gotten a contact high. The sun, the smoke, the walk, the strange faces, all the raspy and squealing fanfare. The block began to carousel around me, or I around it. I wasn't sure.

"We not laughing at you, miss," a younger boy said. "It's just, damn . . . yo."

A few more agreed with him. Yes, this was fucked-up.

"Well, bless your little heart, girlfriend," said Miss Cigarette. "And you know we will call. I see your number, right here. I'm gonna keep your flyer."

"Sit down," said one woman minding a pan of peas and rice. "Eat with us."

"No, no," I said. "Thank you. I'm trying to get a lot of flyers out today."

"You all by yourself?" asked Miss Cigarette, scowling. "Ain't nobody out here with you looking for her?"

"Yes," I said. "And, no. Well, some. But people lose hope, you know?"

I slipped away from their murmurs of reassurance and solidarity. I gathered I inspired a conversation on their hood from long ago, before I was here, when the girls and women and mothers and wives never came back home even then. As they involved themselves in urban legends and tall tales, I inched discreetly up the tall stoop with the flyers and Scotch tape. I had a presumed sincere purpose, but also motive. I waited for a person to exit. I didn't have to wait long. The entrance lock was broken.

Fortunately, Summer and I were resourceful enough to spare ourselves residency in buildings not yet squalid, but ominous nonetheless. This lobby led to a courtyard packed with dumpsters. Mustard-yellow lighting revealed an ornate ceiling and black-scuffed floor men worked hard to create. Desiccated vermin have an odor that wins over incense smoke every time. So does piss. Cornered plants had long died, leaving weak sticks and hard soil in dirty clay pots. My every shuffle echoed.

I could walk down two different hallways, and staircases at both their ends, if I turned right or left. First I crept into the middle of the lobby to look for mailboxes. They were on my right. I guessed Jalyn, like so many sons of unmarried mothers, would have kept his mother's last name: Stewart. And this could be some help in locating his apartment, if in fact he was living with his mother and not a girlfriend. I turned back to the mailboxes to see no names on them, only numbers. But I was in luck. The postman in these parts was not too efficient, perhaps mostly temps. And many boxes were broken. Residents simply piled incorrectly sorted mail on the ledge above the boxes. There was mounds of it.

Just as I grabbed some, a door in the left hall opened. I knew rapid change took place now. No one knew all their neighbors in the buildings anymore. I fiddled to find my keys in my bag's inside zip pocket. I pulled them out and fingered the tinier mailbox key for my brownstone. But I had no need to pretend. The tenant coming out was a graying middle-aged White man carrying a large string instrument, a bass or a cello, on a shoulder strap. He skipped out, spotted his gray cat slip into the hallway, chased it a few feet, and lightly nudged the animal in before dead-bolting his door. He never looked my way.

On a landing or two above me, a baby howled and a laugh track boomed. I ignored my beating heart and grabbed a lob of magazines, utility bills, collections notices, and junk mail. I flipped through it quickly, as dutty wine music pulsed in my ears and charred meat smells crept into my nose. I dropped my hips, maybe out of nervousness, and swayed a bit as the names fluttered by. No mail said "Stewart." I looked at the end of the ledge and saw a box from Citibank. I picked it up and it felt like checkbooks. But the name was Frankel.

I had no choice but to explore the floors, as the story had not listed an apartment number. My Nikes were soft on the limestone steps, spider-webbed and cracked, with dry-rotted blinds on each floor. The mustard-yellow lobby gave way to dull floors with brick-red doors and green tile. I wondered where a mother might plant herself with six children long-term. Corner apartments seemed most likely. They were usually bigger, wider, with more windows and at least an extra room or two. It seemed I was correct on the second floor. I heard the theme songs to *American Idol* and *Barney* playing at one time.

Someone once told me these buildings had "penthouses," full-floor apartments up top where celebrities or lucky owners' relatives lived, for Big Apple mini-mansions—six walking flights as part of the dues. But I never got that far in my search for where Jaylyn Stewart may have lived and a peek for signs of Summer inside.

The super, apparently Dominican, appeared out of nowhere on the fourth floor, carrying buckets and a handful of rags. I bumped into him as soon as I rounded the ledge, up a height that surely only residents or known visitors climbed. Even in my sneakers, I toppled backward. He tried to catch me but was too late.

He gained his balance as I lost mine, reached for me, and asked, "You okay, miss?"

But I rolled away from him, quickly surveying the floor to see what may have tumbled from my bag. I gathered my wallet, body spray, and keys.

He blocked my way to the steps, with his big shoulders and

wide arms appearing to open and swallow me. I pushed him off from trying to help me, or at least I hoped.

"You lost? Who you looking for?"

I tried to speak a lie that did not come as quickly as it should have. And he was coming closer. So, I blurted out the truth.

"I'm looking for where Jaylyn Stewart may have lived, because he's a rapist and a murderer and he's terrorized women here. And my sister might be one of them."

His name tag read SANCHEZ. Sanchez glared, turned green, and then red. Sanchez's shoulders seemed to look bigger, but his arms tightened into clasped hands as if he was praying. Then Sanchez came closer with each word: "You go. Jaylyn no live here no more. He gone! You people can't keep coming around here. I call police on you. Now. You go!"

"Don't hurt me!" I yelled. I circled around to find the nearest stairway. It was to my right. I prepared to tussle with Sanchez to reach it.

I heard Sanchez's buckets fall as I pushed past him and ran down four flights of stairs, through a lobby where the front door gave my only light, out into a line of happy, dancing children I toppled to the sidewalk, past the hollers of their people who guarded them, circling around and around for the direction of north, to home.

MY PHONE RANG FROM INSIDE my apartment. I raced in to it. Already, the mob was calling me. I would have to apologize to them, keep nice with all people who might see my sister out there one day. And, it was only right. Perhaps I was rude, and betrayed their trust.

But wait, I suddenly thought, *isn't it my cell number on the flyer?*

The phone was already in my hand and I had said hello. A few seconds into the call, I exhaled. It was not a vengeful Harlemnite. It was only a little better: a disgruntled client. She yanked me into a conversation I was getting too used to.

"I can give you an extra page, free of charge of course, to make up for my errors in your inventory links," I said, near breathless. "I really, really apologize. I'm so sorry."

Clara McIntyre custom-made personalized babywear by hand and sewing machine on Long Island. Her son was threatening to fire me as their web designer, newsletter manager, and blogger. I had not posted in weeks. Their search engine rankings had plummeted. Nearly every link for a customer to purchase a blanket, dress, short suit, or onesie was broken. Who knows how many customers abandoned their carts without bothering to email that they could not place their order? I skipped through my backed-up inbox as I consoled Clara. Her son hadn't minced words in his email: "Get this fixed or lose us as a client." He had sent it a month ago. I had missed it.

"I don't want an elaborate website," Clara said. "My customers are busy women. All I need is a homepage, my family's page, contact page, product gallery, and payment page. If people get lost trying to spend money, I don't have a business."

"I agree with you," I insisted. I found a napkin from takeout and used it to wipe my forehead and chest. I was dripping in sweat.

"What about a customer reviews or testimonial page?" I asked. "I can personally reach out to people on your mailing list and get that designed for you."

"People are gonna want something for taking time to leave a review," Clara said. "A discount or free gift. I'm barely getting by."

"No," I told her. "They're popular now. People love to leave them. Your customers can do it in a few seconds."

I worked with Clara for three years, cheaply, as I found plenty of stock photos of babies in sunny clothes and soft blankets. She was enough to keep me grocery shopping at Fairway and not Path-mark. She would send a few emails to promote sales, discounts, and personalized options; I flowered them up with sugary words current and potential customers could be sold on. Clara knew I was not from the city, and we had met face-to-face—a rare thing in today's online gig market. She sent me a heartfelt card for my mother, a standalone one, not from a rote pack kept on hand. I never told her about Summer's disappearance. I couldn't do it now. She reached the limits of her understanding. We ended the call nicely.

"Damn!" I yelled to no one. I now had two free jobs to do: one I had already done that I had to correct, and a conciliatory one I would not be paid for. I turned off my computer and turned on *Judge Judy*. If I was not careful, I would be a defendant soon. I had enough to linger on from Mama's life insurance policy. My free-lancing was down to a few small business owners. I needed corpo-rate accounts to pay me bigger money for my eagle eyes, writing, and marketing savvy. I must return to LinkedIn, cold calling, and networking at meet-ups.

I nearly jumped off the couch when I heard the bam, bam, bam on the door.

I was followed from Jaylyn's building. I ran too slowly, failed to look behind.

I nicked my shoulder on the corner of a bookcase on my way into the bathroom, to think of what to do. Hide in the shower? Then I softened my footsteps to tiptoe toward Summer's bedroom, as that room had more doors to hide behind.

But then I thought I heard Asha's voice: "Autumn? You home?"

I stepped softly to the keyhole, and she stood there. I opened up to a man I did not expect.

NINE

"He had your buzzer wrong. He kept buzzing me."

In a blue suit and black tie, Detective Montgomery stood in front of the peace sign sheet over our rooftop door, beside Asha.

"You missed our appointment," he informed me.

"I had an appointment today?" I asked.

"Yeah," he grinned. "We were supposed to check out We Go On together, remember?"

"If you don't want the appointment, I'll take it," Asha said. "Mr. Noel, I do awesome back and foot work. When's the last time you been to a chiropractor?"

"It's been some years," he answered.

"Good! Keep it that way. They mess you up for sure. What's your sign?"

"Aries."

"Oh, so you are prone to headaches and head colds. I can tell just by looking in your eyes you're missing out on a lot of cold foods."

"It's not summer yet, young lady."

"No, I mean you need foods with cold temperatures. They chill your body down when they burn off. Leafy greens, cucumber, melon if you can find it. You still need soup, but something tells me you're running hot."

"Asha, if you don't mind," I sighed.

"I'll bring you back up a flyer," she said on her way down.

I did not remember any plans with Detective Montgomery. I would check my calendar later. It seemed the courteous thing to do now was let him in.

"I really don't remember. I'm sorry."

I shut the door. He started to walk behind me, but I stopped him.

"Lemme get things together. Make sure no unmentionables are lying around."

"Certainly," he said, and retreated back to lean against the front door. "You don't seem like the kind to miss appointments. I wanted to come check on you."

"Thanks," I said from the indentation serving as our kitchen. It stank in there. Yep, I was this grimy now. Blinds closed. Garbage bag I failed to take out days ago. The swill was uneaten salads with rotting onion and broccoli, sticky Utz snack bags, pungent kale. A sink full of dishes soaked in gray water. Fluffed eggs in a bowl, the omelets I abandoned midthought. A melted pint of ice cream. Summer's sketchbooks, journals. Two bags of laundry I'd asked Chase to drop off for me.

"I can go," Detective Montgomery called out to me. "We can talk another time."

"No, no," I told him. "I appreciate you stopping by. Care for tea or coffee?"

"I've had too much tea today. Water would be fine."

"Ice?"

"Sure."

The tumblers scattered around, polluted with lipstick and juice pulp and dregs. I recovered a clean gym bottle, held it to the ice maker, filled it with water. I slid the bowl of old eggs into the fridge. It was spare: condiments, ancient almond milk, a cheddar-hard wedge of Brie, Jell-O cups, and takeout boxes.

"Just gimme a couple minutes," I called out. "A little over-loaded with work now. I couldn't get to cleaning yet."

"I'm in no hurry," I heard.

He stood patiently, alternated his gaze between the bedroom I used to sleep in and book titles on hallway shelves. I saw myself as a toddler, wobbly and bent, not knowing the next steps, reaching out to follow someone taller. Pride recommenced. I gathered Summer's things and my many papers to stack in a corner so Detective Montgomery could have a walking path to the couch without an impromptu Twister game. I did not have to go searching for a lighter to spark the scented candles we kept on the windowsill. One was right there. I twisted open the wood blinds, cracked two windows, washed my hands, and clutched Detective Montgomery's water.

"Sorry about that," I said. "You can come in now."

He took his time, processing the scene of Summer's intimate space. He fingered a rose quartz amulet I'd hung over the picture of me and Summer's tenth birthday in Hedgewood, when Mr. Murphy drove through a tornado warning to bat down our homebound disappointment with our very first surprise party. The gemstone matched the balloons I knew were pink in Summer's black-and-white creation.

"Summer gave me that necklace for Christmas," I said. "I opened gifts without her of course."

"Yes, I know," he told me. He wisped the amulet aside to see the picture better. "I guess this is your mother, grandmother, and Summer, or . . . ?"

"Mr. Murphy gave us a little party that year, and took that picture we kept all these years. He was like my stepfather. My father died when I was five."

The detective stepped inside further and took in even more, intrigued and dazzled.

"Well, I can tell people truly live well here. Nice place. Lot of character."

"Thanks. Summer was the great designer. She worked over there in the corner."

"Did she?"

"Yep," I said.

Montgomery strolled along my personal art festival. Yes, I had actually considered paying the vendor fee to sell off Summer's works at local street fairs. He stooped down to look closer at her small paintings of our old life and house, abstracts of what she alone saw, and portraits of imaginary people. I continued to talk.

"She was a night owl. By the time she hit her stride I was out for the count. But we got along well. She was fancier than me. I got by with simple things, a little luxury when I brought in enough business. Other than that, we fit pretty well. The standard bitchiness here and there, but normal. Women's hormones. The moon."

"Did she have any commissions, people who paid her a lot up front? Invoices . . . ?"

"If she did have new ones, she didn't tell me. When she first got here, she sold some things to new bistros popping up, an upscale hotel, a few hair salons. She was excited. I think she got undisciplined, just the fun of the Big Apple, and slowed down a lot. Shall we sit?"

I guided him to the couch. I went to the wicker chaise we covered with pillows Summer embroidered with patterns and lines. I saw my feet were dusty and my toenails chipped, sharply. Had I bitten them?

"Sorry I'm not dressed for company," I said.

"It's fine just to see you're okay. I like to go to my clients' houses sometimes."

"Your clients?"

"It's a more polite thing to say."

"I see. I like politeness, but I wish people would get more real with me."

"I'm all real. I tried to call first."

"I thought I heard call waiting earlier. I had an angry client on the line."

"Well, I'm sorry to hear that. On a better note, your neighbor's a nice young lady."

"Asha's a good friend," I said.

His brow wrinkled. "I asked her about your sister, what she thought about her disappearance. She clammed up, said she didn't know much about your sister."

"Apparently none of us knew much about my sister," I told him.

"Hard to believe Asha wouldn't know much about a neighbor she had for so long a time, or be part of searching for her."

"Everybody's lost steam on this. And, Asha probably only let you in because you're in a suit. Not that serial killers don't wear suits. And tax collectors, and sheriffs serving evictions for that matter. I think she's heard me mention you. It was only okay to let you in, not tell you our life stories. We look out for each other. She was there that night and I know she talked to police. She's just as in the dark about Summer as we all are."

"Did you get a chance to look through Summer's things more? I'm curious."

"A little at a time," I said. "It's hard for me to do. It's one thing to think of someone and see them in your mind. Like, not outside of myself. I don't want you to think I'm in here jumping at my own shadow or having hallucinations or anything."

"No, you mean in your mind's eye," he assured me. "I got you. May I see some of her journals?"

I walked to choose a spiral notebook and bound journal, both with less pages filled, perhaps faster lanes to a destination. These were pretty ones Mama made nice jackets for: good cloth and fabric from her clothes she just started to shrink inside. Montgomery skimmed as I talked. I related to Summer's handwriting like my own. Montgomery frowned through much of it.

"You're welcome to take them if you think it will help," I said.

"Sure," he said. "I think it would help. Like looking around where she lived does."

Other than her bedroom and its consoling atmosphere of her, I kept Summer's life and things here preserved and intact, my newly disoriented messiness aside.

"It's hard to let pieces of her leave out of here. They're all I have. And the words people leave behind are themselves outside of your mind. It's who they really are in their own minds. I think people deserve that respect."

"And, you feel like you're violating your sister if we look through her stuff for whatever you can find, to help figure out where she is?"

"It's not the only violation I'm giving her, Detective Montgomery."

Asha picked up on Chase still coming by. Fran caught him rush away a few mornings as she shoveled the snow or Swiffered the hallways. He told me later. It was civil. I'm sure they'd just thought he was checking in on Summer's sister, not sleeping with her. Belinda was the only one who perhaps knew more, given her veiled warnings about noise. Had she heard me calling his name? Or just put two and two together? I needed to be upfront with someone about all the links in the chain, for Summer's sake. I took the risk of turning my most fervent ally off.

"Detective Montgomery, I'm sleeping with Summer's old boyfriend," I said.

If a secret is in the open with just one other mind besides the one keeping it, then it is no longer a secret. It is a fact.

"I still don't think she would up and leave everything and everyone without a word," I continued. "But I've thought maybe she sensed he and I slept together once, when they were still kinda sort of a couple. The best-case scenario is she's punishing us."

"Wow," Detective Montgomery said. "Was it the fellow who picked you up when we met?"

"Maybe I don't remember. She kind of put him off when Mama was dying. I don't know. I guess nerves. So, I went away with him on a trip abroad he invited her to, and well . . ."

"You sure he didn't tell her about it? I mean, that could explain a runaway case. She's an adult, and so it's legal to run away."

At this point I had to surrender to trust and hear him out. At least he had a reason beyond indifference and apathy to suspect she could estrange so abruptly.

"Chase never told her. He couldn't. Neither could I. If she knew, she sensed it."

Montgomery looked more off-kilter and uncomposed than he ever had, blindsided.

"Well, Autumn," he said, "hey, you kids are grown. People come together in odd ways. And, they leave each other in even more odd ways."

"Would you like some more water?" I asked.

"Sure."

Okay. So now I seemed phony and maybe only guilt-tripped for a distraction from my own moral injustice. He would probably never see me again after this.

"I've always had attachment issues to men anyway," I told him. "I had boyfriends in college, my twenties, sure. But nothing stuck. When Mama moved out here and she needed so much time and so much care, I stopped seeing men altogether. Chase was just a man I knew already. And he knew me, like a sister I was. He has no family here. He's lonely, too. I trust him."

"You don't have to explain yourself to me. I'm no saint," he admitted. "I just don't think it's wise to rely on him alone at a time like this, if he's more engaged in being with you than finding her."

"He was engaged," I insisted. "So was my neighbor. And our landlords. They did not grow up with her, from just a baby, like I did. It's easier for them to accept her absence. I can't. I need Chase. This independence shit is getting old. It's scary. Maybe I just want a man to be the big man. Like old times. I'll stay home to have some kids, you know?"

"Most women want to settle down eventually," Detective Montgomery said. "I have a daughter. She's in school."

"Oh, what's she studying?" I asked.

"Prelaw. Wasn't no way I was gonna let her get into law enforcement like she wanted to. I survived it myself, by miracle. I was a good street cop for over ten years. Like men in my family. Best job in town, we thought. And we all grayed earlier than the rest in my family for it. I went to night school at Medgar Evers, to move on."

"You do a lot of good. So did my father. He was a fireman. Wasn't many fires to put out in Hedgewood. He was safer at work than play. Daughters like brave daddies."

Detective Montgomery leaned back. Maybe he saw some of me in the women he loved, as he reminded me of men who had loved and protected me in my girlhood.

"I talk to her," he continued. "I'm all for women working and having careers."

"Women cops have one benefit," I said.

"What's that?"

"If a woman walks around with a gun and badge, she won't get called 'Hey baby' or thrown in a killer's van. I should've gone to the police academy just for that benefit."

"True," he laughed. "Yeah, I see 'em every single day. It's like catcalling is their job. I feel sorry for you women nowadays. Disrespect is an epidemic."

I had already told him my secret, my sin so pleasurable and good I did not feel guilty enough about it until I thought about telling it to someone. It felt just right to have that man in bed with me, sharing my heartache and softening my hesitance to sleep. I was tired of having to refrain from my joy. I decided to share more.

"Summer had some past bad experiences," I began. "With men. She told me. Some of it seemed clear in her drawings, sketches, about it. I can show you, maybe later."

"You don't have to now," he said. "Do so at your own pace. Or maybe with that group I told you about, if you've thought about going."

"Look, all that AA stuff and confessional parading isn't for me."

"It's only a suggestion. You deal with things how you want to."

I repeated what had become my mantra: "I'm doing fine. No matter what's wrong with our situation, Chase is here for me. He does a lot. He's bringing me groceries later on today. It's been a cold winter, Detective Montgomery, you know?"

Montgomery nodded. He flipped out printouts I forgot I folded into the journal.

"You must have put these here," he said. "They seem important. And your stepfather was in the NAACP, I see. Good for you."

He passed me the papers. I shuffled its chaos I knew well: Hedgewood Sentinel features on the big fish Cole Murphy, Mama's life insurance disbursement paperwork, and several *Daily News* crime sections I ripped straight from the paper.

"Yeah, he had a high-class reputation," I said, "unlike this Jaylyn Stewart."

I needed to hold the detective as long as I could. He certainly had to leave, at some point. It must be discipline that turned off obsession with cases. When he did leave, I would face a drumroll of footsteps up our stairs, an angry mob come to avenge my earlier stalking. The same flyers I wanted people to use to find Summer could also be used to find me.

"What does law enforcement think of this boy beyond what they say to the press?" I asked. "How many more like him don't we know about?"

"Police can never say everything they know to the press," Montgomery confirmed. "If they do, the public gets facts guilty parties can plan lies and cover-ups about in advance."

"He's confessed to all of it," I said. "He's gonna get the book thrown at him. What difference will it make if he had any more, and he doesn't confess to them?"

"Any more what?"

"Well, more women he may have killed."

"Autumn, the good news is this guy is off the street and you don't have to worry about him."

"So, you don't follow?" I peered at Montgomery. I certainly appreciated his concern and efforts. I knew it was genuine. But I could not let it blind his true accountabilities to me. "I'd be interested to know where he was the night Summer disappeared," I said.

"Hmmm, so would I," Montgomery agreed. "The most heartbreaking part of the job is when these tragedies happen to people, and you walk through a sea of faces every day with no clue who's responsible for bringing this darkness into our lives."

The metal bell clanged. This time I knew it was Asha, returning in hopes of a new customer.

"I know you have to go," I told him. "I appreciate you coming by, and listening."

Asha knocked.

"Okay, Asha!" I yelled. We both stood up, but he turned back.

"Got any plans for Easter?" he asked me.

A Hedgewood trip was probably due, but out of the question. It was too soon.

"No," I admitted. "I need to catch up on work."

"My wife's cooking dinner, and you're welcome," he said. "We're in the Graham Court. Should be ready for company in the early afternoon. And maybe I'll have read these diaries by then and thought of something new. You have my cell."

"Oh, thank you," I smiled. "If I get enough done. What could it hurt?"

Outside the door, Asha campaigned with her shining eyes. She passed my oddly established gumshoe friend a flyer for Sugar Hill Holistic Care by Asha Goddess: NUTRITION, YOGA, REIKI, AND PSYCHIC FILTRATION. COLON CLEANSES COMING SOON . . .

Spring

TEN

At the apartment's threshold lies the frontline of our inner-to-outer lives: flip-flops to dash out in a hurry, then kick off once back inside. Open toed season arrived, yet I resisted slipping on Summer's many fun-colored and neutral pairs. Their soles curved upward in precise facsimile to her feet. Upon closer look each of her toes made its mark still. Their arches sank in perfect proportion to her feet, slightly smaller than mine—as was her waist—ever since we filled out to grown women. Her heels had ground a small bowl in back of each shoe. They appeared desperate to be worn again, waiting by the door in fidelity, like loyal pets, shaped in time to their owner's still-missing person.

By mid-April, I relocated the unsightly pile and dangerous obstruction of gray-speckled snow shoes from the entrance to underneath the bed I never slept in anymore. The flip-flops stayed put.

Noon news reminded when Good Friday came. Chase was gone to Connecticut for a coworker's family tradition. I first remembered only he was not there, not why he wasn't. I tidied up my inbox, sent a few nice responses to feign actual work, and enjoyed a weird movie vortex on Netflix. I was waiting for eight o'clock. Any nuns not at church or the terminally ill's bedside would be eating and prepping for early bedtimes. The convent's answering machine clicked on the one telephone in the whole house, in its living room. I had no message in mind.

Greetings and God bless you. No one is here at Saint Mary's Home of Holy Work to take your call. Please leave us a message and—"Allo? Allo?"

"Hi," I said. "I'd like to speak with Penny."

"Who? Allo?"

"Penny!" I yelled.

"Penny, yes. I think she still at church now. For evening Mass."

Of course. It was Good Friday, second only to Ash Wednesday in nights a Catholic chapel's lights stayed on as long as they did at Baptist Bible studies.

"I no see her today. Leave a message?"

Penny is not Mama. She just isn't. She only helped us care for her, at the end. You gotta be a big girl now.

"No," I told the woman. "I'll just call her back later."

Where we were from, and wherever we went, Easter was and always would be everybody's pageant. Wherever I stood on belief in God in any given year (it fluctuated), nothing canceled Easter. To folks like us, the tall tale of a beaten-down man rising from the dead and defying a monstrous tomb was more relevant than an angel's birth. The preachers finally had the full house eluding them the rest of the year. Old faces were behind the front door. Graves found an audience. Right after Christmas, talk turned to Easter: dresses, speeches, hats, purses, scoring hams, baking cakes, and assembling baskets.

Mama's girls weren't going to carry store-bought straw. I still had a few of the baskets she had given me and Summer. She dazzled us with manipulated clay, yarn, wood, and even dried cornhusk baskets once. Back then their contents were boiled eggs, jelly beans, and homemade fudge. Now they held my office supplies, broken jewelry, pens, and junk drawer things.

I stared blankly at a flowerpot Mama had hand-painted with little bunnies and ducks. I had stored computer cleaning stuff in it for years. I swiped it off my desk and stomped on the shattered, sharp result.

"How could you do this to me?" I screamed.

I had no incentive not to cry so loud and become so disheveled. I curled into a ball against the kitchen island.

Montgomery's was not my only invitation. Penny had invited me to the West Side four-story brick convent, where she lived with the other nuns. They all worked: as church administrators, preschool teachers, or nurses like Penny. They wore tennis shoes, jeans, and trendy tops and skirts most times I saw them. I heard they held customary habit and dress for Mass. Summer and I once joined them for dinner, on a long wood table with manor candlesticks, large bowls set buffet-style, no meat and no talk of fashion or the latest man debacles. By sundown the dining room was again a neat place and the kitchen back to its spotless urban-rustic vibe. Penny used to stop by to hold hands with us, read verses from Psalms and Matthew, and pray before she left. I always insisted I was a believer, despite what contradicted it.

"You're always baptized, for the rest of your life," Penny reminded us.

Thank God.

EASTER SUNDAY SEEMED A DAY for a long walk. My goal was Central Park—about fifty blocks. I'd done it before, when New York was still new enough to give me tingles and wonder. Now it was an old friend. Intimacy speeds things up. I opened my door to a purple peace sign on a hazel-colored sheet and headed down.

"Hi, miss. You look pretty today."

Belinda's teenaged son leaned against the wall in our stairwell, just waking up. How grateful I was to grow up in the spacious heartland, with copious options for the grumpy privacy that finding myself demanded. His hair finally inched into fuller cornrows. He was transitioning from awkward to beautiful. I imagined the stability our quiet, uncrowded brownstone life provided could thwart his transition to a kind of man who leaked his future into a vat full of errors.

"You're getting to be handsome yourself," I said. "Tell your mother I said hello."

He opened his eyes wider, stretched like it was his first morning in years, and patted at his disheveled clothes as he stood to get on his way.

"Glad you been cool since everything went down. My moms was scared."

His voice had a depth it had not before, whether from maturity or seriousness I was unsure. His caring smile disarmed me. I never considered the role Summer played for him and his family, how much longer she knew them, and how much more she engaged them. I hardly could remember the children's names or tell them apart. I confronted myself. I knew I could have stigmatized the one who stood before me as a threat if I did not know him.

I went down to check the mailbox, gambling on a real holiday to guilt Summer into sending me a card or note to say she was okay, or clue me in to where she may not be okay. I slid my fingers through an empty, cold tunnel and closed the box. I moved on to browse for energy food at the bodega. I resigned to a cup of black coffee and bottle of water. One of the bodega cats, a short Russian blue, came from its water bowl and through my legs for the first time ever. I let it twist around my calves.

"Life ain't so bad, sweetie, now is it?"

I set $2 on the counter and picked up a *New York Daily News*. I knew I could flip through without paying, as I often did, the benefit of many years on one block and not knowing the owners' language but them knowing my face. I saw half a page on Jaylyn Stewart. So I put another dollar and quarter on the counter.

The story careened my walk and sank me into my familiar emotional oubliette, where I was not safe, no one cared about my Black female life, and unimaginable things happened to my sister.

New evidence has challenged murder charges against Jaylyn Stewart, 26, who confessed to raping and stabbing DeJanay Little, 16, and Shanice Johnson, 42.

Little was a student at the Bayard Rustin Educational Complex. Johnson was a secretary at a Westchester real estate firm. Their bodies were discovered in Harlem last fall.

A condominium board turned over its outdoor surveillance video appearing to show Little, who lived nearby, getting into an SUV with an unidentified man on the night she disappeared. The man in the video appears much taller and larger than Stewart. The video's quality is too poor to identify a license plate number.

Bite marks found on Johnson do not appear to match Stewart's teeth impressions.

Today, Stewart's attorneys released a statement calling his prior confession to the murders "forced" and "an unfortunate outcome of New York City Police Department abuse tactics."

Police last month arrested Stewart for an unrelated charge and made a preliminary match of Stewart's DNA to evidence taken from the victims. The bodies of Little and Johnson were found in uptown dumpsters just blocks apart.

"We have maintained Jaylyn's innocence from the moment he was arrested and hopefully this new information will push the District Attorney's Office to end prosecution of this innocent man so he can move on with his life," said the family's attorneys, Reardanz and Lowell, in the statement.

Stewart has previously served time as a juvenile and an adult in Lincoln Correctional Facility in Manhattan and Washington Correctional Facility in Comstock for drug dealing and attempted robbery offenses.

"All this is definitely a disappointment," said Johnson's daughter Latisha, 19, a sophomore at Hunter College. "At first nobody was even doing anything about my mom's death, and now they can't get what they're doing right."

Little's mother, Bernice Little, 37, believes Stewart is the right suspect.

"It's probably gang-related," she says. "It's part of their initiation. They have to kill innocent people. Rob folks, rape. Everybody think Harlem changed. It didn't, especially not for women."

Stewart remains held on $1 million bail.

I had no rights to the disappointment Shanice Johnson's daughter expressed. All we had in common is we both lost our mothers. But a real suspect with a name and face gave me the most comfort I'd had about Summer since she disappeared. I was sad for myself. For I was just as poisoned as White women who crossed the street when Jaylyn Stewarts approached or White men who lynched them with no trials in the past. When I imagined who could have hurt Summer, it never occurred to me to imagine anything but a Black man. He was convenient, the distraction from so much more to be scared of in this world. Even I believed in the Black boogeyman I had been told all my life was near, waiting for us at corners and alleys and rooftops.

•

THE GRAHAM COURT WAS LIKE a tall sandcastle moated by the makeshift African village on 116th and 117th Streets, where a few little restaurants addicted me to fried whole red snapper with oto. There, French-speaking Black women I could never find twice micro-braided my hair when I wanted length without chemicals or scalp scorching. I draped a cream pea coat over a pink sweater dress paired with beige boots, because it was Easter Sunday. I added a scarf, my signature back when I lived among regulars I spent more than a moment with. It was a bargain to go to Detective Montgomery's. I could curry favor to spark him into helping me get past this latest catch-22: Boogeymen certainly existed but I may have to look elsewhere, plus beg forgiveness, for thinking Jaylyn Stewart should burn in hell. Whether he was a killer or not, I had scarier questions carried into a whole new season now.

How come Summer wouldn't think of me and how I must feel, and try to get in touch just to ease my mind, if she ran away in sadness after Mama died? Could she be that cold? Perhaps. I never thought I could be so cold as to enjoy a man she had first.

How come Gregory, Fran, and Asha acted like no one vanished from our midst? When did being polite become being insensitive to another person's reality?

How could any woman's body be an acceptable erasure from the world, brushed off as her doing or her wish, but the news treated only prominent or rich women and girls like victims to look for?

I put those questions aside under the entrance's arch. The courtyard's silence stood apart from city racket. The arcade behind the first set of bars waited like a cage, the hoary guard's chamber empty. Through the wrought-iron gate I spotted a baby-blue Easter egg rolled to the oval sidewalk at the edge of the soon-to-be garden.

A breeze fluttered neat bushes. The court's four pavilions seemed protective and stately. I had not called or confirmed, so had no one ready to meet me or give me instructions to the inside. I pulled out my cell phone and dialed Detective Montgomery's number.

"Autumn," I said. "It's Autumn Spencer."

"Oh, goodness."

I could not turn back now. He sounded too boisterously pleased. The buzzer static droned while I let myself through two gates into the courtyard. There, I saw a carousel of open first-floor windows. I turned away from them and up to sky in the open courtyard, a simple circular nest of a private yard Mama would have enjoyed. The eight floors of nearly a hundred apartments was a neighborhood unto itself, like we had back in a carefully wound enclave in Hedgewood.

I paced the circular pavement to thwart talking to myself. Humming took care of it. The door to one of the complex's rotundas opened on my left, and Detective Montgomery appeared. He looked like an entirely different type of man in his blue jeans, red hooded sweatshirt, and baseball cap—kind of thuggish in a middle-aged cornball way.

"Well, hi there," he said. "Glad you made it."

I held out my hand and he hugged me instead.

"I really shouldn't be here," was my greeting. "I have so much to do . . ."

My words echoed in the chunky foyer as we went to the cage elevator.

"There's no rules here," he said. "Stay as long or short as you want."

"Just know it's my work and not my manners when I eat and run, Detective Montgomery."

"Please, call me Noel."

Happening upon these elevators was a rare city delight as

stirring as good restaurant service or a better slice of street pizza. The ascent fluttered my stomach the way I imagined Charlie's did during his adventure in *Willy Wonka & the Chocolate Factory.*

"I've never been in this building," I said at the fourth floor. We were going to the top. "It's a landmark I hear."

"My wife's family grew up in here. There's been some hiccups over the years, but things are quieter now."

"Good."

We stepped into a circular hallway shared with a few other homes, one door open enough for me to have cased in. A few little brown girls, in pastel tutu garb, wobbled and jiggled in a circle they made for a room full of well-dressed adults who paid them or the open door no mind. The gospel music contradicted the champagne a butler poured. Guests challenged his balancing act of the bottle and silver serving tray. Inside Montgomery's place, his landing was rimmed by an ancient telephone secretary, coat rack, winter boot and summer sandal cubbies, tennis rackets, golf clubs, and large studio photograph of a neat family of four—parents, boy, and girl. To the side was a narrow kitchen slot still wide enough to hold a table. Directly behind it was a dining room garnished in flowers: curtains, upholstery, rugs, framed prints, and bouquets in several vases. Clear vases of Easter lilies and baby's breath centered the table setting.

Three women in the kitchen did not risk losing a heavy pan, train of thought, or the right spice to do more than say "Hi." A chocolate face was the same one framed in a picture on Detective Montgomery's desk. In an adjacent living room an elaborate entertainment center caught my eye—with a movie screen and surround sound. An aquarium sat on a fortified stand. Its golden and tropical fish drifted under a pink-tinged light. Detective Montgomery took my coat and latched it onto a twig on the rack. His hand on my back pushed me inside the kitchen.

"This is Autumn Spencer," he told the three, no resemblance between them but a profound fondness shared among people who can whisper in each other's ears or drink from the same glass. He pointed out Mrs. Montgomery, her friend Sybil, and a neighbor Thandiwe. I offered to help. "Oh, no, no, no," "You're a guest," "Sit down," "Make yourself comfortable," "Food'll be ready soon," and "Have a mimosa."

"Jesus would be hungry now, especially after three days," Montgomery teased.

"You want it quick or you want it good?" the neighbor asked him. She fished the tip of her bleached-gold dreadlocks out of a high boiling pot.

"It works either way for him," Mrs. Montgomery told her. "I've been married to the man for almost thirty years, so I know."

She handed me a mimosa.

"I'm gonna pretend I didn't hear that, Noel," Sybil said.

"We all will. Lemme introduce our guest to the sane people around here."

"Sane people can't cook like this, honey . . ."

I was relieved to be there. I felt silly about my prediction of what a policeman's home would look like—doused in out-dated furniture, pistol set at the door, thrift store prints of lakes and mountains on the wall, and a mounted deer head in there somewhere.

"Your home is really nice," I told him.

"Thanks, like yours," he told me. "Has your day been good so far?"

"Well, I didn't get much sleep," I confessed. "I would've gone to church. But it was a long night. I wasn't gonna let that ruin the day."

"Always a new day."

"And yours? Church?"

"If I'm lucky enough to get Easter off, I won't be waking up early for church," Detective Montgomery grinned. He seemed a regular person now, outside the station.

We passed a cologned toilet room. Mrs. Montgomery or another "sane" person had adorned it with real plants, bowls of potpourri, thick maroon and taupe towels, a heavy fan rug trimmed in hieroglyphics, and more smooth affirmation stones like Detective Montgomery put on his desk.

Five people holed inside the family room, and there we stopped before a deep hallway for the private spaces. Three women and two men sat on cream couches and chairs watching a basketball game. A teen girl held a bottle to a baby's mouth. I had not thought about how Detective Montgomery would present me: a victim, a suspect, a nuisance, a "client"?

He was diplomatic.

"This is one of our Harlem neighbors, Autumn Spencer," he told the group, and the women smiled while the men struggled to take their eyes off a full-court press to glance and wave at me. "She's up on Sugar Hill."

I spoke hello to all as Detective Montgomery rounded out the names and associations: his daughter, Celeste; her boyfriend, Marcus; his nephew Shane and Shane's wife, Monica; and Shila, Shane and Monica's daughter, and her baby boy, Christopher, three months.

We watched basketball until Thandiwe rang a real silver dinner bell to call us. There were enough trays, serving basins, and warmers on the dining table for lunchtime at my old Catholic school, leaving hardly enough room for the dinnerware itself. Mrs. Montgomery saw me staring and explained: "Oh, we aren't this gluttonous. People gonna come by here all day and night. This is still Harlem, honey."

The deal became the men would stick around long enough for prayer before they made plates, to finish Easter dinner in front of a basketball game. The women shamed them for this. We bowed our heads and Detective Montgomery said grace: "Dear God, thank you for allowing us to live to another Easter. Thank you for family and new friends. We pray for the safety of those not with us, our passed-on loved ones and Noel Jr., who is unable to be here with us today. Watch over him, Dear Father. Hold him close. Bless this food and the hands that made it. Amen."

I hardly knew where to begin, so I started nearest to me: on cheese grits with shrimp, peas and rice, cranberry sauce, rice pudding, broccoli salad, and sausage links. I wanted to sample everything, including braised chickens Thandiwe informed me were slaughtered that morning at a selling coop on Amsterdam Avenue. The conversation was light and unimportant: mostly complaints about work, long church services, and delays in building improvements. Mrs. Montgomery was a doctor at a Bronx clinic. Her besties were teachers. Monica worked at MTA headquarters and Celeste was studying law, as her father had told me. I was the oddball, accustomed to the fuller job description and convoluted explanation of my professions: freelance entrepreneur, marketing and media expert, language artist, ghostwriter, ghostblogger. I left the two-steps-from-dire-straits part out.

Evidently, Noel did more than ponder who followed Harlem women up to roofs and pushed them into cars and locked them in basements. He tuck-pointed where management did not, buried his tropical fish in shallow courtyard graves, accepted Marcus's work around the home in exchange for his promised loan repayments, and gave Shila rides upstate to visit her boyfriend, serving time for an unmentioned offense.

As promised, Detective Montgomery huffed away from the game to retrieve other people who breezed in on what I gathered was an uptown tour to fill tote bags with plates covered in aluminum foil. The visitors ranged from the kente cloth–clad young

woman whose powerful afro belied her silence, to a sweaty al-
coholic holding a paper bag as he avoided food and filled up on
mimosas. A female bus driver appeared with three teenagers, just
long enough to pack their Easter dinner in Tupperware. They were
all "neighbors" as well. It was quite an assortment of familiars,
strikingly random, like a carnival of dejection. But everyone who
settled in for a while loved the Montgomerys. The game ended and
the men re-joined us. The women won a vote as to which bootleg
DVDs to start a marathon on.

Mrs. Montgomery hugged me good-bye, seeming sincere, glad
to know me, I was a sweetheart and I should come back again for
the Fourth of July.

Detective Montgomery and his nephew Shane walked me
downstairs. Shane flipped out two cigarettes from a Newport box
the moment he shut the cage to the elevator.

"I didn't know you smoked," I told Detective Montgomery.

"Used to, like a chimney," he said.

"How can you chase down bad guys all day with smoky lungs?"

Shane laughed. "Oh, so you told her 'bout our penchant for
cops? Fam almost recruited me into it. No, not me."

"She knows all about it," Detective Montgomery said. "I'll concentrate on getting you a car now. Unless you do that new Uber
thing."

"Oh, no." I shook my head. "I mean, yes, I do. But I'm not sure
if my bank balance needs to do it now."

"This Harlem, sweetheart," Shane said. "You're a pretty
woman."

"Even if she wasn't. Makes no difference."

"This is Harlem," they said in unison.

How nice it was that none of them mentioned it, for surely
Noel whispered around that I was his hopeless and lonely "client"
missing her twin sister. And this is why they were so wise, even

when I wasn't. Thirty-two blocks at night was a different stroll from thirty-two blocks in the afternoon. The gypsy cabs rolled easily from a depot near one of its largest buildings. Montgomery told me to get home safe, and he waved until the cab broke through the next traffic light and turned to take me home.

ELEVEN

I was satisfied. I finally sculpted what I felt was a powerful, eye-catching, and still succinct description for Summer's "Circumstances," ready for the moment the state criminal justice division notified me she would finally be publicized through the Missing Persons Clearinghouse. I huddled on the fire escape and read aloud from my tablet: "Summer is a missing vulnerable adult who may have depression or require medical attention. She was last seen on December 19th or 20th in her brownstone apartment in Harlem. She accessed the building's roof with no trace to indicate she returned inside. Summer changes her appearance frequently. She is originally from Hedgewood, Illinois."

The corner of our living room stood out of its shadows under the streetlights, a mausoleum of unfinished inspiration. I needed to pack up Summer's artwork, books, and things. Her creations sank into the wall like part of the construction. Save for an exposed brick wall where we'd been promised a phony fireplace, my home was Summer's shrine, a place to wait rather than live. This couldn't go on. The most humane, and fair, solution was to give her belongings to our relatives in Illinois at Christmas. Maybe by then they would be ready to bring up Summer. Our relatives never left Hedgewood, not even for Chicago. And, they thought Mama and her girls were so weird for living out in the country over in town. So, two girls living without husbands in New York City—just a movie set for them—was weirder. They never saw us anyway, well before Mama died, so Summer was not a concern for them.

I guessed they would care when she turned up in a dumpster.

FINALLY, SPRING BECAME WARM ENOUGH to keep me from shivering on the fire escape. Chase and I enjoyed the breeze in front of the open windows. We devoured Chinese food off a rolling desk, his Chromebook in his lap and my tablet in my hands. At first we spent our days and nights talking about Summer, until we didn't. It was easier for him to zone off into trending topics, ROIs, and target markets as I ramped up the call-to-action subliminal messaging in a client's latest blog. But finishing Summer's "Circumstances" had pricked me with the need.

"I think I should put all this homemade art away," I told Chase. "Get it out of sight, out of mind now."

Chop suey twisted in my mouth while I talked. It was my special request of him that night, the most greens I had in weeks.

"Why would you do that?" he asked.

"Well, I can start buying real work," I told him. "I'll need room for it."

Then, thinking of how much he'd just paid for our dinner, "When I start to make real money again, of course."

He went to the counter for second helpings.

"I think it's all good for you," he said. "It's inspiring. She really was good. She could've made it to higher planes had she wanted to. I think she was scared, of all the rejection on the way."

"That's what makes it so sad to keep around," I sighed. "Stunted potential. Nobody but the people who really cared about her will ever know how good she was."

"I think it's almost like having her here still," Chase smiled.

"Something to pass down. Save your money, hon. You won't regret it."

We ate and worked in silence, then went to bed together. I had just received a new box of little nothings from an online sale. But he was asleep in minutes. I stayed up replaying how he thought of Summer's art as "having her here still." It could be how he thought of me.

Chase hadn't fled or stopped coming by. Just scooted back from the table a bit. He gave me the sense I was an obligation more than an anticipation. He brooded over long hours and a new "diet." They required him to stay at the gym longer than I liked to wait to see him at night. His explanation was valid: wanting to look good for summer, no pun intended, I'm sure. Indeed, he hardly noticed he said the word. So, he had become insensitive as well. It was enough to make me think guilt was setting into him more than he'd thought it would. I prepared myself for the day one of us got a conscience. Thankfully, he had to do so much social media for work he forgot about it in real life, so I was not constantly streaming around the internet with him. The break would be clean.

OVER A LENGTHY CHAT THREAD, my college buddy Cathy convinced me into a playdate with her five-year-old and newborn—never mind I had no children to bring along to play, too. I had not seen her in over a year. She flew out for Mama's funeral last February and invited me to stay awhile with her that March. I was running late, so the newest bundle of joy had to settle for a gift of uptown dollar-store fare: generic baby lotion that did not smell too off, a pack of Pampers, the surprise of "organic" baby wipes, onesies.

Cathy sat on the steps of the Union Square terminal doing what she was doing the last time I saw her: yelling at her first child to put his shirt back on and stop running so fast. A gray fabric baby carrier was strapped tight against her chest. Her hair was tied in long twists she bundled atop her head. She wore a wrap-around skirt with totem poles stitched down the side where it cinched. The tie was now unknotted. She held her skirt up by hand.

"Your skirt . . ." I told her. I grabbed up its edge just as it almost came loose.

"It's totally okay," she said as she kissed my cheek and hugged me at my neck. "I've had two kids pull my boobs out and tear off my clothes all the time. All my modesty left a long time ago. Here. Take her."

Inside the tight fabric was a delightfully creamy face. Raven eyes and wheat-colored curls marked that Cathy's mother was a by-product of a Brit's discovery of Japanese women during military service. Her father was Nigerian. Her Baby Daddy was Haitian—not in the country now, but on his obligatory expatriate term of a few years after marrying an American, to assume legitimacy. With the first kid, Cathy was fine with a "spiritual ceremony." After a second, she demanded he get a real job—not selling weed. The four-month-old was a jumbo water balloon in my arms, not even as heavy as a bag of potatoes. I knew her name was Sara, and may have been able to pick her out of a crowd due to all the photos Cathy sent over email.

"I'm gonna go ahead and proceed with getting my tubes tied now," I told Cathy. "I'll just take this one and be on my merry way."

"No," Cathy said. "Take *him*."

Her oldest had joined a gang of anonymous playdaters about his age in a game of chase for a Nerf ball. I indulged myself in a compulsion I found calming in spite of its grueling reason. I scanned the crowd of pretty mothers sporting activewear and bags under their eyes for a soft and hopeful face like Summer's. I concocted a nonviolent story in my head: Prince Charming is a rich widower, he makes the best hot chocolate ever (with marshmallows), and romances Summer to sip it on our roof, they speed off in a limo and he proposes to the new mother of his sad children. And the limo crashes before the proposal. Survival, but amnesia. So, Summer forgets to tell him about her family and her life and me. She is slowly remembering.

"Autumn!" Cathy yelled. "Don't believe anyone who tells you having a newborn is stressful. If they've said that, then they've never had a kindergartener."

She marched off yelling, "Oscar, get over here, kindergartener!"

I was glad I came. It is restorative to see faces you've known for fifteen years. Cathy's plans to be a doctor, via a Romance languages concentration, did not materialize to much beyond tour-guiding Manhattan and teaching English in Liberia, where the natives spoke French like she did. But Cathy was lucky. She was an only child of a tenured Pratt professor father and an older mother who almost gave up after many miscarriages. They disapproved of her choices but still bought her a two-bedroom co-op in Park Slope. Her son had gone to private preschool and was now in private school. The sandy-colored boy called me Auntie Autumn. I reached in the cheap gold gift bag.

"I didn't forget . . ." I told him.

I pulled out a box of Sour Patch Kids, his favorite. I could always bring candy to playfully spite the mothers of my growing number of "nieces" and "nephews." He screamed "Yes!" and started to tear open the box. Cathy confiscated it.

"You will not have one Sour Patch Kid until you eat lunch. Stop that crying and tell Auntie Autumn 'Thank you.'"

We waited for the time it took Cathy to grab the newborn and stuff her back into her warm felt nest. Oscar stood in silent protest.

Cathy and I used to spend more frequent days together lolling through sidewalk traffic in Union Square or Fort Greene with her disinterested son giving us pause to catch up with him, or for him to catch up with us. We drifted through block after block in a couple of hours, talking about where we should go and what we should do next and if we were hungry and what we had a taste for, until it was dark and time to go home. We wandered to subjects her background made important to her, while I could not have cared less for them than the price of all the corn in Illinois. My worldview was limited to a $20 auto-pay to Children International each month to sponsor an orphan girl in Sierra Leone. Her name was Fatu. But Cathy was knowledgeable about Syrian crises, sweatshops, Mexican Chihuahua mills, and sex trafficking. She was involved in Black immigrant rights protests and crusades, down to marrying one who overstayed his visa. Maybe this is why, even though her living space and children were taken care of, her allowance was slim. We wound up in a McDonald's to split a box of thirty-two chicken nuggets and packs of $1 fries with her son, swapping new theories of how our America was going to hell in a handbasket.

"We don't have jobs because White America is mad about a Black president," Cathy said loud enough for a White man near us to look twice. "We would have been better off with Hillary. No big huge threat like him."

"Looks like we're about to get our chance to see," I said.

Cathy fussed under her shirt to finagle a nipple out for Sara, and the man nearby glared more. "Yes, and finally women will breastfeed in public without stares."

The man turned back to his Big Mac.

"Cathy, woman president or not, nothing will change the fact this is a White man's world and we're the bottom caste," I said.

"Well, can we at least go back to the days it wasn't so blatant?" she said. "I can deal with covert racism. You're a nutcase if you can't. But right in our faces like this?"

The White man shifted and scrolled his iPhone. She changed the subject.

"How's Chase?" Cathy asked.

She only brought up Mama or Summer if I did, and she must have guessed Chase—that loyal man until the end—was the nearest to family I had now.

"He's good," I said.

I would not tell her a thing, although Cathy was probably one who would have suspended judgment in the name of Black love, African heritage multiplication, biodiversity, and educated Black two-parent householding.

"Well, you see him a lot? Do you see *anybody* up there all by yourself now?"

"We still see each other." Cathy wasn't the judging type, but still I held back.

"Well, good. I worry about you. I can't let you wind up a Joyce Vincent."

"A who?" I could not keep up with all the stars overdosing and dying young.

"A Joyce Vincent," she insisted. "A British woman who was a skeleton in her apartment by the time anybody found her. Three years she sat alone in there. Pretty, educated, popular. Even a singer once."

"Well," I said, "it's a shame people totally neglect their older relatives, but they do."

"She was only thirty-eight. Three sisters! Real boyfriends. But nobody looked for her for three years. Her mail piled up and her television played the whole time. When people are going through stuff, they cut off. I can't let *you* go missing, too."

"Stay out of creepy YouTube, Cathy," I advised. "That shit gets you twisted quick."

I should know. I'd poured a whole printer cartridge into violence and crime.

She shoved her breast under her collar. She patted the baby's back urgently.

"Cathy, I'm totally fine." My rote saying. "Some Blacks have to stay in Harlem, even with rapes and murders and women's disappearances no one cares about. I know the Jaylyn Stewart situation has not escaped you."

I left out my foolish attempt to track down his apartment for signs of Summer in it, only leading me to that scary super named Sanchez.

"He's being framed," Cathy said.

"Why would you think that?" I didn't pretend to hide my shock.

"It's not what I think. It was on the news. Wrong DNA or something like that."

"No, wrong teeth impressions. His DNA is still there."

"One woman comes from a family that knows how to make noise. They had to arrest somebody. And, you know I'm all for Black men's rights, but . . ."

"So am I. It just seems there's never any uproar when it's about Black women's rights. We riot when Black men are shot. What about those women?"

"It's not about taking sides against Black men for Black women, Autumn. It's about plain right and wrong, always."

I loved her too much not to agree to disagree. I expected too much of her to know how I felt. She was married, after all. Her parents lived just blocks from her. She couldn't possibly know what it was to live with no nest. If a Joyce Vincent really existed, this world must cough up some blame that a sky-high percentage of pretty, educated Black women settled as unmarried spinsters. Out of those I knew across my real-life-turned-online networks, most didn't marry even if they wanted to. But it was not a choice. Many married and found themselves the breadwinners. Or they married men who were not Black. The rest seemed frozen in time. They kept gambling in the "What's our status?" game with all their chips on the table and nothing stacking up.

"And, you can't marry any man if you're against them. Or afraid of them."

"I'm not against them, and I do see men," I said. "We can't all be mixed and light-skinned with long-hair Miss Cathy."

"Wait, I'm darker than you."

"You are not."

"Oh, you just wait until summer . . ."

I heard the tap-click of a camera's shutter in the back of my mind, and the room went still like a photograph. And she just kept on saying it.

"You've seen me in the summer, half brown, half red, like a spoiled apple."

She laughed while I drifted off, away and away, thinking of Summer . . .

"And, you can hardly call this rat's nest 'mixed hair.' I have to schedule a weekend just to comb it out. We are definitely locking Sara's hair. Oscar won't let me near him with a comb, but I'm getting him to a real Rasta woman on Fulton to lock it—tight as she can. I don't care what Haitians say about dreadlocks being low-class. I'm not doing it anymore. Autumn? Autumn?"

The last New Year's Eve with my mother and sister was a foreshadow of what this next year might be like. Summer came in coked up hours after the ball dropped: speed talking, sniffing, and glassy-eyed. I didn't know what to do about my sister mixed up in the wrong crowd in her thirties. Her switch was so pronounced she slashed her shoulder-length mane Mama slaved over until we left home. She chopped it to a raggedy, lopsided Mohawk. I thought that was an attempt to fit in with the artsy crowd. But I knew the Mohawk marked a new moment in things. Mama mustered strength to sit up on her elbows and rattle out her disgust through an oxygen tube.

Chase came around that weekend. He graciously took over Mama's care for the night. He did not think the Mohawk was a big deal.

"I guess it's something radical," he said. "Happens if you're going through a lot."

"It looks absolutely awful," I said.

"I think it's kind of cool, in a Mr. T sort of way," Chase grinned.

He slithered two thick cotton washrags around in cold water and set them in our ice bucket we once kept around just for fun. Now, Mama needed it. He lifted the washrags with a pair of salad tongs. Mama liked the cold on her forehead and chest to reverse fevers.

"I thought it would be cool, too," I said. "But now. It's just too big of a sign. There's enough death and disappearing going on in this house."

"Maybe that's why it was a cool thought," Chase said. "Coping with a mother disappearing by accident, so make something disappear deliberately?"

"Okay, Dr. Phil," I said.

Chase left me alone with only my reflection across the mirror. My black turtleneck stretched against a roll across my belly. The gym hadn't seen me in months. At that point, this group of oddball friends was a little secret between Summer and me. Chase was largely in the dark. She warned me not to tell him. He just thought she was spending more time "networking." I just thought it was a phase. Summer always needed her crews to leave me out of, like her own primal push for a separate identity after a lifetime of forced association with me. But about a month later she wanted to be so separate she rejected Chase's trip to Grenada, sent me off, and was the last daughter to hold Mama's hand.

I WAS CRYING IN THE middle of McDonald's. Oscar stared. The White man finally had enough of us. He balled up all his food paper and left.

"Thank you for coming to Illinois for my mother's funeral," I whimpered.

In my meltdown, Cathy turned to wipe barbecue sauce off Oscar's shirt and whisper it was time to go pee.

"Of course," she said. "I was happy to be there. I know you'd do the same for me. I loved Miss Spencer. Remember she came to the dining hall yelling, 'Where are all the Black boys?' It was hilarious."

"It really, really was." Cathy's goofiness was a defense mechanism few could understand let alone tolerate, but it had come in handy for me the last fifteen years.

"Oh my God. No men for us there. And look at us now. Some men are so lucky."

Cathy and I stayed to gossip through Oscar's complaints of boredom. To extend our woman time, we rationed him Sour Patch Kids in exchange for quiet. So-and-so did not get married like she was supposed to. The other so-and-so quit her law firm to join the Peace Corps, disillusioned she was too plump and needed a weave to make partner. Yet another so-and-so did not call us when she came to New York for a trip we saw her post pictures of. The whole time, Cathy never mentioned Summer. She specialized in being cheerful.

I already knew I would slip into the corner bodega before I got home, to buy "wine product" labeled Merlot. I told this to Cathy. She asked if I wanted some weed she had in the diaper bag instead. I declined. I felt sedated as it was. I walked down to the platform at Fourteenth Street to wait with them for the F train to Brooklyn, where they would come up after dark, and my friend would keep one child at her breasts and her eyes on another far ahead of her, not thinking again about Auntie Autumn until I next appeared with sweets.

TWELVE

Soon, I wandered back to the Union Square Barnes & Noble on my own. I landed in the Psychology section. I thought here was where I could find books comparable to *The Art of War*. Devils and angels on earth. No in-betweens. An angel never does rude or fucked-up shit to another person and just says, "Oops, I had a bad day." And a devil does not apologize. If I was an angel, then I must figure out how to handle devils without killing anyone because this is not what angels do. My manners will be better. How do angels win if they do not carry long swords?

Copious choices in Barnes & Noble dizzied me. Book titles leaped out from spines packed in tightly; *Smash Your Competition* and *Climb Over, Not Up, the Ladder* both arrested my interest. I whittled them out. I wanted to find the books where the authors had fangs, horns, and blisters on their knuckles. Or a glob of blood on the right side of their shirts. I would know they had bleeding hearts. Then, I might be able to trust what they had to tell me. I clutched the books under my arms and continued along the shelves.

I saw a tall woman on a ladder, to help her just one step up to higher shelves. She did little more than make sure tightly packed books were still tight. She climbed down and rolled the ladder a little to her left. In the crook of the section, she flipped through one of the books for enough time for me to notice she was reading it—not handling it for work.

What kind of job was that? Where could I apply? How much was this woman paid to go up and down a ladder like she's on the StairMaster? And read books for free?

The woman wearing man-size brown penny loafers met my eyes and smiled. I guessed I was supposed to smile back at her. It was not my responsibility to hold the hopes of Team Kindness on my little shoulders. One thing Summer's self-absorbed discourtesies showed me is I cared too much about what others needed even when I do not need it back.

"Can I help you find anything?" she asked, glancing at the titles under my shoulders. "Something with a more *positive* approach?"

She said *positive* the way a debutante cotillion coach might say *virginity*. I went from being a worthy adult contributor to society—enjoying myself in privacy and freedom—to a charitable Team Kindness catch of the day. She looked at me, with her glasses parked low and eyes peering above them, and finally walked away.

Something felt heavy in my hands. I needed air. I threw two $20 bills at a stunned cashier and walked into Union Square. A baby-faced freckled boy, probably in college and dreaming of being the next Jay-Z before this world comes down and tears dreams out of your mind, ran onto the street. He called me "Ma'am," not "baby." He gave me the change I left. Then I looked at a book in my hands with a title just as true as *The Art of War*. It was *The Myth of Sanity.*

I WAS OUT OF FOOD. And wine added up. I had to pare down from Manhattan's prices, even though those prices seemed to include only coffee and junk food unless Chase supplied a real hot meal. I decided on a fresh start, maybe even detox. Between Asha and me, I was the only one who had enough credit, or an intact driver's license, to reserve a Zipcar for a cheaper stock-up in Jersey. One Sunday I got a Mini Cooper, not the most practical for bulk shopping, but well . . . compulsions.

Just like a long-term love, past the point of surprises, Chase gave a familiar list from his SWAG office phone: "Those snack-bag thingies . . . you know, with Doritos and Cheetos and pretzels all mixed in together? Twenty-four pack of Corona, a big Tide, a twelve-pack of Zest, and as much toilet paper as you can stuff in without blocking the rear window."

"A hundred pack of ultra-thin condoms?" I suggested.

"I got that one covered, sweetie. Drive safe."

Asha knocked so we could go. She had totes for us, to save the world in recycling. I suddenly felt queasy and not up to it, as wine and toast was no real brunch, but the car was already reserved. We walked to 145th Street to wait for the number 7 bus down, to get nearer to the car's reserved parking space. As usual, inside the bus was colder than outside. We had a nice pick of seats. Asha and I sat in the furthest possible back. She read a natural hair-style magazine. I brought along *Night Wind*, drawn to it for the first time since the trip to meet its author, refreshed on the curves and grooves of Gabriel Johns's writing, episodic and saga-like. I opened it to the section devoted to his lost wife.

Anna was a beautiful storm, as lovely as a woman could be when she arrests your loins and your mind. She required patience and ability to still, like a portrait subject as the painter searches out her angles and shades. For those whom she passed quickly and at first, in mercy to unhear the tre-ble of what would come next, she remained an astonishing figure. I know the sway she brought upon the boughs of our spice trees, the scent of it all one a child could have

remembered as the most heavenly he ever knew, for igno-
rance of the malevolence it was. I squashed a leatherback
turtle, and many fish, when I ran to her near the sea, hoping to sell her sewing and her singing so I could write. We
had not known. Water pushed me back, not my vigor and
will. Certainly not my heart. Her hands, like a child's with
no hairs and lines yet, reaching out to me as gray water
lashed at our sides and bucketed our bodies from above. I
could swim, but I could not push hard enough. This is just
one way my mind will see it, forever maybe. She simply
disappeared.

Then the bus veered onto Columbus so sharply I lost my place
and thought. I looked out to the coming street before us, with
Central Park at the fringe of Harlem and the traffic slimmed down
to fewer lanes.

That's when I saw her.

On the east side of the street, in the doorway of a stone house
with high steps behind an iron gate. Summer. The coffee cup in her
hand was no surprise. She wore jeans and a gray hoodie. Her hair
was a puff-bun on the top of her head. She leashed an orange poo-
dle. The bus jutted forward away from her. I strained to look back
through the window across from me. Warmth seeped through my
midsection. My eyes watered into a blur. I dropped the book in my
lap, grabbed the handrail, and leaped up. Asha looked up from her
magazine. Her mouth was moving. I stepped over her knees onto
her toes, reaching back to press the yellow strip to stop the bus.

"Summer!" I shouted.

"What?" Asha yelled.

I reined in the angry tirade furling in my brain, the insults and
shouts Summer deserved for finding her way out of our sadness
but leaving me here, the abuse I would heap to return the anguish

her insensitivity and irresponsibility created. What the hell was wrong with her? How could she have run off to a new life right uptown without even explaining? I ignored the Upper West Sider wearing large black sunglasses. My tennis shoes may have plowed through her tough Chanel loafers to mash her toes, as her "Watch it!" indicated they had. The bus did not come to a complete halt but I pushed the door open.

"Autumn, wait for me!" Asha scrambled to collect our tote bags.

I turned to see Asha smashed between the doors before she wriggled out after me. The driver cursed us out as he passed. On the quiet block, the houses all looked the same behind their iron gates. I jogged two blocks. My eyes stayed on Summer and her dog, now hunched in a gated grass patch around the lone tree across from the house they left. I was so intent on catching her I almost ran past.

She did not look my way at all. So I stood and caught my breath before the pretty woman's eyes angled into my direction. And I was so sure. Then, embarrassed. Asha came up to me, expectant and poised. But I had no one to show her. The woman was not Summer, not even close to a lookalike, up close. I could not name her a hallucination, because an actual person truly stood before me. Rather, she was an optical illusion.

"You look like somebody I know," I told her anyway.

As I felt Asha's palm in mine, my illusion frowned and rushed away.

THIRTEEN

I tumbled off the edge of the George Washington Bridge and barely escaped being crushed on the West Side Highway or flung into the Hudson River, drowning and disappearing like Gabriel Johns's wife, the water pushing in until my car became as uncaged as a skeleton freed of skin. I don't like the bridges or tunnels anymore. They are too unpredictable and sly, it appears to me now. I am lost, in water. I will never be found.

Where is the car? My bag? My bag. My purse. I need it. I need it . . . right . . . now.

My feeble arms seemed matchsticks with skin, too tired to raise. I looked down at my body, cloaked in white. My toes were freshly manicured, a sparkly magenta. I felt no itchiness down below; my underwear must be fairly recent. I checked my underarms. Just a little musty, not much. What made me understand I was in a hospital was the television mounted high up, rather than in front of me. And my arm hurt. I was wearing a gold tennis bracelet, a gift from Chase. A little bathroom was in my peripheral vision—but I didn't see a bathtub to boot. I saw a steel rod on the side of the toilet.

My tongue felt bloated out of my mouth. Judging from the taste, my breath was repulsive. My behind was sore. When I lifted my arm and slightly turned to rub it, it felt like a raccoon leaped to rake its claws across my forearm. No. I just had tubes in my arm. They ripped out.

I knew there should be an alarm button to press, for me to get an explanation. I was not going to spend a second to find it. I was just going to holler.

Two women in cartoon-character scrubs run in.

"Missus Spencer," one of the women said.

Her hair was curly waves she corseted into a bun, and her breasts were soft and full and plump as she leaned over me. Still I struggled. I hollered. I was too weak and tired to throw her off. The other woman had run out.

"Let me go! Let me go!" I yelled. I kicked my pretty toenail feet against the bed. The woman held down my arms. She talked to me.

"Missus Spencer, you're in the hospital. You're okay. You—are—*okay*. Please. Please. Your heart rate. Relax."

I pitched a tantrum and an imaginary fistfight I was not too ladylike to have. I had something I needed to take out on someone. She just happened to be there—alone, until the other nurse returned with a male nurse. Working together, they subdued me, one nurse on my chest and the other two at my feet. I yelled and cried. I was not supposed to be anywhere without lipstick, with bad breath and funky armpits. That aspect of the moment, more than the lacuna as to how I arrived, was more upsetting than feeling chained. I was pinned. There was nothing I could do. So I stopped. I breathed.

"That's it . . ." the male nurse said. "That's it, Miss Spencer . . . breathe."

I opened my hot mouth and pulled air in. *Wheel of Fortune* was on the television. It was the bonus round. Another couples' week. No vowels on the board but an *E* and an *O*. More than enough there with the three *T*'s, one *S*, one *N*, and one *P* to figure it out. Two people on TV couldn't see what I did from a hospital bed? It must be my life wasted on words.

"'Thing of the Past,'" I blurted, and I huffed and puffed and squirmed.

"What? What did you say?" one nurse asked me.

"Thing of the past," I said again, just as the couple's ten seconds passed and the short funny buzzer sounded.

Pat Sajak announced the answer to the puzzle.

Thing of the past indeed.

SOMETIME SOON AFTER, CHASE RACED up from SWAG's offices to Harlem Hospital. When he appeared at the door with the neat, circular Styrofoam containers of food, I was instantly relieved. He brought in sugar-free Jell-O, mashed potatoes with extra gravy on the side, creamed spinach, coffee, and Neapolitan ice cream.

"Why'd you bring me this?" I asked him.

He looked disappointed. "I thought these were your favorites," he told me.

He kissed me on my forehead. Then he rolled the room's extra chair closer to the bed. He peeled open the plastic utensils. He poured water from the plastic pitcher into our plastic cups, and was careful to keep the ice at bay.

"I haven't eaten these things together since Mama died," I reminded him.

"Oh," he said. "Sorry. You used to send me to the hospital cafeteria for creamed spinach and mashed potatoes. You keep Jell-O cups in the fridge. You know, your diets?"

"I do?"

"Yeah."

I could only demonstrate my apology when I picked up the plastic spoon to swirl around the coffee and pick through the mashed potatoes. I would try.

My mother is dead. And so is my sister. She is not in New York City living a new fabulous life without me. She is in a garbage dump, or the woods, far away.

"You were asleep when I came this afternoon," Chase updated me. "A nurse called to tell me you woke up."

"It's my sugar and dehydration."

I would not entertain one accusation of hysteria, nervous breakdown, mental illness. All the cop-outs. Most people could do so much better, if they wanted to. My life had proved me way too resilient to be unable to control my own spirit and mind.

"They're balancing my fluids now. My sugar's already leveled out. The doctor told me I was just a few insulin grams above hypoglycemic shock when I spazzed out."

I winced at the awful clack, just Chase's hard-edged brown briefcase on the tray. He smiled an apology and snapped open the brass shutters. He set my copy of *Night Wind* on my tummy. The book curled upward to release the sour smell of its yellowing pages, in aging metamorphosis like a teenaged book kept since college.

"You dropped this," he said. "Thank God Asha was there. I took the car back for you already. You need me to bring you anything?"

"No," I told him. "I need to be out of here tonight."

Weakness astonished me when I lifted up to get ready. Chase patted me to stay down.

"I don't think that's a good idea," he said. "Autumn, something's going on with you. And it's more than stress, which I understand. I'm not minimizing it. I'm just saying this has gone on a long time and you're wearing yourself out."

Mine was a silent pout. I let it go. He did not understand. His mother and sister did not disappear in the same year. He had real-job health insurance. My lowest-rung Obamacare plan covered emergencies somewhat, but extended stay would cost. I thought about a deadline I had for Norma Roth, my temp-agency client. She needed to pull in as many resumes as possible before other agencies snatched up college kids free for the summer. I needed to distribute her marketing flyer to regional university career offices. I could not afford to have another client quit me. Two had already.

"You gotta eat better, and back away from that coffee," Chase smiled. "I wasn't supposed to bring you any. But I know you."

I was glad he brought me food. I was enormously happy and settled just to see him. He had known all of us. His presence corresponded me to Mama and Summer, together.

"I got an email from Mr. Johns," he continued. "Well, from Olivia. She said it's time they caught up with the rest of the world and posted a website. She wanted permission to use some of SWAG's photos. She said we really got him. And . . ."

"What?" I asked.

"I told her the beautiful young lady she met can design websites, and I'd ask her if she would do it. She was thrilled to know you were back at it, considering how you left."

Perhaps he thought it was a favor to me to disassociate the vacation where we'd consummated our relationship from the place where I found out my mother passed on.

"I'm just worried about keeping up with everything I have to do," I sighed. "I can't go making promises to people all around the world now."

He looked let down. He soaked all day in a world where connections and networks were so fragile no one could kick too many gift horses in the mouth. This was not how I wanted it to go. He had already been unappreciated by one of us.

"You're doing good," he answered. He put his palm on my forehead. "I know how much you've lost. You're still seeing Noel Montgomery? He helps, right?"

So, Chase still got it. Somebody else still did want to know. I was not completely alone. Somebody else revered the cause—and no matter if it was because he had loved Summer or because he believed what I believed. I was not stranded on an island of deranged worry all by myself.

"I had to be honest, the past few months totaled me," Chase said. "It isn't just you. It's all hit me too. I asked to slow things down a bit at work. Nobody could make any promises, but I'll be around a bit more, 'kay?"

I did not answer him. We were past the point of walking away from each other. I did not think I could. He tricked me to think he wanted to. But, now we were stuck and at some point we would have to show ourselves, come out of hiding. What could anyone say about it? Summer was gone. And I think a strange woman I chased on the street was God's sign that Summer was not a woman I could expect to run into again anymore.

FOURTEEN

Contrary to what he told me in the hospital weeks before, Chase remained late at the office. Again. And again. According to his message, I had no need to cook or bathe, or do anything remotely satisfactory for him that another red-blooded woman would be compelled to do for a man. It was getting to be more like roommates or siblings or, well . . .

Hey, babycakes. I'm just calling to tell you hello. I know I'm calling kinda late. So if you cooked something, I'm sorry. I may not be there until late tonight . . .

Delete.

I had picked up a whole roasted chicken at Fairway, with French bread and pasta salad. I filled his plate and left it on the stove, not only because it's tradition and a woman's sage wisdom to know her place, to keep the organ above the male member full too. And I really wanted to. Ugh. What a sorry feminist I was. It was bad enough he found *The Myth of Sanity* book, and could have guessed I must be questioning mine. I only left the book in the bathroom a few days for tub and throne reading. It wasn't my cup of tea.

But Chase asked, "What are you doing with this?" almost like he was my father and he found a used condom under my princess daybed.

"It looked like an interesting read."

His condemnation didn't last. He started on it in bed. Then he threw it in his bag for his work commute. He liked it, the bastard. He wanted to discuss it, rather than make love. I scuttled to my desk and its threatening contents.

Macy's: $967.

Rip.

Discover: $2,249.

Rip.

Sallie Mae: $21,934.

Rip.

New York State W-9 2013–2014 taxes: $3,236.

Rip.

I kept Children International for Fatu in Sierra Leone, coloring well now she was: $21.

No more booze, I promised. I exchanged wine for my cabinet stash of tea, less raucous company without the same power to dust dreams from my nights. With the windows opened to the moist, crisp breezes May brought down to Harlem, Belinda had nothing to complain about her children hearing. At least not from my bed.

But I found a bottle in a paper bag behind piles of wheat pasta and brown rice I never made for that romantic dinner I planned a few weeks back. A glass tranced me into the ability to make an essentials list, write out all the checks, and stamp all the envelopes.

I AWOKE ALONE ON MY side of the bed in a blot of Merlot on the mattress, the grownup style of bed-wetting. My alarm hadn't gone off; that only happened if I remembered to set it. Luckily, garbage trucks ran behind Uptown this morning. Today was Roth Staffing's annual photo shoot. I was to write new website bios for them. The photo shoot started right after their lunch. It was after noon. If I took advantage of spring fashion—maxi dresses hung straight in the closet (no ironing required)—I would have time to grab coffee and a bagel at the bodega.

I went to the kitchen to down the last of the orange juice. I was parched. I grabbed a carton of almond milk to chase it with. My face was swollen; I looked mad on one side and baffled on the other. I had no clean towels. Chase had yet to pick up my laundry. I grabbed an exfoliating mesh ball from the shower caddy. I scrubbed my tongue until it may have begun bleeding. Then, I switched the shower to as cold as I could stand it and held my open mouth up to the faucet. I reached outside the shower into the medicine cabinet so I could get to the Bayer, dislodging pill bottles and a container of Nyquil that spilled. I washed down aspirin with hard water. I didn't dry off. I swiped deodorant and sprayed a mix of old Victoria's Secret body splashes. I pulled my damp hair back with a scrunchie.

A long royal-blue dress would do in a business-casual setting, a good fit over my bloated tummy. I was wearing small gold hoops still, two days now. My earlobes itched, but I didn't have time to debate it. I threw a wooden bangle over my arm. I did not bathe enough these days for my last pedicure to lose luster, so I slipped on nude peep-toes. I could buff and file my fingernails on the train. I could lotion my hands and face, and do my makeup there too. Dark women could get away with bare face, a little mascara, Carmex, and lip gloss in a pinch. All were in my work tote. I would organize all the paper into it on the train ride too. Twenty minutes after garbage trucks knocked me out of sleep, I was locking my apartment door.

On the second floor, a mattress and box spring bunched in with tall brown shelves. It all blocked my path. I could see through that a U-Haul box propped open the second-floor apartment door. Down the stairs, a box propped open our lobby door near the mailboxes as well. So did one at the outside door. What . . . ?

"Hello, hello?" I called out. No one answered me. "Hello!"

I stood to no answer. I pulled out a travel-size lotion I stocked from Chase's business trips. I could at least shine my face and legs while I waited for a person responsible for this to materialize. I moved on to a vat of Carmex. Finally, I heard voices near the door on the second floor.

"Help! I need to get out up here."

A pockmarked pink face peeked between the shelves and box spring. "Oh, just one second, ma'am. Hold on."

I saw another man shuffle out and ease his hands between the shelves. He scooted one back and slid it down the hall in a careful rotation through the door. His partner did the same with the other shelf. The mattress plopped against the cleared wall, the box spring against it. I crouched through a triangular clearing.

"Sorry about that," the man who found me said.

"No problem. I wasn't expecting anybody to be moving in today."

"Hope we weren't too loud. Folks got a lot of stuff. We should be done by . . . what, 'bout three o'clock?"

"Don't bet on it," his coworker said. "See how many trunks they got? We should have had another man for this."

"Who are they?" I asked.

"Couple coming from Connecticut. They got a kid. Guy's a lawyer."

I took a wild guess they were White.

I saw Fran at the mailboxes, wrangling out her mail that always piled to the point postal workers chastised us tenants when they could not fit anymore in. I'd hardly seen her since her dramatic effort to prove to me that our rooftop door, and all possible entrances, were secure.

"Excuse me," I told the men.

Fran saw me and waved.

"Fran, I didn't know anybody was moving in," I said.

"Oh? We left you a message."

"I must have missed it. What happened to my neighbor downstairs?"

"Oh my goodness, Autumn. Belinda left months ago, after the New Year."

"Fran, I would have heard a move," I said. "I'm a bit touched but not out of touch."

"She must have done so little by little, until it was empty. Section 8 didn't cover it all. She rarely paid her part. We kept it out of court, but couldn't keep working with her."

"Wait a minute. I just saw Belinda's oldest boy last week, maybe."

And I heard Belinda's door open and close all the time. That could have been familiar safe memory. I was used to it after so many years. She and her children must have been sneaking in to sleep. I had been stumbling out to the bodega for a late-night snack, about a week ago, when I saw her tallest boy. As usual, he called me "Miss" and offered to help.

"Dunno. Maybe they still have keys. I'm not sure she had somewhere set to go."

I was enraged at Fran's lack of concern about security, as if we'd learned nothing from Summer's debatable abduction or bad luck but certain disappearance from here.

"So, they have keys and they don't live here?" I yelled. One of the moving men peeked down to see what the fuss was about. "How can we keep people from trying to break in? If she's that hard up, what's to say she won't send people to rob us? Two women have been alone in this building all this time with keys wandering?"

"I apologize we haven't changed locks yet," Fran pleaded. "We waited because of all the commotion from the rooftop incident, so you and Asha wouldn't have any more changes now. We've dealt with a lot of situations recently we aren't used to, Autumn."

"Well, I apologize if missing someone I love brought undue attention to your property."

"It was not a bother to us, more than concern for you," she replied. "But we did have to think about how we can serve the most unpredictable needs that arise from tenants, so that included restricting them to those who can pay us."

I was not dumb. All the pretend liberalism and social activism ended when it came to the bottom line. Fran noticed, just like we all did. The same prewar space going for $1,500 a few years ago went for $3,000 now. The block was cleaned more often. More expensive shoes tightroped through the dog shit on the sidewalks and balance-beamed around glass from broken forty-ounces. New chains were coming to 125th Street, beyond Starbucks, MAC, and Old Navy. My landlords were good to me. They fixed what little needed to be fixed. They were patient with me on the rent, courteous sympathizers to the ordeals I managed. But I had to stand with the sister and her kids. The owners of our home inherited it, from their family who paid for it long ago. Now, it was just profit. Who was next—Asha? Me?

"We're doing the best we can, Autumn," Fran insisted.

"Have I ever said you guys weren't?" I smiled.

"No, you haven't. And we don't worry about you for it. Belinda was here for years. We stuck with her until her babies weren't babies anymore. We had to take a stand."

Woman to woman, I understood her. Her family gave her property to rent, not a mission, for her livelihood, not another woman's. Fran and I were both businesswomen. If I was in the red, it usually wasn't my fault. Up until recently, that is. But at my peak self, I saw money struggles after late payers threw me off when I needed it most, or non-payers assumed I didn't need it at all. I felt sorry for Belinda and her kids, but I understood Fran's perspective. Freeloading is always the training for more direct thefts.

"You should meet the new people," she said. "They're your kind."

"Oh?"

"Yes, into arts and culture. Hang out with them, Autumn. We think about you over here, all alone."

"I am *fine*," I interrupted her. "And I'm sure everybody'll get along well. But I'll miss seeing those kids in the hallway. And smelling Belinda's fried chicken."

"I know. So will I."

"Okay," I stammered. "Well, I gotta get going. I'm late for a meeting. I'll leave the rent on top of your box. Early. I'm on a new budgeting plan."

"That's not necessary, but do what you wish."

Asha sat on our stoop in a purple kimono, reviving dreadlock wigs and puffing a cigar. Across the street, the couple leaned into the back of a long moving truck, laughing and talking.

"Girl . . ." she said.

I couldn't afford to lose a step. Then, from the curb, my gaze racing for anything yellow or old black sedan, "Hey, did you know Belinda and the kids left?"

"I hope my complaints about all the music they blasted didn't have anything to do with it," Asha sighed. "I guess we better get used to Celine Dion."

I could not get into it with her now, not gentrification or rising rents or even Belinda. We would gab on it all later. Plus it seemed the couple was starting to walk toward the house and I wanted to avoid them. A gypsy cab slowed to a crawl around the moving truck. So I ran to its back door and let myself in before the driver could pull off. The trip would cost $20, plus tip, to get through Midtown traffic.

NORMA ROTH, THE TEMP AGENCY owner, didn't even notice I was late. Her photographer finished only a few of her placement managers before I flustered onto the sixteenth floor of the Forty-Seventh Street skyscraper. I immediately proceeded to a back office where a stool, plain gray backdrop, and lights were set up. The company employed eight full-time staff, most in recruiting and accounting. Norma's receptionist ordered doughnuts, coffee, and bagels for the time. Norma caught me clutching a cup of black coffee.

"Oh, Autumn, you have to get your picture done too, honey," she insisted. "You're our web designer and marketing girl. I got a lotta good kids 'cause of you."

"Oh, no, no. I'm just here to interview you guys and update your bios," I told her.

No pressed powder in my bag. I knew my hair was a mess I only got away with because the "native" thing was on-trend.

"No, I insist," Norma insisted. "It's the right thing to do. We're all a team. And you look lovely, dear." She pulled a compact from her purse and opened to its mirror.

Norma paid me well and she never once complained about my shortcomings this past year, like all the others had. If only to appease her, I wiped shine off my face with a napkin, plumped up my lips, and smiled for the camera. Then, I went on to finding out if any more happened for the staff since I last charted the hobbies, hometowns, college majors, and local schools that led these more reasonable adults to full-time jobs in New York City. It took me two hours of tight smiles and quick catch-up. I discovered I mainly had to add "proud mom of one" and sometimes "two or three" to a few bios. And dads. And dogs and cats. I made careful notes not to mix any of them up. Then, I would have my rent money.

"Autumn, thanks a lot," Norma told me. "Now, if you could get all this up as soon as possible, honey, I'd so appreciate it. I've lost fifty pounds since they shot us last year. I want to show it off."

"Yes, I noticed. But you know, it's rude to comment on other people's weight."

"Oh, I'll take it. Pour it on."

"You know, you weren't big before."

"It started when I had to sit shiva for my mother's brother. I stayed in the kitchen. It was easiest. But I had no excuse to keep it going."

"Well, I have to figure out your secrets."

"A lotta water and salads, some special vitamins my doctor cooked up for me, and walking out of this place a few times a day to join the rest of the living world."

"You deserve it."

I left her office suite confident I still had at least one major client.

Maybe that lured me down Seventh Avenue, and entitled me to a stopover at Macy's to see spring sales. I knew I shouldn't have. Because I really didn't need anything new: not one purse, bag, pair of heels, lipstick, or perfume bottle. However, I wanted to be waited on and pursued, seduced to give over what little I had to offer.

My wares soothed me: a fresh cucumber hydrating spray, a Guerlain eau de toilette in the perfect size for a clutch purse, silver teardrop hoops. All on sale . . .

The duets and packs of women could have been friends, or mother and daughters, or sisters, as I most imagined them. Yes, little girls were lured from their mother's fingertips in shopping malls and pretty women disappeared from their lots. But I realized how comfortably safe and secure I always felt in stores. An army of women—clerks, managers, shoppers, and even food court servers—were Foxy Browns in our own rights. We were, altogether in our consumerist bliss, a daunting fortress for crafty men. How fun to think Macy's, and everywhere like it, could be the last nunneries we had left.

•

ONCE HOME, I DID REMEMBER to transfer a payment to Children International for my "child." I fiddled with my online portfolio, only to switch its font and some colors really. I updated my title from "Business Writing & Media Specialist" to "Tired Ass Ho," saved it by accident, and had to go through the trouble of switching it back.

The *ho* part was opinion but the tired part was plain fact. I'd pushed through to make the rent and make it to Norma. That helped. But at some point I had to tackle the credit and stop sending utility payments late. I couldn't do the roommate or Airbnb hustle. My home was still Summer's home. If she reappeared to erase this mirage of the rest of my life without her, I'd have to put people out after I spent their money. I opened the pictures from Norma of me and the Roth staff. It turned out my hangover face was not as gruesome as I envisioned it. I looked fresh, actually, candid and honest. It was just how I needed to look to seek out new clients—soon.

FIFTEEN

There was a redwood rocking chair. Grandma's maroon crochet blanket hung over it, in front of a china cabinet full of bottles we couldn't touch and their Kool-Aid we couldn't drink. The rocking chair was no one's in particular. But the adults told me and my sister to stay out of it. We rock back too hard, and we'll fall and break our necks—and "My good chair too." But when Mr. Murphy sat in it, the legs bent. He didn't rock in it. He jiggled from side to side and that's not the way it was supposed to go.

We had his *Sports Illustrated*s and *Newsweek*s on top of our *Star* and *Shape* magazines now. We had his "Gimme that!" big underwear. His long, loose, dark socks in the laundry room. We didn't have to worry that the dryer and air conditioner ran up the electric bill. He paid them. We had liverwurst and hog head cheese in the fridge, next to hot peppers and open tins of sardines. We couldn't go in Mama's bedroom any more to watch her TV, because her door was closed and a man was snoring. Mama wasn't downstairs to fix us eggs, toast, and juice. So we made cereal with too much milk. Stomachaches attacked us later. We saw Grandma fall asleep every night in the living room chair, and not go upstairs to her room. We stayed downstairs with her. We left bones and scraps for the abandoned cats Mama didn't notice anymore.

We made Father's Day cards like every year, for our daddy. Mama told us to make Mr. Murphy one too, to be "nice." We didn't put as much time into his. We left out the flowers and hearts. He read the words Mama told us to write: "Thank You Mr. Murphy" and "We Love You Mr. Murphy." He said, "Call me Cole." We called him "Cole" for a few days. It did not fit our mouths that well. We went back to calling him "Mr. Murphy." It seemed he was at our house all the time, or she was gone for days away at his. We saw how quickly Mama ran after the mailman with stamped envelopes ready, rather than bill envelopes lingering on our lazy Susan. Still, the general rhythm of our ways shifted into a partitioned life. It was a division of the quartet we once were, not a multiplication of it.

Mama stopped taking us to see my father's family. She spit when she talked about them. "They forgot us," she said. Instead, we went to Mr. Murphy's family things. One time he brought his son and his son's wife to our house. They wore army clothes. Mr. Murphy took over the kitchen to make their coffee. We had to wait until the wife got out of the bathroom with her kids before we could go in. But as soon as we got a turn, Mama called us. She cooked a big lunch for them. We had to set the table, but not from this drawer and that cabinet. We had to open the china cabinet, and pull drawers underneath to get the heavy red napkins out. We put the big white spoons and forks in the food. We took the little kids to run through the new sprinklers Mr. Murphy bought. They were too little and they got scared. Mr. Murphy's son's wife was upset we made her little girl catch cold.

We fixed back our hair, like ladies, when the strangers left. We played in the lipstick and eye shadow we bought at Kmart, with dollars Mr. Murphy slipped us to go find something as he and

Mama grabbed the large bundles of toilet paper and racks of paper towels we never had before. We could do our homework all on our own, now, even though it was much harder in the higher grade. We were expected to do just as well. We were big girls, smart girls, pretty girls. And it was our job to be good and help Mama out.

"She been through enough with y'all as it is . . ."

We went out on our own, became murky and clandestine. The training bras cut into our skin, but we did not trouble Mama for new ones. We shared our clothes. We traded our shoes. We cleaned up without being asked. We said "Okay" when Mr. Murphy was there and Mama told us we can go to public school now.

There, we withered under the boys' comments and interest in our fresh new faces. Their spitting remarks about our asses, deep throats, and torn-up pussies were common. The other girls grew up creeping past boys and men who talked like that. Our smiles diminished. We became cozy with the counselors and secretaries. They would cut short phone calls or temperature-taking to find out what was wrong, again, with the new girls.

We were not babies, together, anymore. And we were growing apart. She wanted different things than I did.

But some things stay inseparable, frozen in time, permanent. We buried some of our stories underneath broken cement in the shed. We wrote about how life was scary the bigger you grow, but we'd always be together. We rolled the papers with our words and jiggled them inside the bad bottles Mama left out in the shed, and other places. And we put the tops back on and knew we would always find each other there, no matter what.

"I'M SO SORRY," I INTERRUPTED myself. "I didn't mean to tell you all that."

"No problem," Detective Montgomery said.

His pages of notes waited on the table, for what I guess he

expected would be real clues and information. But it was more of the same: conjecture, speculation, useless nostalgia. I needed him as uproared as he was at the start. As more time passed, more hope faded. My new batch of FIND SUMMER SPENCER flyers sat on his desk. I copied them for ten cents each at a nearby pharmacy. I knew better than to pay too much, like the one thousand color ones I soon saw floating in garbages on our block, even in drains.

"So, this Mr. Murphy seems like he kind of just took over everything, acted like he owned the place," was Detective Montgomery's summary of my extended report on how Summer and I drifted from each other. New York City brought us back together.

"He did," I confirmed. "I don't ever remember struggling, or starving, or tension. Maybe it was there. Mama was only a secretary at the water plant. But she got us a house in a good place. We stayed. She wasn't gonna have us all moving around like vagabonds."

"Does this Murphy know you're out here searching for Summer?"

I laughed. After his stroke, Mama went to see him every single day. He had a big old ranch, two properties with wooden stakelike fencing around it. But not one of his relatives wanted to come out to tend his needs or mash his food or pretend to understand what he said. He wound up in a private room at a senior living and elder care facility.

"I saw him in February last year, when I took care of business for my mother's life insurance policies. I had to see Mr. Murphy's son. He had taken over things."

"How'd that go?"

"I got to his senior community and it had an approved visitors list. I thought surely I wasn't on it. I was. He put 'Autumn Spencer. Daughter.'"

"It sounds like you all were the only real family he had in his older life."

"Mr. Murphy was not a humble man. He put a lot of people off, I think. It doesn't help me now, but I found this old article Summer printed out about him resigning from a position . . . Local NAACP, I think. I recall, vaguely, gossip about him being a flirt. Pushy, complained about, before Mama met him. He told her high and mighty Black folks were jealous of him, wanted him down a peg. But he never seemed unfaithful to her."

"So, you're not close to him as a stepfather now?" Montgomery asked.

"He's demented, now. This was a fancy place. These people got dressed up for dinners. It smelled like Glade, not pee. They had nice chandeliers. A big enclosed patio off the dining hall, with a courtyard and garden and geese and greenhouse. I saw a bunny. Mr. Murphy was in the courtyard. In a wheelchair. An attendant was helping him eat. When I went outside, he lit up. He said 'Aum . . . Aum.' And the man helping him saw me, said he'd get out the way. I told him to go on. I wanted to see Mr. Murphy get spoon-fed. So many years bossing us around, pushing my mother to walk on eggshells. I told him Mama was gone, and I was on my way to bury her. I haven't spoken to him since."

I took up so much time Detective Montgomery could do little more than jot down the original reason I came: My downstairs neighbor Belinda was not who I thought she was, or even where I thought she was, for a long time. I needed to know why she left with no good-bye, where she was the night Summer disappeared, why she left so soon after. Her son shot up like a redwood in just a few years, surely capable of overpowering one of us women he grew up past. He kept using his key to come back into our building long after they were evicted. He never mentioned they no longer lived there.

"But, back to why I came," I said. "Don't you think it's odd Belinda didn't say good-bye? After everything this winter, I thought we were all a team around there. Now I don't know whose team she was on."

"Autumn," Montgomery said, "It feels like we're running out of our options to keep thinking about Summer. I've helped you push police to do more than they wanted to do. I've been to your home, met neighbors, read the journals. My hands are tied with how much privacy I can invade to question others further. It's time for you to think about yourself, and how your life can go on with or without Summer, beyond looking for her."

There was no beyond for me. I would remain unflinching, strident.

I could not walk two roads: one intact and cleared for my progress, another detoured and blocked by my past. I picked my road. Every vision I had for what life could have been had to go off the side of it. My only compass was strength and force, for the rest of my life if necessary, in my drive to guarantee someone answered for my sister's disappearance, even if she was that someone. Even she was going to have to answer me.

Summer

SIXTEEN

Summer may have forgotten Chase's birthdays by design. I did it by accident.

We certainly discussed it. I had to do better. He deserved it. I tried for a table at Red Rooster on Lenox. But with Fourth of July weekend and its tourists, my effort was moot. I got on the months-long waiting list in hopes to make it past the velvet rope on my own birthday in September. It would be my independent woman treat, to compensate. We settled on Red Lobster on 125th Street instead. I had put together a belated gift bag of cologne, new underwear, and socks. And lingerie, for me. But birthday sex was pat, dry, and quiet, even with the assistance of the Quiet Storm on 107.5 and the lingerie. We took everything off neatly. I even folded my dress.

Chase had stopped picking up my laundry. I had stopped picking up dinner to have ready for him after work. We stopped emailing during the day to take our minds off our jobs. It was hot by now, yet we hadn't been to one outdoor concert or festival. A few times, I met him at his office for nearby happy hours. He put me in a cab uptown after. Then it was the solstice: concerts, full beaches, and blankets spread. We were nowhere near them. We barbecued on his tiny patio on the Fourth of July. His older balding roommate scared up a younger blonde to talk to; she and I waited patiently to eat while the men showed off their grilling skills.

"Let's go on the fire escape . . . I have this bottle of wine," I suggested one night.

"No drinking for me tonight, babe. Booze isn't on my diet, remember?" he said.

So I slipped into his boxers and T-shirt to go drink Riesling outside alone, barefoot, staring ahead at an ashy moon and squares of light from so many Hamilton Heights windows. When I came back into bed, Chase was engrossed in *The Myth of Sanity*, with its subtitle *Divided Consciousness and the Promise of Awareness*.

"I'm really digging this," he told me. "This lady knows what she's talking about. We're all going through life with something, wearing these masks, to cover it up. I wonder if I'm doing that. A Black man, everything on my back. I never thought of it as trauma."

I shrank away. It seemed he talked to me personally and I didn't like it. He didn't want to do anything about my traumas. His great American Dream was always so much more important. When our mother was dying, he wanted to network in the tropics and visit his boyhood home. The honeymoon feast cooked down to the gristle of grief responsible for the first time we fell into each other's arms, and the next times, and the upcoming times.

He threw salt in the wound, reading straight from the book: "'The survivors I see in my practice have known undistilled fear, have seen how nakedly terrifying life can be, and in many cases have seen how nakedly ugly their fellow human beings can be. Listening to their stories, no one could be surprised that they consider the possibility of not going on. In the struggle with the power of their past experiences, even the biological imperative to survive is puny . . . No. Their choosing to die would not be surprising. What is so extraordinary about these people is they choose to live.'"

I did not know how to fill the space of his pregnant pause. He reached for my hand.

"Yes, we do," he said to me. "No, we have. Whatever it takes, babe, we'll make it."

There was safety in his touch. The beauty in his face drew me into it. When we started kissing, just like the first times, I knew he wanted me—purely Autumn, not Summer packaged in a new way. And what bothered me most, more than how true what he said was, is it was that easy. It was easy to forget her, put her away. Just like the world had.

I pulled away from him. "I can't read that pompous, cathartic shrink stuff. It's too much information to trust."

"You bought it." He pulled away with me, to the edge of the bed.

"I was looking for something else."

The maroon blanket was handy, gnarled at my pillow. I put it over my body, then slipped it up over my head.

"Autumn, I'm sorry. I guess I thought this would help. I'm having a hard time figuring out how to be with you, with everything going on."

Chase closed the book, pitched it to the floor, and pressed not too gently against me to reach over to turn off the lamp.

"What're you trying to do, smother me?" I yelled.

"Good night, Autumn."

I slapped his arm. "You really hurt my chest."

"Autumn, I said good night. Damn!"

He jumped up from under the covers with his pillow. He slammed the door so hard small wall hangings shook. I could not believe he did it. It was bad luck to go to bed angry. I did my best to stay silent as I walked after him. He was comfortable on the couch. I flipped the light switch. He twisted up with his arm over his eyes.

"Turn the lights off, Autumn," he mumbled. "I don't want to talk about this now. I have to get up early. I have a real job."

I tried, but couldn't hold back the anger. "You don't care a thing about anything I go through. You pulled me away from my mother knowing she was on her last legs!"

"Oh, so there you go. Autumn, that was not my fault."

"You cared about none of us. You were just thinking about fucking me then, right?"

"Me? Me? You were the one with panties on from Asha's sex party bullshit. While you wanna talk about me, I wasn't packing that kind of shit on a business trip."

"I was busy, taking care of my mother. It was all I had clean!"

"Yeah, right."

"You were the one who didn't let them know you needed your own room," I shouted. "I was just supposed to be going to get away and rest, not fuck your brains out."

"The travel department messed that up. You know that."

"You could've had the balls to demand those sons of bitches pay for my mother. And Penny. And all of us to come along! For your bullshit campaign."

"There's no way your mother could've come with us in the state she was in. And my bullshit campaigns just paid your damned rent this month."

"My mother's grave paid for my damned rent."

"Okay, look, whoever paid for the rent, I'm not gonna keep coming here to be your whipping post any longer. I haven't recognized you in months. I've tried to be there for you. No, I have been there. I'm outta here, Autumn."

He flew down the hall. I stood there. I felt like both cracking him upside the head with a bottle of wine and drinking what was left. I chose to do the latter.

In my old room, Chase pulled out the luggage he stored there because we had more space. A group of button-down shirts stuck on their hangers and flopped over the extended handle. He dumped a mesh bag of his socks and threw balled-up pairs onto the floor next to the luggage. He turned to the Lane cedar trunk at the foot of my four-poster bed, its covers bundled to near-human form. I had not slept there in ages. We rarely opened the trunk. Summer received it as a gift from a college friend's parents. They sent it straight from the manufacturer in Altavista, Virginia. Now, the trunk's baby-smooth wooden top was piled with my and Chase's hoodies, sweaters, and gym clothes I forgot to send to laundry. It explained the mustiness.

Chase hurled everything off the chest in one heap. Then he tore open the lid. The underside of the smooth caramel-colored lid snapped down gently into a folded-in, velvet-lined shelf. There he kept a watch, cuff links, and a few pinky rings I had forgotten about. Now I wished I had pawned his stuff. For what seemed like the first time, I glimpsed the diamond clusters and trinkets he gave Summer and me these past few years. The compartments in the trunk held the assortment with meticulousness. With his back to me, he picked his baubles from ours and pretended not to know I was at the door, swigging.

"Don't you put one finger on my stuff. They're gifts," I reminded him.

The tenor in my voice belonged to something else, not me. It was a woman barking for a part of her already gone, and another leaving soon. The part of Summer I carried with me readied to smash the wine bottle against the wall and carve our names into his back. So he would never, ever forget me and this chunk of our lives he tore into.

"I've been the only one here for you!" he yelled. "When you were in the hospital, I was the one who was there. All this madness this past year. I've been here, Autumn!"

"Fine, you don't have to be here for me anymore," I said. "Get out!"

"I'm going."

Chase feigned examining the jewelry—slowly and surely, with close-up inspection as if he had never seen it before, just like I barely had.

"Autumn, I told you to stay in New York. They wanted you to go to Grenada."

He set his jewelry inside a soft suede pouch that came with the luggage. He went on to slip each button-down off the heavy mahogany hangers and fold it. I stared at the luggage. I totally forgot. I bought him that luggage, as a platonic thank-you for the Grenada trip. It was half off at Barneys during the massive winter clearance. How could he think I did not care about him, or appreciate us together? We had risked our reputations to be with each other. We had moved past the shame and guilt. It had to mean something.

You can apologize, I thought to myself. Or beg. Or say: "I need you. I really do." As I was thinking about saying what I did not, Chase was talking to me. He stopped.

"You're not even listening to me," I heard him say. "You never listen anymore. I'm just here. Just a warm body. I don't know how to, what to . . . Fuck it."

"Do I really want to hear what you have to say to me?" I asked him. "You're leaving me. You said it. Why do I wanna listen to you now?"

"I tried to cancel the trip. They wouldn't let me. They'd already promised the client the timeline. They knew about Missus Spencer. It was all in motion. I tried to move it back, Autumn. I did. Then, you all made it seem like it was this great thing, for you to get away."

I never said out loud that I deduced Summer set me up to have time with Mama all to herself, precisely because she sensed an end that maybe I just did not want to. I never wanted to mar his memories of Summer, to put it in his face how calculating she had been.

"No," I told him. "I'm an adult. It was my choice, and fault. I shouldn't have gone. And maybe if I hadn't, she wouldn't have gone either."

I was trying to talk to him about our shame, humiliation, and lowering of our standards in this affair that needed to evolve into honesty and openness, not lies and hiding.

It was too late.

He sat down on the side of the bed, poking at the Timberlands he wanted to stuff his feet into. He struggled. With his head bent, I could see a colony of gray hairs at his crown. In my mind, I saw myself mount him on the bed. I would stroke his chest and jiggle my behind on top of his hardness, and squirm and twist until he reached for me to slip my panties off and bring him into me. But he shot up before I could reach him. He was on to one of my laundry bags now. Its contents were his random effort to pack enough clothes for a pouting period I was now nervous about.

He was really and truly getting out of my apartment. With him gone, I would have no other motion or sound in the house to remind me what day and time it was. Even the alarm of the refrigerator door shooshing open and shut or the soft pound of his feet on faux hardwood could do the trick. He kept me alive each time he put the shower to use, clicked on the light switches, or burdened the teakettle. And, his oblivious late-night snores had taken the place of Summer tapping around in the night. If Chase had caught me last year, before I came home to the end of my childhood, before I regretted not cherishing it with as much pride and celebration as my mother gave to my baby teeth or drawings, I would have hurled myself in front of him and fought. I would have come out of my corner ready to knock him out in my home, our home, so he would awaken so happy he would stay.

But now, I was spent. To have a man walk out on me would not be the worst thing that happened. To feel this way was thrilling

and poignant and disappointing all at once. I had entered the
"I've seen worse" category of jaded human beings. Before innocence goes rancid, we fight for perfection and guard against the
worst of any outcome. We know how to hunt down optimism in
the darkest trenches, to retain those goals of purity young eyes
depend on. But after long, grown-ups have so many checked boxes
add up along the sanity-insanity divide: bankruptcy, home loss,
divorce, defaulted loans, unemployment, health scares, dead parents, quicksands into adultery, faded looks, slowed metabolisms.
The bar is so lowered that more is tolerable and "worse" does not
terrify like it used to. Maybe Chase felt this way too. He was me-
thodical, pragmatic, organized, unemotional about another lost
thing.

"Do what you want to do," was the last thing I said to him.

It was the time in the night when preachers talk about God
above toll-free numbers on many channels. One year ago, I would
have used the time Chase was still snoring or Summer was just
going to bed to do those things Emily Post, Iyanla, Dolly Parton,
and my mother told me to do: meditation and yoga, journal out
my thoughts, touch my toes, visualize the expansion of my orga-
nization and my name in lights.

Instead I was head-split drunk from a bottle of wine tucked between my breasts. Spit rolled down to land on the cucumber-green
pillows. A gray-haired and twinkly-eyed preacher shouted "You
can change your life!" at me. He had humming and a choir in the
background of his lecture. I turned around to be more comfortable. Then Chase smashed his lips onto my stinky-spit cheek with
a whisper: "I do love you, Autumn. I really do."

It was the thing that put me to sleep. But it was not real.

CHASE CAME TO THE UNITED STATES to live with illegal relatives in a Black and immigrant depot in Miami called Liberty

City. He was only ten. He traveled here by boat, starting from Venezuela. The relatives told him to forget his real name and his home. He was put in private school by a White woman his uncle's wife cleaned house for. New paperwork was created for him at the school; old paperwork was "lost" or "missing." The woman kept him in schools that sped him to a high ACT score, a scholarship, and in-state tuition. He moved to New York later to work at the college buddy's marketing company. Summer temped there, a necessity for her. It was where they met.

All this time, I had seen him as one of the few constants of our lives. Near family. I never considered we were the same for him. I knew he wouldn't go for long.

He'd miss me.

We are framing a new school picture from our "daughter" Fatu, in Sierra Leone, and thank God these do-gooders have given me an African child smiling rather than in stereotypical pain and suffering for being $20 richer every month.

We are headed to Far Rockaway, last stop on the A train, squirming with our knees pressed together, trying not to laugh, as wine coolers in our thermoses run through us until we get to his coworkers' house on the water, where cool women turn roasting s'mores over burning branches into a teaching moment for their toddlers, and spectacled men bob to John Coltrane and Tom Petty. We are anonymous adulterers, in separate disparate friend groups who know nothing of our secret history.

We are on the fire escape, counting the number of White people who walk by or through nearby doors.

We are under the covers, and I tell him I think I want to be celibate but it is not true because we laugh and use the last condom.

We are watching *Saturday Night Live* with the lights dimmed and too much butter on the popcorn, complaining it is not as funny as it used to be and waiting for Lorde to wail "Royals."

We are tasting the freezer-burnt ice cream we just bought and blaming the bodega.

We are wobbling on the bed to swish dust off the ceiling fans, pollen off the sills.

We are yelling at Asha to "get yo ass in the house, girl!" out of an open window.

We are making sure the rooftop padlock is secure, that I am safe at home, always.

We are dreaming in familiar arms. We are in love. And I missed it.

How?

SEVENTEEN

I awoke short of breath, relieved to unshackle a nightmare where Summer was screaming in back of a truck-stop killer's semi. I tumbled to the toilet, retching. Once in the kitchen to ignite my teapot, I remembered it was scorched. I'd left it on during a nap. Chase must have used something to smash my framed poster of Gabriel Johns's SWAG Marketing ad to itty-bitty bits of glass. I cut my feet when I stumbled upon them.

Without Chase I had one less guarantee I would not become a Joyce Vincent, a very real fact of urbane singledom. I found a Netflix documentary about her. London, England's sister city to my New York, swallowed her alive in its overpopulated galaxy, just as Cathy had said. She wilted to teeth and bones in the unfair grave of her flat, absent of visitors. Her sad biopic, *Dreams of a Life*, paraded intelligent, articulate associates who falsely concluded an active member of society not yet forty would choose to go missing. Some expressed guilt. Many, without self-blame, came up with reasons to blame her for her own neglect: She was moody, she disappeared often, she rushed away when she ran into friends.

These were similar smears I heard poured onto Summer. I felt how I had slackened with her disappearance, caught in a maelstrom of my own crises: financial, romantic, emotional.

And this laxity and paucity is what doomed Joyce. Maybe Summer. Maybe me.

So I broke down in a few days. Online, Chase showed no new updates. It remained that way, so I just liked an old picture he first uploaded of him with college friends. Then, I called after I knew he'd be sleeping. I did not want to put him on the spot.

"Hi. I was just thinking about you. I know we have a lot to talk about. I'm ready to listen now. Can see each other this week?"

I eagerly checked his voice message the next morning.

I have a conference in Boston to get ready for. I'll call you when I get back.

When a few days passed, I tried texting.

"Hi. How was Boston?"

"It was productive."

"Great. Any new clients? Your roommate find a new job yet?"

He left me hanging.

I went the professional route.

"Good morning. I been poking around on other Caribbean bed-and-breakfasts websites. The Johns's job could take a while, but I'm up for it."

"You didn't seem interested at first, but I'll pass Olivia your info."

Desperate, I emailed him a nag: "We're supposed to go to the Nicki Minaj concert at the Barclays Center."

He got back to me after the end-of-July concert took place. "I didn't think you still wanted to go. I sold the tickets."

I tried email again, and decided to play the weaker sex. "Look at this email Clara McIntyre sent me. She says her company wants an expert 'more equipped' to handle their needs at this time, and she wishes me the best in my future endeavors. You think it's worth a try to meet with her? I really need her business."

"It's up to you. Do what you want to do."

He hit me with the last words I had spoken to him. Those were his last to me. For now, at least. So I made like my taste for sushi at this one place in his neighborhood had nothing to do with passing by his apartment. Neither did window-shopping for gold pens at a store I could not afford near his Chambers subway stop. I kept my apartment free of garbage and the counters clean, in case he showed up. I cooled beers in the fridge. I picked up a man's terry cloth robe, slippers, and sweat suit at Marshalls. He'd need something to wear if he stayed overnight. He had run away without leaving a sock behind. I Googled "love spells." This led me to a number in New Orleans, on a website picturing a long-bearded pink man standing at a straw-roofed storefront, in a swamp. His spell casting started at $300 one-time and $500 for a package.

"I won't do anything negative," he cautioned in a Creole voice laced with coughs.

I felt scared and hung up.

Determined, I improvised. I bought red, pink, and white dollar-store candles. These were the common colors of love, passion, and purity according to many spells I condensed into one all my own. I chanted several verses compiled from different versions. The August waxing gibbous moon wasn't totally full. I chanted twice to make up for the inconvenience. Had it not been for my dwindling bank balance, I would have called a psychic.

I did the next best thing.

NO WOMAN COULD CONSOLE A downturn she had never known the upside of, so I called Asha over other friends who never really saw me with Chase. Our usual watering holes, St. Nick's Jazz Pub and the Lenox Lounge, had both closed in recent years. Neither their fame nor the lingering spirits of all their past regular jazzmen (and women) could surmount Harlem's rising rents. Asha and I settled for Red Rooster's upper circle bar, the last-ditch fort against folks with no reservation. We crunched next to a dance floor the size of a small farm pigpen, full of aging B-boys and house dancers. We stole our seats only because the DJ got them moving.

"I'd take the bartender home tonight if I couldn't tell he's gay," Asha said. "Why waste such a thing? Look at him . . . A vision from above."

"I don't know," I pouted. "He's cute." Then, "Chase hasn't been around lately. Seems like since I got out of the hospital, he's been busy with his job."

"Girl, let the man work," Asha told me. "Then marry him so you won't have to."

"Well, I've lost enough people. It's rude of him to disappear like this now."

"Don't let your qi spin out of control again from worrying about it. Girl, you were a mess. He'll be back around. If I had money, I'd bet you. You know, I screwed two dudes last month. Not one had money for a movie. I had to tell one I wanted an orgasm, too."

"I told you to leave those broke brothers alone."

"They're good men. Really, good men. Fine. Talented."

"Good men have money for the movies, certainly the matinee," I told her. "You're a beautiful, good, hardworking girl, Asha. Love who you want, but raise the bar."

I waved my PayPal card for business expenses. The cute bartender seized it.

"You have no business messing around with any man who doesn't have a good job and education or can't take you to the movies," I lectured, ironically. Apparently, I didn't have business messing around with a man who worked a good job and took me to movies.

"Well, they're working on their educations. One is studying

welding. The other was getting his associate's in business. He did some time, you know."

"Now, what did you expect? Do these men even have names?"

"Solomon and Jay. But Autumn, Black men are hurt and lost. The only way we can come together is to abolish these standards set up by establishments who've left us out."

"Just get drunk on me to get yourself good to call up Mr. Right Now when we get back but only the one who gave you an orgasm, please. You can't marry either one."

We avoided looking at the mostly older men and young boys in caps. In a pair, it was easier to look like lesbians in love, so the male species kept a distance. We took our minds off not belonging here with Cokes, caffeine for the road, before I closed the tab.

"I will definitely take your advice, though it means I have to raise the bar when I haven't lifted weights since college," Asha said. "But so long as you keep taking all my advice, I'll do the same. I'm proud of you, lady."

Her tone was not the usual: the rehearsed parody of a holistic quack to the stars who gets a book deal, infomercials, and glitzy website. Her expression was one to stop the conversation. I did not understand it, or my reply:

"I'll be glad when I'm proud of me too," I said. "I can't get there if I'm losing everybody."

"Even if you keep everybody, it's no good to you if you can't find yourself," she smiled. "So long as we stay off rooftops and out of hospitals, we have a shot."

I pretended I was not worried PayPal would not come through. It did, though probably from giving up on that balance and going directly to my bank account. Uber was out of the question though. Asha and I wobbled away. My blurred vision made out a subway entrance and its directions: UPTOWN & THE BRONX. We felt the sidewalk quake, joined hands, and ran down as best we could to meet the 3 train uptown to home, a nice thing to say we had. On the way, Asha dozed. I just felt happy, at peace.

"What did you say?" I heard Asha giggle, as I gripped the railing inside home.

In my head, I thought I had said I would get hard at work on her website soon, and it would be tempting with tons of juicy citrus colors and subtle call-to-action leads. But I would have failed a sobriety test at that point and could not clarify.

I staggered to the top floor. I smelled the new neighbors' weed smoke. How audacious, for these people not even here two months. How entitled, to just know we would not complain to our landlords. What if our mothers were visiting, if I had one? I guessed they saw assumed we were "down."

I timed my entrances and exits wisely to avoid an encounter. I could not muster polite pleasantries now. If I heard their conversations or bags whisking through the halls or keys turning the lock, I hesitated at my landing. If I glimpsed them detained in hellos or good-byes or deliveries in the foyer, I continued on around the block until I was sure they were gone. The few times I crossed one of the three on the street, they barely looked at me—the most telling introduction. Colonialists weren't known for warm greetings.

But I would remind them we were here first and they needed to play by whatever rules we indicated they should. I would do it subtly, quietly, and in so many other words—the way Summer taught me to handle ones who thought the whole world was theirs.

EIGHTEEN

Control. I had to find it.

Excuses to give up and check out wouldn't stop. I had just wrapped my head around the possibility of a Joyce Vincent, perhaps worse than a Shanice Johnson and Dejanay Little. A family mob missed them. Not Joyce. Not Summer either. I understood why she wouldn't endure the abrupt family reunion Mama's funeral became, knowing we wouldn't see most of those people again until our funerals or theirs. I was an army of one for her, scanning every public face and voice until I had headaches. I counted my blessings, for at least every time I thought I saw her, a real body was the cause. The woman just walking her dog was no hallucination, but an illusion. Asha saw her, too. Still. At the rate of getting myself so worked up to land in a hospital bed, hallucinations were only a matter of time.

And now a young Black woman, Sandra Bland, got stopped somewhere in Texas for changing lanes improperly. She somehow found herself fighting with a White male cop over this. Or rather, her failure to put out a cigarette when he asked her to. She was only in the hick town to start a new job at the college she graduated from. I could identify what broke in her mind: your reward for a job offer is a struggle with a man, then a weekend in a jail.

How's that for irony? Only time would tell if her "suicide" in her jail cell was really foul play. I watched her confused mother and sisters, dignified women under pressure to be professional mourners, without rage, in press conferences. I remembered all the times I also strut the high road over my own living hells.

But the high road was sinking in the fleeting comfort of a spent life insurance windfall, my average woman's dependence on a lost man, an overextended term of mourning, and a losing battle for justice I was all by myself in. The most alive thing in my space now was a desktop IBM. It had chips and wires—no blood, teeth, or bones. The only thing here who could make money was me. If I had to, I would show up back in Hedgewood, the alien planet of small-town middle America. The mall was always hiring. Residents had nowhere else to go. My deadline to make that decision lit a fire under me to get control in New York.

Today.

Right now.

I started with a call to Fran under pretense of a complaint about marijuana smoke.

"I'm not related to Bob Marley, though I wish I was part of his inheritance kingdom today," I told her. "Just because I'm Black—"

"Oh, no, Autumn," Fran interrupted. "Please don't imply that. I would never assume you should be automatically comfortable with marijuana because you're Black. I'll let it go this time, but let me know immediately if it happens again."

"Cool beans."

Then I took another matter into my own hands: "Have you heard from Belinda?"

"Um, no, Autumn. She didn't exactly leave on the best terms."

"I know she owed you money. She borrowed a lot of money from neighbors, too," I lied. "Maybe I could contact her at work to see if she plans to pay us back."

"We tried that, Autumn," Fran sighed. "Several times, trust me. But . . ."

I knew my old neighbor was a nurse's assistant at a rehabilitation facility in Queens. After we hung up, I searched for the address. It was quite a train trek. No wonder she always rushed out at the crack of dawn only to get home in the dark.

With the information I had, next I had to plan how best to approach her. I should probably start off slow, with some friendliness and concern about how she moved without telling us. Then, I would not beat around the bush. First responses are truth.

"Did you put somebody up to trying to rob us here, for your money troubles?"

Only her swift, vehement denial or utter confusion would satisfy me it was not possible. A seemingly rehearsed pat answer would not.

I wanted to consult with Detective Montgomery first. I went to the precinct in the morning, unannounced.

"No, I have not tracked down your old neighbor," he answered me.

"How could you not take this seriously?" I asked. "I'm saying maybe this woman is untrustworthy. She couldn't pay rent, left in the middle of the night, like a thief. Those kind of people do set up robberies. We never went up to the roof. Why was my sister up there?"

"Belinda fully cooperated with police and gave a statement. Did you see it?"

"No," I said. "I'd like to. Look, I'm not accusing Belinda of murder or anything."

"It sounds like that's exactly what you're doing."

"She had motives to send someone, a stranger we wouldn't recognize, to three single women living alone. She knew our habits, our comings and goings."

"She did," he agreed. "But in this case, her knowing all that saved your life."

"My life?"

"She was the one who got the fire department there the night you reported your sister as missing. Without her, nobody would've ever shown up for you."

"Nobody called the fire department. I called 911."

Detective Montgomery looked at me, started to say something, and stopped. He delved into his desk mine of mail, papers, and notes. He excavated Summer's two journals. I trusted him with Mama's handmade gifts to search for clues, not to question clues I found.

"I want you to read through these," he said. "I think you're missing some things."

"What?" I asked.

He shook his head, and then he spoke quietly.

"Autumn, you know, I was thinking you would come clean with me. You seemed to be getting to that. Now, you've paused. I want to get you some help."

"Help? Oh, how convenient. Everybody's a psychologist these days."

"No, everybody's not. But I am."

"Oh and you just happened to take a pay cut, and risk your life every day, to work for the NYPD?"

He should have been of more use to me by now. This wasn't working out.

"I'm serious, Autumn," he droned. "My work with you hasn't gone anywhere. You're just using me to indulge yourself and go deeper into this than I thought you would."

"I'm gonna go as deep as I have to," I said, "to find my sister. Even if the detective assigned to her case doesn't care."

"I am not assigned to your sister's case. I'm assigned to yours."

Control. I had to find it.

I had to get it. I threw up an instant wall between Detective Montgomery and myself. No more walks down my memory lane, hand in hand with my confidence. No more relaxation. No more long conversations. And, he certainly could never show up at my door again, to recommend anything to me.

I would end things nicely. He would not have a clue how I felt. It was easiest.

"Thank you for all your help," I smiled. "I know you care. But I think you've done all you can and I need to move on to people who can do more for this case."

"Autumn," he said, "we met at Harlem Hospital, right before New Year's Eve."

I had not been a patient in a hospital in years, before this spring. After the bus ride with Asha. For dehydration and exhaustion and low blood sugar. He kept on.

"A police officer was with me when I first interviewed you, yes. But police often sit in on volatile patients. Especially when a patient is suicidal."

His voice drifted. The room spun.

"Patient? Suicidal?"

"You wanted to believe I was a detective. I thought you were joking. Then it seemed like how you wanted to open up to me, so I allowed it. It's my fault for not correcting you sooner. Which I've tried to do, by the way, as you've had me and an overwhelmed precinct look for a woman we found no signs ever existed. I've found some truth in these journals you told me were Summer's. Like why you told me they were hers."

"They are Summer's! And I need them back. They're heirlooms."

"Yes, please, read them. I've marked pages I think tell us why Summer isn't here."

I seized Mama's work, Summer's thoughts, my possessions. I

unzipped my purse to drop in the journals. I looked around the office. On the table was an hourglass, something I'd never noticed before. Near the smooth, round, shiny stones and picture of his family. The water cooler was in the corner, as usual.

"I need to talk to your sergeant," I hissed.

"I don't have a sergeant," he said. "I don't even have a boss. I do pro bono work here when I have time. This is just a Police Athletic League. They loan me space."

"What're you . . . ?"

"All this time, you've been thinking you were visiting a police station?"

He reached for a manila folder on his desk, pulled out the same gridded sheet he always pulled out when we talked. It was clear. He stopped talking to make several notes in a top grid. I reached over his desk and snatched the paper away.

"Autumn!"

I was a fast reader. I had a near-perfect verbal score on both the SAT and GRE. I read for a living, mostly shit that needed to be fixed. I blogged, blabbed, without a comma out of place. I could glance at a page for a few seconds and know what it said, interpret meaning, harvest context clues. I needed no time to grasp his notes: "Client is in advanced stage of derealization, bordering on full disassociation. Client is in fuller characterization of an altered personality, a woman with a missing twin she calls Summer and has possibly presented as before in therapy or with others."

He reached for the papers. I threw them onto the floor.

"I can show you all my notes," he said. "I have nothing to hide. But you need to be prepared for what they say and ready to hear it all, to move forward."

"Client? Derealization? Altered?"

"Autumn, you threatened to jump off your roof. Had it not been for your neighbor downstairs, you might have done so. The lady saw you pacing the roof. She called 911. It was too tricky for them to come in behind you, so the fire department set up a landing apparatus while you carried on. They said you sounded very angry. But, you never jumped. You climbed down their ladder on your own."

"You're getting me mixed up with my sister, Detective Montgomery. Of course," I laughed. "Of course. Our father was a fireman. She would have listened to them. All this time, you knew my sister climbed down a ladder and you didn't tell me? Where is she?"

"*You* climbed down the ladder. *You* claimed to be 'Summer Spencer' on your intakes, insurance forms, everything. But your IDs said 'Autumn.' Police clarified that."

I heard him, but nothing made any sense. I paced around the office.

"You said you were only up there to look for your sister, Summer, not trying to harm yourself. There's so many cases in that place. Your insurance only allowed so much, so hey. That's the system. Your word was taken and you were released. I agreed to treat you for free. You went home with Chase. He was very upset, so we never got to talk."

So now Chase was in on it too? No wonder he dashed out and never returned.

"There's no twin," I heard. "You pretend you have her, but there's no evidence of her. *You* walked out up to your own roof. It was only you, Autumn. I know that now."

The water cooler was in the corner. Was he giving me water or vodka? Was I getting drunk to let this go on this long? It would have no smell, but the taste . . .

"You're trying to make me go crazy," I said. "You will not. If everything I've been through hasn't done it so far, you're not gonna start me to it now."

"And we need to move on to everything you've been through so this part of you can speak of why you created Summer, and why you need her so badly."

I grabbed my purse so fast everything in it spilled. I captured the journals first. I panicked to put it all back in: my Carmex, my creamy lipstick, my perfume, my travel-size lotion Chase always gave me from his business trips, my things—not Summer's, or some woman who thought she was Summer, or some woman who made Summer up.

I knew who I was.

I put my purse over my shoulder and used the chair for balance as I stood again.

"As a professional," Detective Montgomery went on, "I wouldn't be doing my job if I let you go now. Please, Autumn, just stay. I really want to talk some more."

The softer he became, the louder I roared.

"I don't need hospitals or doctors or talking," I shouted. "I am *not* crazy."

"You're not crazy at all. You're remarkable, one of my most high-functioning clients. But that doesn't mean you don't have some traumas to address. I can help you do it, but not by hiding behind Summer anymore. We must talk about you, Autumn."

"I'm never talking about anything with you again."

I ran around him to the door, looking for someone else in the hallway through the see-through glass. The days, weeks, and months I wasted thinking Montgomery was an ally skid across my mind like pages in a book and kept landing back to this page, here now, and the words on it.

"Autumn, please," he yelled.

He moved his back against the doorknob.

I had never fought with a man. I never thought Montgomery would be the first.

"I can help you," he said, glancing out of the door's window. "I *want* to help you. When your mother died, a lot of what was pent up inside came flooding out—"

I battered him with my purse, at his face and chest and stomach. He put up his hands and would not move away. I had nowhere to go. I was trapped and cornered. He could grab me before I broke through the window. I ran behind his desk.

"Just let me out of here. I have to go home. Please, just let me go home."

He kept on, away from the door and toward me with large hands, a big face, and a chest so wide I could not see beyond it anymore.

"You needed someone. A sister who could paint and draw. The artist. The one who was adventurous and risky, while you stayed quiet and routine. A protector . . ."

"I'm not listening anymore."

I pounded my palms at my ears. The whole room compressed to nothing but his voice. And I couldn't quiet it even as he fell to a near whisper.

"Who talks about Summer, but you? Who else asks about her?"

"It's all still fresh," I cried. "She only went missing in December."

This demon went on.

"Do your neighbors mention her? Why hasn't your family come to New York to help you look for her? Outta all the men in New York, you just had to take your sister's? I've been to your home. I only saw pictures of you, not one with a twin or any other woman who looked like you. Not one. I glanced at a recent life insurance policy, I assume your mother's? You were the only beneficiary. I did not see why your mother would leave Summer out. Up until then, I believed you, Autumn. Then, well . . . I didn't. I just couldn't understand why you were only talking to me to find a woman who was never here."

I moved under the window. I stood on weary legs, cold and shaky arms holding me. I pressed one ear against the wall to muffle this man's voice, his lies, his wickedness.

"How come nobody but you ever tried to push an investigation? Not one friend."

"They're failed artists," I sobbed. "Climbers. They can't climb someone who's not here. They're just users. Druggies even."

"Were those your friends?" I heard, like an echo. "The ones who never called back about an investigation in a woman named 'Summer'? You were the one with cocaine in your system. I have the medical records. Your name is on them."

The hard wall hurt my shoulder as I pushed into it. I could not bust through concrete and pour myself out onto the street.

"All right, Autumn," he sighed. "Let me see you home now. If you can show me a piece of mail or bill for Summer, and not for your mother or you, I'll believe you. If you can show me a picture of you with your sister, I will believe you. I make mistakes, too."

"I'm never showing you shit again."

"Autumn, please listen to me. Sometimes, people dissociate from themselves. Altered personalities sometimes take years to come out. When your mother died . . ."

"Split personality disorder?" I talked into the cinderblock wall, rubbed my cheek on its textures. I could have beat my head into it. "That's not even real. It's just phony people on talk shows."

"It's not called *split personality* anymore. It's called dissociative identity disorder. A fragmented identity. A multiplicity of selves. Amnesia, from one part to another. Or, the forgetfulness you have in extreme. Impulsive behavior. Flashbacks. And yes, self-harm."

I started to choke. He left me and went to his water cooler. He brought me a plastic cup of water. But I wanted myself to choke it out. I coughed, sat down on his chair, and held my stomach. I clung to my purse, the only thing in here besides me that I knew well.

The awful man sat on the edge of the desk. I turned his chair around to the wall, to keep my back to him so he would not talk anymore. I had letters, cards, presents, and pictures from my sister. I even started and ended my period with her. It's just how symbiotic and synergized we were, sepia skin and auburn hair, size 8 feet. Only our personalities, resumes, and dental records looked different. A monozygote, just split off into two beings. I was here, still, to keep our cells moving around the world a little while longer.

Grandma sat in the rocking chair and she crocheted the maroon blanket I couldn't wait to have, but Summer took it always without giving me a turn.

"Your mama's water broke in my front yard when she was squat down eating dirt. She was like my Aunt Cassie down South. But we ain't have no iron pills back then. We do now. But your mama threw down those pills from the doctor and went right back to digging that dirt. I let her go ahead. She carried you over the summer, the worst time.

"It was so hot the day you was born your mama almost laid in that hospital by herself. Summer supposed to be over, but seem like it was just starting. Wasn't enough money in the world to get us out from under them fans. Top of September and your daddy ain't have no air conditionin' in his car. I don't even know if they had it in the cars back then. So I wanted to name you Summer. That fit you best. Your mama said it sound like a porn name. I wouldn't know. I ain't never seen no pornos. But she said Autumn, close as it was, could make sense. That's how you got your name. I love both just the same."

Summer even took my name.

"Autumn," the man in the room with me interrupted, "there is no Summer. I thought she could be a delusion, and you'd need medication. But you don't hear her or see her. You've been saying the opposite. You only identify with her, and sometimes even as her."

The man in the room smiled at me. We were still and calm, together.

"I can help you find Summer, so you can talk to her again. That's what you want. Thank you for trusting me, to share her with. So, can we talk about you?"

"No," I said. "No." And then, "Never."

I caught the man off guard. I do not remember turning the doorknob.

Maybe I ran through the door. My Foxy Brown inside could do that. Where was my pistol? A lady officer was alone at the front desk. Then I heard her and the man calling my name. But I ran and ran and ran. Across 151st Street an ice cream truck almost struck me. I did not stop to check the direction of home. I did not need to. I could walk Harlem in my sleep. But I couldn't go home. Not now. So I just ran and ran and ran and ran . . .

Nineteen

I ran in a maze between St. Nicholas and Edgecombe before I tripped forward up a sudden hill. I didn't know I busted my bottom lip. I knew I hit it, and it hurt.

I ran past stares, snickers, and wide-eyed gazes. Cathy's Park Slope co-op was near the Days Inn of Brooklyn's downtown, off a few trains I was sure branched off of the F, which branched off the D, which was waiting for me down in the 145th Street station.

I wasn't totally sure of Cathy's address. My phone was dead. I would walk until I recognized it: by a waterless fountain in a taller brown building's courtyard. The upper apartments had outdoor balconies. The grass was always neat. Maybe the gardener would be out, and allow me in. People of all colors and ages would come by. Some would have little dogs. One of the people would trust me . . . *Cathy Adeosun, you know? She has a son and just had a little baby girl?*

She lived on the ninth floor. I knew this from the number of birthday cards, holiday greetings, and gifts for her children I mailed. I would knock on every door in the hallway. If she was behind none, I would go back down the elevator and start on the other side. Or, maybe I would put my ear to every door until I heard her tell Oscar not to run so fast and to put his underwear back on. Sara would be crying. I would hear Fela Kuti, Miriam Makeba, Manu Chao, or Onyeka Onwenu. I would stay on her carpeted floor with pillows beneath me, underneath fabric with winding histories Cathy would tell me. I would fetch her breast pump, warm bottles in slightly furling water, change diapers, unhinge the stroller, and take Oscar to a Disney movie or to McDonald's for a Happy Meal. I would go with her to visit her parents in Bed-Stuy, where their brownstone sat on Gates Avenue. We would drink wine while her mother approved of everything I said, and eat lots of bread and rice and lamb.

I walked off the D to wait for the F at West Fourth Street. I gave $5 to a fervent bucket drummer and took a pamphlet from a Jehovah's Witnesses team. Then a train with a dull orange bullet flew to the platform and stopped. I pressed my lips together to dull the pain. White collars rushed on at Delancey and Broadway, to stand at the sweaty poles. The train came up above ground across the bridge I did not remember from my previous trips to see Cathy. I guessed it was the Manhattan Bridge. After the bridge, dark suits departed in clusters at Marcy Avenue and Hewes Street. I blended in with the people left behind with me, mostly Black and Latin. I kept my eyes on the city gliding past the window, moving as if it had wheels and I were stationary, fixed, constructed, indestructible, and eternal. I waited to hear Seventh Avenue. The train would plunge underground again at some point. Fewer stops then, more gliding. I needed to close my eyes, to forget this whole day.

I wouldn't let that outrageous man up in Harlem get to me.

THE CONDUCTOR ANNOUNCED MYRTLE. I opened my eyes. Bushwick Shop and Save in the train window. A laundromat popped out below the platform. A market on the other side. A row of restaurants. The rush-hour people. Percolating blight.

I needed to get off and find somewhere to use a toilet. The ride was so long.

The Myrtle Avenue noise made 125th sound quiet. Four thoroughfares crisscrossed the intersection. The density of storefronts, hair salons, beauty supply stores, markets, bodegas, furniture stores, and apartment buildings engulfed my attention. I ignored the men who stared at my face. I did not feel my Foxy Brown any more, to suck my teeth or roll my eyes or share my offense with a glare. I felt limp and trounced.

I saw a nail salon. I needed a pedicure, but was in no mood to sit for one. I would be doing too much to circle back to one of the dollar stores to buy flip-flops or sandals to keep my toes uncovered. I could go for an eyebrow wax instead. I had let them go so fuzzy. I'd let myself go in general. Running was time-consuming.

The soft acidic smell of the salon soothed my sensation of an inner dismantling. I knew it well. A boy stopped applying acrylic silk wrap to a little girl's fingertips. Her mother sat nearby with toes inside the quick-dry lamp. He walked over to find me examining the poster of prices near the door, and its blessed Mastercard label at the bottom with other credit card insignias—for a minimum of $20.

"What you getting?"

Eight-dollar brow wax. Five-dollar lip wax. It would add up to enough for whoever took care of me to get a better tip than most left. An unoccupied older lady in a blue smock came smiling up behind the man, her arms outstretched to me. She beamed.

"Hi, no see you long time . . . Come!"

She glided me to the "wax room," a curtained spare closet with boxes stacked at its edges, and a cracked rubber spa bed covered in wrinkled tissue paper she did not replace. She only smoothed it out and pulled up to where my head would rest. She gave me a tissue and held a hand mirror in front of me. Plum-colored lipstick smudged one corner of my mouth.

"Lie down," she said.

I pressed the tissue into my lip and saw it turn pink. "Can I use the bathroom first?"

"Oh. Yes, yes."

The woman pointed past the curtain to a door with the last of its former brown paint still evident in hanging peels. My knees touched the toilet seat soon as I walked into a bowl of backed-up toilet paper and red rust stains. A box of Kleenex sat on the tank. I latched the hook into a nail stuck in the doorway, dropped my jeans, and sat down without wiping the seat first. Pee flushed out in a large burst. I felt the sting of more in my bladder, mashed my elbows into my thighs and squeezed my stomach slowly in and out until two more streams came down. When I wiped myself, I saw blood on the tissue. I checked my purse. I did not have my usual stash of liners in my pocketbook. I curled half the tissues together and bunched the creation into my panties. Someone knocked before I could debate the risk of flooding if I flushed. I did not. Women were used to seeing these things and the men would just have to deal.

"Wait a moment."

I wiped my fingers with tissue, not wanting to walk to the main sink where the workers poured out noodle broth and filled hot pots for tea, customers washed fingertips free of oil before their nails were polished, and everyone washed their hands for the bathroom. When I unhooked the door, the mother was before me. She stood on the edges of her feet with cotton balls still stuck between her toes in her paper-thin pink sandals.

"Sorry," I told her.

"No worries," she said. "I been holding out until my polish got hard. They charge you now when you smudge on your way out, even if you tip. They want to do the whole nail over. Can't even give you a decent bathroom for—"

"Would you happen to have a pad or tampon on you?" I asked.

"Geez Louise, I don't think I do." She put her hand on her forehead.

"It's okay. I'll just have to stop at the store. And, uh, it's clogged."

"Gotcha. That's the hood for you. Excuse me."

My brow stylist leaned on the spa bed smoothing her smock. She had no look on her face until she saw me. Then she clinched into what seemed to be the same automatic smile, no in-between space for her lips to part or cheeks to work.

I lay down on the bed and closed my eyes, listening to the pitter-patter of wooden sticks in a pot of warm wax. Normally, I stopped workers in these joints and asked them to open a new applicator for me. But I trusted she was clean enough. A sense of something swirled, serenity for me to zone out as I had on the train. She came close to my face with warm breath in even sighs. My head slipped to the side.

"Oh, no, no," she said, her dark eyes squinched on me when I opened my eyes. "No move, or wax come down. It burn you bad. You should know."

"Okay," I said, and she giggled at me.

She pat on the paper strips and rubbed me right where I needed it, each gentle mash at my temple and atop my eyelids releasing a knot in my head, clearing it up. She removed the strips on one eye quickly and adequately, with no smarting. When she came back with more wax on the wooden strip and a new paper applicator in her hand, my eyes opened briefly and then fluttered back down.

"Long day?" she asked softly. "Lot of work? You shouldn't stress so."

"I know," I whispered.

After my brow stylist removed the last bits of paper, she mashed above the bridge of my nose where Asha did as well—to open my third eye, Asha would tell me. The woman kneaded the area with her thumb before she lifted the paper. She wiped around my mouth and nose with a tissue paper, before she set warm wax down above my lips. Her pull was gentler there. She patted at me to look at my reflection in a mirror she held for me. I saw my new face: bright, alert, and competent now.

"You like?" she asked me.

"Yes, I do," I smiled. "Thank you. I really like it. I'll have to leave your tip on my card. I don't have any cash. I came all the way from Harlem, on a whim."

"No, fine," the brow stylist said. "Keep growing them in. Next time, it'll be perfect."

"Hey, chica," I heard behind me.

I turned to see the mother. She took my hand and pushed a hard plastic wedge in it.

"Had one in my makeup bag," she said. "The oddest places we find these things."

"Well, you're smarter than I am," I told her. "Thank you so much."

"It'll hold you over."

She looked at my stylist and gestured to her brows and above her lip. The stylist grinned that same automatic grin and led the woman to the old tissue paper and cracked bed. I waved good-bye to them.

"Go home to sleep now," the stylist said. "See you next time. Don't be so long."

I went back to the bathroom and let the bundle of tissue slip away. I washed my hands in the communal sink. The entire front wall of the salon was glass, a familiar foreign land through it. The boy who had been on tampon lady's daughter was now stationed at the door for the next ghetto princess to fall in line—a steady stream of customers all day long, morning or night, hot or cold, rain or shine.

"I must charge $20," he said to my Mastercard. He did not even remove his blue face mask as he talked to me and punched in the numbers.

"Yes, and please make sure to give her the balance," I told him. "She's good."

"Oh, sure, ma'am. You write it."

He handed me my customer receipt and his to sign. I inspected both like I once did obsessively for all my receipts, when I was more forward-thinking and responsible.

Control.

Start now.

I saw my name on the receipts. Autumn Spencer. Of course. It demystified all that was escaping me since I first boarded the D train in Harlem. Cathy and her place. I laughed at myself for being as clumsy in transit as I had been when I first ditched my car in new Big Apple life.

A bright aperture emanated in the salon's thumbtacked corkboard littered with takeout menus, *Se Habla Español* services, and amateur musician pluggers. I interpreted the light for the eye chart we read from the time we are young until we no longer see, an advertisement for an optician perhaps. As I moved to the door I did not see a huge *E* helming a tower of shrinking letters. This white paper included a picture, familiar telephone number, and directions: FIND SUMMER SPENCER.

My body seemed to spin around the smells, noise, chatter, and robotic workers of the salon. I failed to breathe for some time. I resumed my breath. I tore down the flyer. I crushed it into my sweaty palms. Then I pulled the glass door back, and the customer bells crashed to the floor. I was queasy but numb and in a fugue, at a loss to recall when I had ever thought this remote region was hunting ground for Summer.

I reasoned with all the trending news of Bushwick: a burgeoning frontier for the underground galleries, affordable artist live-in studios, cheap cooperative loft spaces . . . It was my job to know these things, stay ahead of the curve, predict the cultural temperature. I would not have to be a sleuth to think Summer could be here. Of course I must have marked this territory at some point, to raise awareness of her.

Ahead I saw another elevated train platform. First, I needed to find a starchy, portable meal. To hold me over for tonight and the next two days. I would stay inside, with phones and computer off until at least the weekend. I would just work on more hot zones people like Summer burrowed in these days. I would plot out the rest of August, to my September birthday. I would redo my resume, and try not to tell anyone who burst through my safe quarantine to go to hell. I kept heading east down Myrtle and crossed Bushwick Avenue, with my arm tight and my head down.

"Miss Spencer! Hold up, girl!" The voice was male.

I did not turn. Was I followed? I could not have been, not all this way. I envisioned a swarm of white coats to overpower me into the back of a medivan, or officers to pull me into a squad car. But I had the flyer now. The business kept it up all this time. How long? I did not know. Still, it was proof many people wanted her found. The train was just a little further. It was a trick. I did not turn. I stepped up my pace. A full-fledged sprint would attract attention. I could not outrun a gang who found me, to tear me away into places with more men like the one I left in Harlem.

"Hey, lady! It's me, Raymond."

I didn't know any Raymonds.

But the voice was right behind me. I could feel it closer than it should have been, right at my back. I needed to see how far it was. And it was already there.

"Hey, girl, what's up?"

The light man with five o'clock shadow and curly brown hair

pulled me into his arms. I leaned back from his try at kissing me on the cheek, to stare at his face. I knew the face. And yes, his name was Raymond. Or, Ramon. Raymond was his American name.

"Wow, haven't seen you since . . . Well, a long time," he said. "How you been?"

"I'm fine," I said. I looked around, behind him, and at the train ahead.

He aimed for my cheek again. This time he didn't miss. I mapped my brain for how I knew him. His face lay impressed somewhere, I just knew it. I met so many people, always, in New York. I had a tote bag's worth of business cards I indexed in Outlook when I had motivation—by profession, neighborhood, claim to fame, and future use if any.

"So whatcha doing down here in Bushwick after all this time?" Raymond asked. He had the curl and turn of a native Romance language on his English.

"Nothing," I told him. Then, "I don't know. I'm headed back to Harlem now."

"You know, I was just talking about you the other day. You remember Calvin and Stacy, right? They still have open gallery every Tuesday on Broadway."

"Oh, I don't go out much these days," I said. "Manhattan's gotten too expensive."

"No, Broadway here in Bushwick. Remember? Free tequila and whiskey, all the chips and salsa and guac you can eat, other munchies on the patio . . . know what I mean?"

"No, I don't remember." I turned my head down and pulled at my puff of hair.

"You were there every week, back in the day. Stacy bought one of the paintings you were selling. I was at their place few weeks ago, looking at it. Your name came up."

"Raymond, I'm sorry," I interrupted and put my hands out.

"But I'm really hungry and it's gonna take me forever to get back uptown from here."

"Well, let's go grab some food, girl," he said.

Now his arm was around my shoulder and he was walking me down the street.

"You know this is my hood," he kept on. "I know everywhere there is to know. I take care of you, girl. Just tell me what you want. I got us there in no time."

"Whatever I want?"

All he talked about drew a blank for me. I could not remember selling pictures to anyone down here. It was a mistake I was here now. I only fell asleep on the train.

But his smell went to my head and dropped it down into a scene of low blue lights, faces made of colors across an entire crayon box, chairs packed tight in a smoky room, and nice wind from an open door. His scent was a particular cologne, with sweat and doll-smelling hair I remembered close to me. I walked a whole block with him. I listened to him: how supposedly overjoyed he was to see me, how much I was so missed by people who had not missed me enough to reach out and find me, if this was so true. The more he talked, the more I recalled: Somewhere around here, with more salons and laundromats and takeout spots, I would see him. I smashed bummed cigarettes down to the sidewalk with giggles, my nights long, and my companions for the evening shifting each time.

I sat down on the only bench inside of a familiar Chinese counter-serve. The menu stood over me like the show time list at a movie theater, where sweet-and-sour chicken was still #28. My eyes went straight to it. The shrimp fried rice was still #16.

This was like déjà vu.

Raymond gripped the counter and yelled our order, several times, to the woman who finally showed up to scribble it down: six egg rolls, two shrimp fried rice, sweet-and-sour chicken, extra sweet-and-sour sauce, broccoli and chicken, egg foo young, and a lot of soy sauce. I heard him crunch bills.

He came to sit across from me at the bench, still and calmer now.

"I still can't believe I ran into you. Man, it's like you just fell off the face of the Earth. Must be making all that good money in Manhattan. Too good for us now."

"Hardly," I told him. "I'm struggling like everybody else."

"Man, no doubt. I'm still at the jewelry store, part-time though."

Whether it was fate I ran back into Raymond, an old "friend," remained to be seen. I know I ran to the train in Harlem thinking of one friend. I was out of breath when I arrived as the train did. It was a man, the detective, back there. He chased me. I wanted a friend. To help me. Why was I running? I couldn't recall. I woke up at Myrtle, soon as it was announced, like it was my stop. A friend popped up, as I wished. I took it.

"My sister disappeared," I said. "And, I thought to look for her down here."

Raymond paused, as anyone would if I told them, to scramble for a distinct comeback not as trite or pedestrian as a simple "I'm sorry" or "How are you?"

"I didn't know you had a sister," was his.

"Well, you didn't know me too well now, did you?"

"I thought I did. Wow. When did all this happen?"

"The end of last year. She's the painter, not me. But I know people mix us up."

"Ohh . . ." He frowned. "I don't remember her. I only remember you."

He had solved a gnawing paranoia I certainly never wished to put on anyone, no matter how small or insignificant I was to people. I knew, firsthand, disappearances hurt.

"Well, I feel bad for you, kiddo," he sighed. "What are the police doing about it?"

"Raymond, thanks, but I don't want to talk about it," I snapped. I was too depleted for a spoken dissertation on women's disposability and interchangeability in today's class-divided urban landscapes, multiplied times five for women of color.

"Okay." He stopped talking and rubbed his knuckles in my cheek, flashed his easy smile. But he did not bolt from the table.

Three men walked in and started shouting before the cook came to the order shelf. I caught the dull aroma of clothes marinated in weed and Newport smoke.

"Yo, lemme get the fried chicken, fries, chop suey, and . . . hurry up, man!"

"Uh lemme get that beef broccoli on brown rice," another said. "Veggie egg rolls."

"Seafood combo," yelled the other, halfway in and out of the door. "And don't play me on the shrimp, yo. Y'all always play on the shrimp. Hold up, hold up . . ."

"You got that?" the first man said.

She hadn't gotten it. He huffed and moved up to the counter, repeating until they debated what I gathered were his frequent orders and complaints to go along with them.

"You pay first or you go," the woman said. Then she whisked back to the grills.

"Come on, ma, don't play me like that."

Raymond grabbed my hand and mixed his long fingers in with mine. The man who couldn't make up his mind blew back through the door. Their voices carried on about how long it was going to take. In between all that, Raymond saw the cook motion him to the counter to jiggle our virtual buffet through to the rolling carousel for pick-up.

"I don't wanna stay," I told him.

"Understood," he said.

A liquor store was up past the train station across the street.

I was the one who said we should get wine to take to his nearby apartment in this urban pocket of service uniforms, misspelled signs, and crooked heels. A phone charger. I needed one. That justified my following him. Surely he would have one. I could call Cathy to say she's right about Harlem. I wasn't safe up there all by myself.

I'VE BEEN HERE BEFORE, instinct said.

I stepped over mop buckets and around an unanchored toilet on a tight stairwell. Beige doors on either side of us at each floor contained loud music and televisions. Once inside, I found clues to recollect Raymond a little. He was from the outskirts of Rome. We met at a non-credit live drawing course I paid too much money for at Parsons continuing education program. A few hours with one naked girl inspired male students to ask out any girl with her clothes on after class. Yes. I guess Summer convinced me to take that. It must have been another costly whim.

Raymond had coerced me to a few sets in Lower Manhattan, way back when. And I kept going out with him and new people. He was a DJ, acoustic guitarist, and backup for poets and singers who practiced in front of a nonpaying crowd at the small weekly set nearby. Though I meandered here on a wrong train it was a familiar route, tied to a fresh euphoria when my apartment was still a bachelorette pad, not a sick room.

I was giddy, and expectant. I'm sure he only needed his memory jogged, as I did. When he recalled Summer, he could tell me more about her: whom she sold paintings to, partied with, and went home with. He'd know where they all lived, or could be found. I was so stupid to concentrate on searching Manhattan alone.

Mounds of records filled his living room. A small eat-in kitchen faced a brick wall. A makeshift studio of turntables, a soundboard, and several guitars posed in the opposite section of the apartment. He separated himself a bedroom with sheets. One had a peace sign. The two rooms were neat, with scented candles and two ceiling fans spiraling madly into a quiver I thought would turn to a crash. When he started his music, I forgot them. He left it to me to uncork and pour the wine. He served me on plastic yellow plates. While night fell I caught up to all Raymond reminded me of me, interred in the marked grave of my past life: my newbie New Yorker penchant for all black, night owl days spent in bed, Hed Kandi nights spent in bars, summer breezes on blankets in Brooklyn parks where hard bread sopped up Brie and hummus and our chopsticks poked snips of tuna from in between tight sushi rolls.

Oh yes, I am eating meat now . . . I was anemic.

When I knew him most and best, I held dreams of a different life, a new whirlpool, to flush all the shine off the goody two-shoes I wore all my life. I met many people, they did not scour to know who I was before, they thought I was talented, they were just as interested in my plans as my jokes, and we coexisted with millions across bridges and tunnels but somehow found each other in the same rooms to talk to. Then, we went our separate ways unless a reason to make more plans arose. New York was not a place of random visiting for anyone but the natives. The rest of us needed an occasion, a party, or an exchange. I had all four with Raymond Fanucci.

We filled up on our Chinese food buffet. A second bottle of wine opened over the plastic cartons scattered across the top of the table. I was forward about it, so he played "Black girl" music: a house mix peppered with Sade, Kelis, and Rihanna. We eased to his couch with egg rolls in greasy hands. It was the most I had eaten in at least a few weeks. We spoke our fortunes: *Those grapes you cannot taste are always sour. Try everything once, even the things you don't think you'll like. A well-aimed spear is worth three.* He never said "Italy." He called it "my country." He told me he would take me to meet his friends, his New York *familia*, in Little Italy tomorrow. I laughed at how he thought I'd be around tomorrow. We both confirmed what we suspected: "No, I no longer do art."

Then, at the time I would have joined the graveyard shifters on a walk to the bodega and unnecessary purchases through a bulletproof walk-up window, Raymond went to his kitchen for what I thought would be sweets for dessert. I heard the rumbles and bumps of blocks of meat and packages in his freezer. He came back with a chilly plastic bag. He dusted a flat saucer on the table with the white powder inside. He breathed it up with short brown straws I normally stirred my coffee with. He scooted me to it next, in his place. I followed, just once. I bent down and sniffed like a bad smoker who wastes half the cigarette. Control. Raymond bent down four or five times. He stood up more excited each time. His hands tore off pieces of egg foo young he stuffed in his mouth. He picked up pints of fried rice to pop straight in his mouth with no utensils. He drank wine from the bottle.

He was on top of me on the couch. I pinched between my legs from more than the tampon I knew was inside. Somewhere in my galloping thoughts, this wad of cotton was insurance against going the whole way. But my shirt lifted above my head. His did too, and maybe I helped him undo my jeans button to slip my pants off. And I told him we could not, because it was that time. He saw the blood on his fingers but did not care. He put my legs around him to pick me up, pushed aside sheets hanging from the wall, and dropped me on top of his two stacked queen-size mattresses, and pushed in and out while I cried out from far too much inside me at once.

TWENTY

I smelled coffee and bacon, but I did not wake up. I heard the door close on the dark rooms with no sunlight past the curtains, in August. I listened to salsa from across the hall, maybe from a room below. Still I did not move. The door opened again, and a strip of light from the kitchen crossed half the apartment. I kept my eyes closed. I heard plates slide around in the kitchen. A microwave slammed before it beeped and whirled and beeped again. I smelled grease and brown sauce. I pressed my face into the pillow. The television came on. I heard them say Sandra Bland, suicide, protests. I slipped away again.

I dreamed of a mob in white coats and fast shoes, outside Raymond's window.

I startled up past one o'clock in the afternoon, according to a dusty digital clock perched on a bathroom towel rack, just one tip or brush necessary for it to fall into a sink of water I had my hands in. I could have been shocked to death. I'd gotten here half asleep. I moved it to the end of the rack near the wall. My clothes were somewhere in the apartment, still dark, with my old friend open-mouthed and shirtless on his couch. He dozed under a fan with dust bunnies coiled throughout its wires. Warmth passed over me when I saw him.

Raymond would not let anyone take me away.

That man in Harlem did not know this place.

In the stained mirror, I saw I was fortunate to have awakened alone. My eyebrows were the only part of my face in place. My first good sleep in weeks, yet my eyes puffed and creased. My swollen lip and nose held a carmine hue. I splashed water in my dried mouth. I pulled back a clear shower curtain to step into Raymond's small, chipped bathtub. On his windowsill: shampoo, shaving cream, a few razors, and generic shower gel. I used it all. As I shaved my lower legs, I resented a man had seen them so hairy. A first. I saw pink tint to the water on the tub's floor. I squat down with my left hand steadying me on the windowsill until I could feel the jammed string of the tampon. The borrowed tampon was so flooded by now it plopped out into the rolling water and rushed down the open drain before I could grab it.

I would have to move around him to find my panties and jeans so I would be able to slip out before he woke up. I saw the top of Raymond's head over the couch when I opened the door. He was up. Lucky me. Now I had to talk about it. I decided to leave nothing to chance. I took awkwardness by the throat and into my hands.

"You've lost all respect for me, and that's okay," I announced.

My rolled pants indicted me, in front of his couch. I bent down to pick them up. The coffee table was back to the neat compartments I was first impressed by. Raymond flipped his chin up to motion me to him. He grabbed the back of my knees to put my legs between his. He had dictated my body from almost the moment he called me, on a Brooklyn street I never planned to be on. In more prudent circumstances, this would be chemistry. After a night of coke and sex with an all but recent stranger, it was just fair.

"I have not," he said to me. "I lose respect for women who know what I want and give it to me anyway. You, I just bump into. Coincidence. I respect a pleasant surprise."

"Yeah, right," I said. "Coincidence indeed. I can't recall why I came down here."

I jumped at a banging on a door so near I thought it was his. He gripped me.

"Relax," he smiled. "No boogeyman is here."

My body had not felt right for a long time, obviously, since I wound up in the hospital. But this "not right" feeling was more pronounced, as if a layer of thin steel encased the whole inside of my body, with stiff bones under taut skin. I wondered why he assumed I would be so agreeable to snort up. I would go see Asha for a detox tea. She would boil it from twigs and sticks and herbs so I shit until I had nothing left and felt ten pounds lighter, degutted, and restabilized.

"I always liked you, beautiful," Raymond said, and my body bridged on top of his for him to kiss my mouth. The blood and wetness between my legs gathered.

My lips spoke on top of his: "I have a boyfriend."

"Oh," he said, his lips still near mine. "Now I lose all respect for you."

I pulled his hair at the side of his face and he loosened me. I wiped at blood that had slipped down my leg. He had seen it, known of it, and found a way around it anyway.

"He why you disappeared?"

"Not only him. I told you what I'm going through."

"You do not love him," he said. "He bore you."

"I can't get dirty again," I told him.

To claim a boyfriend, rather than a rebound off one, was some redemption. Then the pall of pity and loneliness dissolved to a gloss of power and choice. I pulled away to take a roll of paper towels off the holder on his kitchen counter, for another makeshift solution to my ill preparation. A fortune cookie rested on the floor, probably spilled while Raymond clamored for his stock. I slit its plastic and cracked it open to a slip that read: The ultimate test of a relationship is to disagree but to hold hands.

I flipped on whom to apply the statement to: a man I barely knew or the one I thought I did, who left me because he claimed he didn't know me anymore. It would come in handy to keep this new man if I chose to pursue it. Unless Raymond had fallen so in love with abrupt period sex he would treat me like I was brand-new. I was never a one-night-stand girl, until now. This was a refreshed virginity loss for me. I would leave Bushwick crossed over the threshold of recreational sex with no way to turn back. I resolved to linger for the time it took Raymond to hit the Family Dollar for women's underwear and box of tampons.

Two days later, I was still there.

RAYMOND THOUGHT I STAYED BECAUSE I liked him. I stayed because no one would look for me there. I finally comprehended it was no use to keep peeking through the blinds. He had an iPhone charger that wouldn't fit my budget Android, so I had an excuse to pretend no one was trying to reach me. God works in mysterious ways.

We still needed two bottles of wine a night, but takeout of choice crept down to Little Caesars; he worked only part-time, and $40 for mini–Chinese buffets stole his daily bread money. The conversation and messy sex wandered to his front room couch. I slept in still, making brunch for myself as he punched the clock. My options were instant coffee, butter and toast, eggs and browning avocado. I watched news updates about justice for Sandra Bland, now marked by her history of depression and miscarriage and Angry Black Woman Facebook posts, to blame her for her own madness I wouldn't blame her for. Raymond came home. He snorted more coke. I did not. We talked. Summer came up. Chase did not. His phone rang. He looked at numbers and letters. He answered what sounded like men. I teased him, pressed him, to know her name. He said it was no "her." He did not ask about my "him."

While sequestered safely in a hazy acquaintance's T-shirts and boxer shorts, I gave him the details: I came home to my apartment after a late evening out, our rooftop door was open, my sister was gone and I went up to look for her, her footprints were on our roof but she was not, I filed a missing person's report, I haven't seen her since, and everyone treats me like she just walked away, like she wasn't missing at all.

"I cannot imagine you have to go through such a thing," Raymond told my breasts, which he enjoyed most. "No wonder you just disappeared."

"I've been so distraught how no one is up in arms about finding her. She didn't just walk away."

"So was this . . . ?"

He could not say *murder*. Who could?

"My sister was happy. She had a temper. She liked to be by herself. But once she got around people, all was well. We had our differences. But, to just leave me?"

"Sometimes we think we know people, and we don't. Oh, my poor sweet . . ."

The risk of it all now, at our ages, was all the concealed and lost baggage we carried on these flights. Still he comforted me the way men knew how or thought was best, and anchored their self-esteem to, and saw as the best carriage to any load on their shoulders. I was unsure if he catered to me because he was a good host or because I was giving him sex: He fixed our plates, washed the dishes, cleared the table, poured the wine, and offered more blow. I shook my head no. I was not ashamed of him or any of this. I was not as afraid the shower curtain would peel back to a butcher knife as I was of how many emails and voicemails I missed, and what I would see in my apartment that a confusing figure claimed no one else ever lived in.

One more day at Raymond's and I would have looked homeless and destitute, not carried away and swept off my feet. He did not ask me to leave. I only calculated the length of a long weekend naked or in one outfit, on the spur of the moment, as the tip of an overstayed welcome and sign of a fatal attraction. He offered to walk me to the train—not ride the whole way to Harlem with me. Perhaps I had worn him out, too. Still, the offer would have been nice. Without it, I knew I could wake up one day to a minor pain, like stalled internet, a declined debit card, or dog shit on a flip-flopped toe, and burst into tears of latent humiliation. For now, I wrote my number on Raymond's skyline calendar still showing April—he had not flipped the pages in months. He bear-hugged me until the train pulled into the elevated station at a weekday rush hour. Other people's bodies blocked my view of him watching me go away through the glass.

I was marked in his scent. Raymond had jimmied himself up into my nose hairs to make me self-conscious everybody in the car knew what I had been doing for the last seventy-two hours. For this, I had a new friend once old, a mishap turned experience, and a teardrop of perfume left to bring my own smell back.

I needed something to do with my hands. Pens and lipstick—fail safes I felt naked without—and these journals in my purse I could not remember carrying them with me. I traveled with less pretty ways to take notes. I opened one of them to scribble. The teachers had called this automatic reflex "creative," the family called it "strange," the friends called it "artistic," and the men called it "interesting."

A quartet of A-cups and nonexistent waists, robust weaves, and pronounced fingernails came in the door nearest me. The girls soaked the train car in loud gossip and sass about boys it seems they just saw. One of the boys was a punk. Another was sorry. One or another was weak. Maybe all. The friends' chiseled faces looked at one another square when they dipped their fingers in and out of their whole assortment of crinkly chip bags. I recalled the days when I was not above stinking up a room with Cheetos and Doritos, had no interest in the difference between vegans and paleos, and did not need to think green tea and coffee would speed up my metabolism in lieu of nicotine. My purity rung lowered along with my slightly fallen face, just a bit, as I saw my reflection in smeared windows after the car fell underground in Manhattan. Just another woman in just another car in just another town only bigger than most, but still just another and no different for us in any of them, in America, where the privacy of what made us girls could only be guarded for so long.

Twenty-One

I escaped my orange line scam at West Fourth Street for the warranty of the blue. The A train, or, God forbid, the C local, always meant home. No matter the time of day or night, where I was coming from or what had ensnared me there, the sight of a blue circle in the subway could compose me like a sip of wine. The peaks and valleys of Hamilton Heights were just as bony and predictable as I knew them to be. Yet the sky seemed closer. The trees had filled out. I felt shorter than my five foot six, plumper than my 150 pounds. I walked up 149th Street with my head turning back every few addresses. No car was just a car. No footstep only a footstep. The bodega cats, however, were just the bodega cats. I rushed past them. A man on a boy's bike crossed ahead of me. He kept his eyes on me all the while, him waiting for me or me waiting for him or us not knowing who was waiting for whom, until we intersected at his hip and my bag. He called back, "Yo, sorry, ma."

How sweet: a nice one.

I had to search through several keys—to storage, an old gym lock, and the house on Trummel Lane even—for my penny-colored one to the brownstone's lever knob. Normally I felt it on the ring in the harmony of the jingle without looking. My stairs appeared straighter before me than they ever had before. Reflections in the hallway's framed prints obscured their images behind glass, and I had to come close to remind myself what those images were. Maybe Fran and Gregory, or the new neighbors, dusted. I did not smell fried chicken, weed, or Asha's incense. The climb to the top seemed steep.

There was no peace sign on the tie-dyed sheet at the rooftop door. It was a star.

At my door, I tussled with jet lag, if I was behind or ahead of myself. I tried the same keys before the right one let me in. A scent—my body lotions, perfumes, sandalwood incense, Swiffer WetJet pads, and warmed trash—acclimated me back to my space. Along the walls were my bookshelves interspersed with photographs and art and collages. I walked past the kaleidoscope. In the back of the apartment were canvas and cans and supplies stacked like junk, the outline of contents jutting in standoff and imposition. On its other side, my desk, printer, fax machine, and desktop. I tapped the space bar. The machine began to breathe. My screen lit up a window to my inbox, topped in black lines of unread messages. Another window was a classy hotel's website; its nutmeggy colors inspired me to jot ideas for Mr. Johns's online branding. The kitchen island counter teemed with crumbs and shreds of cheese, olive oil and vinegar vessels, canisters of brown sugar and oatmeal and flaxseed meal I never set the tops back on. The answering machine blinked orange. The microwave door was open.

I set my jacket and purse on the counter. I walked to Summer's bedroom. The bed was weighty and still, with no canopy anymore. I knew it was gone. It was too much maintenance: unlatching, folding, dry cleaning, more latching. I just did not know who had dismantled it, and when.

The Myth of Sanity lay on the nightstand, atop other books I meant to get through. A We Go On pamphlet was a bookmark inside *Night Wind*, on my pillow where Chase would have been, for his country and our trip. The bedroom's fire escape gate was open. I ran to check our closets. I thumped on the floor as I raced to each one with no weapon or defense strategy. I came back to the bedroom out of breath.

No intruder.

Perfume bottles glimmered on the overstocked lingerie chest. I remember splurging on Juicy when it first came out. But I never took to it. I went back to Red Door. Quaint pewter frames possessed small photos. A maze of beads, silver and gold ropes, shells, clasps, bangles, and balls made everything on top crooked and vulnerable. I walked around to look at all the pictures on the walls.

Grandma's only time in her life in the newspaper: a black-and-white photo of her young on Easter, in a yellowed obituary clipping I've kept since college.

Mama's cursive "love you baby," razored out of a Hallmark card and set off by papier-mâché.

Two college graduation pictures: me and Mama standing in front of a table of champagne glasses and silver trays with strikes of sunlight, and a silly close-up of me with my tassel blocking one eye as I sipped bubbly.

A dainty, super-glued collage of remnants Mama passed into my hands one by one, her every explanation accented by a wheeze: my first three fallen baby teeth, a braided lock of my baby hair, the hardened button of skin from my fallen navel, the cross from my christening locket, the ribbons from my cream baby christening gown.

All was mine.

I saw a peach stone statement necklace from Avon, mail-ordered in secret and delivered to my hands. It was Mama's last Christmas present to me.

Hoopy and dangling and big earrings, all false precious metals. I remembered when and where I bought them: Claire's, Walmart, Carson's, Ricky's, a vendor on Fifty-First.

A black velvet box of diamond studs, from Chase. To me. My last birthday.

I opened the closet, to a disarray of shoes unpaired in Rubbermaid containers and a shoe rack of smashed heels, laundry bags packed so thick they could have held hidden bodies, blouses with the tags still on them.

I began to yank clothes off the hangers in examination and identification and recall.

Poncho: J.Crew. In Chicago. Sometime during that one job that actually paid me well, but was boring as hell and the blond supervisor sat too close to me.

Le Suit sets. Four of them—in neutral colors, for that deprecating fling with interviewing I gave up on. Pre–"business casual" jackets: muddy tweed, pinstripe, houndstooth.

Khaki sundress, beads at the bottom and a matching hat pinned to its straps: Jamaica, that trip where I screamed at the atmospheric distortion that was snorkeling.

Black Michael Kors blouses from the editorial department's sample closet at *Noire Magazine,* the one time I was let in before I was let go.

A sleeveless mahogany satin A-line dress for my cousin's wedding.

The cotton candy–pink cowl-neck light cashmere sweater I wore on a date with a high school basketball coach I met at the gym, who took me walking on the river near Battery Park and bought me fruit we nibbled in his Jeep before he tried to take my panties off while the wife he told me he did not have kept calling his cell.

The black and blue Gap blazers, button-downs, and soft

V-necks I stocked up on with a blessed employee discount from one of my first jobs in New York.

The thin-striped and flower-touched church dresses, forgotten and stiffened behind club clothes with sequins and sparkles. Monochrome, patterned, polka-dotted, blocked.

No matter. I knew it all well.

I tore it all down, hanger by hanger and piece by piece. The more I presented me and only me to myself, the more a concavity opened inside my stomach. For each piece, I told its story to myself: all mine, none Summer's. The garment's history never had her name, her hands, her money, her lingering, her selection. I saw my hands, my fingers, and my smiles. I saw symbols of everyone but Summer: my friends, my mother, my grandmother, my aunts, my uncles, my cousins, my neighbors, my coworkers, my exes.

I heaved the laundry bags onto the floor, crushed sports bras and crumpled yoga pants and sticky T-shirts. All mine.

Suspended purses and bags on hooks—leather, pleather, and vinyl together with straw, fabric, and hemp separate—netted together by the straps. I jerked them all loose at once. I tore them open one by one as I recounted the class, festival, date, party, job, gala, barbecue, beach, vacation, and situation each represented in my life.

My wardrobe covered the floor, from the wall to the bed. I dragged the next laundry bag and a container of shoes near the windows. I upheaved both. I sat in the middle of the mess of mildewed clothes and funky shoes, identifying each piece. I launched a stiletto at the sheetrock wall. It poked through. I beat tennis shoes onto the floor. I flapped at my shoulder with flip-flops that smelled like my favorite lotions. I hurled rock-hard square heels of work loafers at the windows. A pane cracked. I continued with softer shoes, bags, and belts.

I writhed in the middle of it all, holding up shirts with stains; I remembered the exact wine or tomato sauce spill. The moment the buttons popped skittered across my mind, usually a man or my failure to be on time responsible for it. The promises to sew the tears here and there played back in my head. I smelled the moment when I made the wedge and dots of a hastily set iron pucker up rayon and satin. Even some tulle. It was all me, and all mine. None of it was my sister's.

Control.

I had no taste for ice cream. Meat would have to be thawed. Pizza would require the oven. Hot Pockets and chicken potpie boxes tumbled out of my freezer. I threw one of each into the microwave. I put my face under the faucet and ran the water into my mouth, wetting my chest and shirt. The stewy, cheesy smell flared my hunger. I opened the microwave to resettle my dinner. I closed the door and restarted the microwave.

Go look in the storage, I heard Summer say, just like she was calling from the bed.

"The storage," I said back to her, the sister who loved her canopy bed and walked our halls and woke for water in the middle of the night and straightened picture frames.

She was all in there. She had to be. Everything we put down there together would be there still: primer and solvent jugs, the warm-weather clothes she never got a chance to pull out again, the paintings, the extra bedding. Fran never changed those locks. I just had to put on some shoes and climb down to the cellar to see it all. I breathed, finally: once, hold it, let it out, again, hold it, let it out, again, hooooold it, let it out. Breathe.

Of course. I laughed out loud. And I turned to my door with my presentable self intact and composed. I opened to a woman standing squarely in front of me.

I staggered and cried out. Shock obstructed what may have been a piercing scream.

"So sorry!" the woman said. "We're just wondering if everything was okay up here."

And then I recognized my downstairs neighbor. Or rather, her voice I heard outside their door and through my floor.

"Why wouldn't I be okay?" I stammered.

"Autumn, right?" she said

"Yes."

"We heard a lot of noise."

She held out her hand. I crossed my arms.

"I've been here almost two months," she continued, "and it seems we've never formally met. I'm Maria. I've heard a lot about you from Fran and Gregory."

"I work from home, so I stay in a lot," I said. "I'm cleaning out my closets."

"Oh, I don't blame you," she chuckled. "For both. You know, staying in or cleaning out closets. We still haven't unpacked."

I pat down my shirt. She saw me with no lip gloss or public face or other preparations.

"Well, I'm Maria. My husband's Charles. Our son is Sean, and if you ever—"

"I'm sorry, but I've got something cooking."

"Oh, sure."

She backed down the landing, waved good-bye, and stopped once more.

"Glad to know you're okay."

"I'm perfect."

I shut the door.

My microwave hissed from its corners. I tapped it open and grabbed the food without potholders. I burned my fingers. I shook and sucked them quietly. I did not yell or stomp. Maria was most likely shaking up a martini now, to give a full report on me—down to my nipples through a wet T-shirt and hickeys on my neck. I had no desire to add to it.

After half the food, and with awareness that my every move was background music to strangers beneath me, I quieted. I slowed. I stood in the middle of my living room and inventoried its auras— of me, only me in body. Anyone else was in spirit and mind.

The living room window overlooked 149th Street and all its windows. I heard shuffling below, light and normal, like I awoke to on mornings in the house on Trummel Lane. Bamboo cubes, piled in the corner, stood out in a grim living room. Light bulbs felt too harsh. Moonlight would have to do. It was a late August night when the humidity was high. But the breeze still gave me chills. I wanted the maroon blanket Grandma crocheted for us both but Summer took all for herself. The blanket was in the Lane cedar trunk, in my old bedroom, rolled up with mothballs and waiting for the winter.

I walked down a hallway lined with overstuffed bookshelves and picture frames in the spaces between, holding sets of eyes I was scared to face.

Summer came back. She was here, in my bedroom. Back. She'd slipped in so quietly. And I wasn't even mad.

She stretched my sheets tightly over the top corners of the mattress for me. Then she patted the mattress like an old rug in need of a good beating. She didn't have to turn to know I stood in the doorway, watching her.

She stopped tidying to go to the cedar trunk, to pull out the maroon blanket.

I gathered it. She turned to peeling off grimy pillowcases for crisp ones. I stared at her there, unafraid, only interested. I waited for her to turn to me. She kept on her merry way.

So I went near the kitchen edge, to see a color photo of me, Mama, and my grandmother. Grandma looks off-camera. Mama blows up a balloon. The balloons are not pink. They are darker. Blue, or green. I know it is my tenth birthday. By myself, I blow out a single candle on a birthday cake. Mr. Murphy took the picture.

I walked down the hallway with the blanket around my body, then underneath me. I sat on the hardwood floor with sketchbooks, fat and skinny journals, and loose papers.

This corner I sat in now had been my mother's private nook, her version of her shed back in Hedgewood, when she had her own home and a car and other things to do besides pass away.

My mother was the artist in the apartment, the maker of so many pretty faulty things I kept out and put away and wanted to create also, in her footsteps but also in my own way. And, desperate for money, I had peddled them to fair-weather friends.

Now, my only support was a tough exposed brick wall. I opened a neat little journal with a crocheted jacket. Mama made it for me, out of a thick scarf Grandma once made for her. I read my work.

"Summer is a missing vulnerable adult who may have depression or require medical attention. She was last seen on December 19th or 20th in her brownstone apartment in Harlem. She accessed the building's roof and never returned inside. Summer changes her appearance frequently. She is originally from Hedgewood, Illinois."

The handwriting looked familiar. I chose to trust it, and read and see more. And the more I read and saw, the more I came apart to know.

TWENTY-TWO

I was a bad artist and not-so-bad writer, so the latter became my predilection, if not my downfall. But I really wanted to be like my mama, Grace Contessa Spencer.

My father's motorcycle was off-limits to me, parked between misshapen boxes and old furniture in the backyard shed, left to rust and collect webs I tore off at the start of winters when the spiders started to dry up or die. His helmets were gone, because a cousin took the collection without Mama's permission. We heard my aunt pawned the helmets. The cousin further offended Mama—he would still ride a motorcycle knowing her husband crashed on one. Daddy's rescue rope, breathing apparatus, boots and vests rested neatly on a shelf near his fishing poles, and luggage full of the better clothes Mama never got to Goodwill.

She explained she was out there making "art"—on a Kmart easel, with Farm & Fleet house paint but real sable brushes, palette knives, flea market clay, an old kiln, and a pottery wheel her old community college art department gave away. She said an artist is what she was supposed to be, before she married. Instead she started at the water plant, joining my father to backbone the world in the working class. By the time he died, she had moved from the tunnels to the phones. She showed me how to run the wheel because I liked *Ghost*. I wanted to do that Demi Moore thing, too. Single-serve booze bottles trolled the shed. Virginia Slims butts covered the floor. She sometimes came in from the shed crying to her room or obnoxious ranting and pointing at Grandma. A retired day care center cook who looked like she would have been fast friends with Quasimodo, proud to sport orthopedics or sit with her legs open to slumped stockings, Grandma always won the case.

"I ain't gonna argue with you, girl," was the judge cracking the gavel, to adjourn us until the next time.

The only constant man in our lives was Mama's brother. But he stayed in the bars after he left the water plant tunnels Mama started in. He still picked my mother up to go to work every day. He stopped coming in to say hi to Grandma every morning—just honked from the curb. My mother saved up enough for a Chevy that would be more reliable on our rural roads. Then, we never saw him at the house but on Mother's Day. He brought a new woman with him every year. Her sister Aunt Mae was haggard with five kids, two jobs, and one mysteriously employed husband I gathered was worse than Mama having zero. The oldest kid, a girl, was on "that shit." Her two little sons lived with us once, before the state of Illinois came to monitor them back with my aunt. More often than their names, I heard Grandma call my aunts "them heifers." My uncle blanketed under the lowered expectations men enjoy. He never called us, but Grandma never called him names. If he was on the phone, my mother or grandmother would talk to him for hours and hours like his biggest fans.

So my place was in the shed if my mother was not there. In it, I sat on top of the motorcycle and made the *vroom vroom* noise, until I dribbled spit. Then I climbed down to make shapes on any scrapped canvases or with wet clay: butterflies, unicorns, hearts, and stars. I gave the shapes to Mama and Grandma, along with uprooted dandelions I eventually figured out became slimy stems and browned puffs right after I presented them.

Once in a blue moon, a shoved-off cat knew the direction but not the way home, and became my pet for a while. No one else with me—no friend, no tagalong, no sister. Girlhood was lonesome.

I am a good student. I am quiet in church. I know my Easter speech. Yes, I brushed my teeth for real. Yes—ma'am—I washed off my feet before I got in the bed.

We three moved out of "town," away, rifted and elusive in a wily threesome combined to one baby lotion, White Shoulders, and Bengay scent. The back kitchen rotated its smells: hot dogs and Salisbury steak TV dinners on Mama's bad days, pound cakes and Crock-Pot chili on her good ones. Nobody ever stopped by for long, if Mama wasn't giving something for Grandma or me. And those gatherings always started and ended in daylight. Our two-story stucco house was off desolate roads with no street signs— just little white posts with tiny black letters a driver had to turn on brights to see. Mama met her old friends from high school and the community college at bars, basement parties, and barbecues in town. She went to the Y to swim, but she wouldn't take me because if my hair got wet, it would ruin the crinkle or the straight she spent her Sundays on.

Our neighbors were all White, a few Indian and Hispanic. We recognized their children when it was time to trick-or-treat. Otherwise, seasons determined our relationships: waves and hellos when the temperatures revolved into times to plant flowers, trim hedges, water lawns, rake leaves, clean windows, clear gutters, stretch tarp, and shovel snow. Mr. Johnson, widowed and married to his two girl German shepherds now, came from across the street to help if Mama and I struggled with shovels or the lawn mower, even though he was old and ancient with blue dots and green lines in his ghost-pale face, and we did it faster. But, he said, "I'm a man."

Mr. Murphy's entrance to life is fraught with presence, stiff with blocks in space, a sudden cutout in my storybook house. Mr. Murphy shifted the terms of our life. We rearranged our gentle bickering, brief silent treatments, rollers in our hair all day, open bathroom doors, shoes left here and there, dishes unwashed, same TV channel for days, toenail clippings, wind passing. Mr. Murphy retouched our life. He made us women: primped, pruned, on polished toes, dressed, and never not busy.

At first, he stood up in our living room. He called my mother "Missus Spencer," her married name still. He stuttered when he presented prices for his wares: much better life insurance and burial insurance, at a special price, supposedly just for us. We could even buy our caskets in advance. Grandma sat in the rocking chair beside the china cabinet. Mama and I sat at the dining room table with the man.

He was "Mr. Murphy," not "Cole."

If he sat down, he asked if he could sit, at first. He asked for everything: water, another piece of cake, more coffee, the telephone, the bathroom. Somewhere along more visits they started to tease him: "Gone on 'head" and "You know where it is" and "You know better now to get it yourself." "Help yourself," even. He was not married to another woman I knew, or family by way of kids who called him "Daddy." I never saw him at church. And he went out with my mother without me, without Grandma, and maybe I was too young and Grandma was too old to go. Mama began to disappear nights. Grandma started the maroon blanket on one of them. Grandma never explained or accounted for the absences. I would have to ask: "Where's Ma?"

On days I wanted to spin the pottery wheel or see what I was going to wear for the next week, to messy the closets and drawers and put them back together again, my mother was not there. Grandma was unanimated at night, with her housedresses open and the phone in her lap. Color drained from the big television; she watched *The Honeymooners, Twilight Zone,* Alfred Hitchcock, *I Love Lucy,* and Andy Griffith. So we, too, separated. I stretched over my homework and notebooks on Mama's queen-size bed, to absorb her in all the shows we would have been flipping in color: Carol Burnett, *Good Times, The Jeffersons, One Day at a Time,* and *Laverne & Shirley.* Sometimes I awakened to her next to me watching the news, sometimes in the morning. She still drank her Lipton's, with no bottle next to it anymore.

When Mr. Murphy started to set down his hat, Mama kept her door closed and I stopped going in. If we left home in the evenings, we took his car: mushy leather and not-soft cloth seats, lights instead of dull dials on the dashboard, a phone with an antenna set in the console. The first dinner together, and not without me, was at Red Lobster.

That year my name went from Autumn to my nickname: *Get me my . . .* Pill case. Water. Plate. House shoes. Rubber bands. Socks. Robe. Cover. Yarn basket. Needles. Thread. Flask. Grandma mentioned her locked knees and hands more. She settled into indented space in the easy chair more hours of the night, then the day too. I settled outside more and more in the shed, at the kitchen table alone, or in the yard to wait for a kid I knew from school to step up to our grass. We would talk in the road until a passing car's interruption reminded us we were not good friends.

When I turned ten, and the tornado warning spoiled my Pizza Hut plans, Mr. Murphy gave me the tall doll on a round base. Mama and Grandma gave me cotton training bras. I pounded at my itchy chest all the time, for what they saw that I had not seen because it was so gradual in coming. The knowing smiles and placid conversations about "your time" and "those boys" and "your little thing." Three whole inches in one year, too. I was distraught about pimples emerging like my chest and behind. Grandma bought me

Ultra Glow, to smooth hyperpigmentation on the smallest little bump left behind.

Mr. Murphy told us I should go to the skyscraper—the twelve floors of Hedgewood's tallest office center building near the courthouse. I was to go see the doctor there, one of our neighbors, one of his town business associates. We never saw inside the doctor's house, but I stayed in his office: for creams, pills, shots, and burning peels to clear up my face. The complexion I recognized showed up just in time for middle school. Mr. Murphy claimed I was so pretty now. All due to him.

By then, he lived at our place or Mama at his. I was told to call him "Cole." Cole showed his round belly and wide arms in plain T-shirts tucked in his night pants in the mornings, now, as he ate eggs and toast in the living room, and watched sports. At night, he switched to Coors for the news stations. If I wanted to watch *The Golden Girls* or *A Different World*, I had to ask him. Cole shooed the stray cats away before I could name them by color and personality like I had before he showed up, stray in his own way. He did not want me or Mama to toss them the scraps or the bones.

"They bring rabies," he warned.

He was Mama's "boyfriend." I asked if that's what he was. I knew what it meant. Because he bought her gifts. And he paid some bills. Plus he pulled out his wallet at cash registers before Mama reached for her purse. A couple times, he drove us to society stuff, in town. At these nice parties, Grandma talked very, very proper through her dentures. She told people at the table all about Hedgewood when she was young, coming from the South, and Black people couldn't live here or there. Mama announced where she bought her earrings and her dress. I got to tell people what I just won in school.

"Call me Cole, darling," Mr. Murphy said when Mama was upstairs or out back, and Grandma slept in the La-Z-Boy.

I was in the house alone with Mr. Murphy sometimes, because

he showed up before they got back from the store. Or I did not want to go to church, and they ran late to come back to our dinner he thought would be ready by now. I went school shopping with him alone; Mama was sick, and I could not wear high-waters for another day and still call myself her child. Mr. Murphy roamed tools and electronics. I tried on skirts and shirts in a cubicle in the middle of Kmart. He took me home from a funeral repast. One of our great-aunts died; our people down South were in town for the first time in many years. Grandma wanted to visit as long as she could. Mama wanted to take pictures to mail to everybody later, after she made collages and frames, to show them she was still doing her art. The emptier the beer cartons and Boone's Farm jugs fell, the more and more pictures she snapped. I did not know the people. Neither did Mr. Murphy—her "old man" now. He and I left together.

I laughed at his stories because my mother and grandmother did. I did him favors—hung his coat, brought him a plate, moved over—because he was older and I should.

"Call me Cole, sweetie," he said, when he met me at a bus stop off the main street. The roads branched long ways apart. It was raining. And he had flexibility in his work while Mama had to stay overtime if sewers flooded, even if her daughter would slosh home in thunder and lightning in the part of town without awnings to wait underneath.

I could have walked. I liked the taps and pressure on my head from drops onto my yellow vinyl hat. I liked to see what designs the puddles would flow into when I splashed my galoshes in the middle of them. A dim coating spanned the horizon, to make every cornfield and house around it feel closer than usual. The pending drone of any car up ahead or behind, and the equalizing of color, gave more certainty to life in storms over the sunnier days, Technicolor false. The gray palette was fair. I knew the pulled-over Cadillac was for me, so I shuffled and got in.

Like outside, our house dimmed inside with the blinds tightened, a wet smell although the windows were closed. Mr. Murphy
helped me shake out of the drenched coat, useless hat, and clumsy
boots.

He came too close.

Grandma had herself in the kitchen, with the wood doors on
either side of it shut, because she thought lightning could sneak
inside.

After he came too close, next he started hugging me "Good-
bye" or "Good night."

I thought—but said nothing—about how his big, hard hand
fit over my heart breast for seconds and he pressed. I thought. I
knew I was getting big where I was once small, so maybe I got in
his way. I thought about it a lot, once for a whole night. I received
a detention for sleeping in class.

Next, he reached over to the dish rack to grab a beer mug or
coffee cup from the other side of me as I stood doing dishes. He
could have just gone in front of the dish rack. We had enough
room in the eat-in kitchen, with a wraparound counter too. But
he reached all around to get across, so he meshed into my body
for seconds. Maybe three. Finally, he came behind me in the pantry. I tottered on my tippy-toes to reach the good Orville Reden-
bacher popcorn on the high top shelf where he put it, because he
bought it.

"I'll get it for you," he told me. I didn't even know he was in
the kitchen.

And I felt a long hard line against my rear when he reached
over me, for a long time that was not accidental now, because he
never touched the popcorn box. He just switched himself from
side to side and side. I held the bottom shelf where we put the
canned goods that would kill us if they fell on our heads but only
hurt us if they hit our feet.

A crooked smile it was, a little laugh arose in me, almost a burp. I said "Ummm . . ."

I was eleven.

That night we had meatballs, baked potatoes, canned asparagus with cheese, and frozen biscuits I pulled apart in too-thin strips. They burned on the bottom. Nobody ate any but Mr. Murphy. Grandma and Mama teased I could not make the biscuits ever again.

For a couple of days after this, Cole Murphy was gone away.

Now I was getting phone calls and answering machine messages from my cousins and classmates, all floundering in our own ways we never declared. Our chats surfaced at famous upperclassmen, the next big movie, music awards shows, hairstyles, unfair teachers, and other kids' secrets.

I took it past "See you later."

I had a postscript: "Can I sleep over your house this weekend?"

And Mama hissed: "No, cause I don't want to drop you off and pick you up. It's too far to drive."

When I kept asking for these short getaways to another house and place in town, where I had girls my age for double Dutch and hairstyling and talking on the porch, rather than curt courtesies to the kids around me who could still afford the Catholic school, Grandma stood up for me. She said I was not a little girl anymore . . . I should "Go, go, go!"

Then, Mr. Murphy offered the favor. So I changed my mind and stayed home. Or, I went with others straight after school, girls I wished were sisters. I came to relatives' and friends' houses, inspecting for their needs: leaves to rake, extra hands to clean out the garage, a new baby to sit, a senior to pick up prescriptions for. I could manage three nights a week I did not have to see Mr. Murphy.

If I had no excuse to be away, he found ways to stand behind me and come close. He came when I loaded clothes in the washer, took them from the dryer, stared into the fridge, organized groceries, put towels in the linen closet, and swept the front porch.

"Would you call him Cole, Autumn?" Mama started to say.

In the blessed school days, I sat in classes tracing the lines in my notebooks or the figures in textbooks I was to return at the end of the year. My papers grew much longer than everyone else's. My English and social studies teachers praised them as "best." I finished the math chapters quicker than the rest of the class too; I could go on by myself at my own pace, and finish the whole book. The librarian knew not just my face but my name; I checked out more books than any others, she said. When I doodled and drew, on grass and in secret, I lay on my belly. But when I read at home in the open, I was on my back. If I stayed on my back, Mr. Murphy would stay off of it.

Mama said she was sad I grew out of making stuff out back in the shed.

She had a better recommendation from one of her YMCA swimming friends than a new insurance plan and the salesman who came along with it: summer camp, a military-style departure, sequestered in Indiana cornfields. She begged Mr. Murphy to pay for it. I could go live with other girls and make new friends. I saw friends as useless. They would not come home with me, or take me home with them.

I wanted to march, salute, manage bows and arrows, swim as if my life depended on it, and most else but the strict instruction in the riding halls. They wouldn't let us do any real stallions. No pony could match my daddy's motorcycle.

I met Summer the last day of camp.

The night before the family arrival barbecue at camp, when Mr. Murphy would drive Mama to fetch me to return to Hedgewood, Summer slept beside me in my bunk.

She was waiting in the rocking chair when I came home. She

looked like me, grumpier though. Same height, weight, and notes in the face.

She took over my father's motorcycle, sitting in my place, moving and swaying with the *vroom vroom vroom* sound I used to make, only hers came out in silence.

We didn't like the shed so much anymore. It was too messy, full and weighted. But, we found a patch of broken cement to dig through.

She told me, in a silence I just knew the words to, *We can bury our notes to each other, always.* We stuck them inside all the little bottles Mama used to throw out there.

You are pretty. You are strong. You aren't a bad girl.

She told me, "We can put them in the house, around where he walks and sleeps, to weaken him."

So we used dimes to screw open the heating vents above the skirting boards and snuck in our notes, to dry out and discolor until no one could read the words when Grandma investigated the oven smell long after she last used it.

You can fly. You are going to grow up and get a good job, and be so rich and famous, and you will pay the mafia to kill him.

She told me, "We can put them in our books and lunch boxes and lockers, so someone will find them and know."

We put them there and forgot, so the counselor called Mama to talk about them.

You will be Foxy Brown and She-Ra, to shoot him and chop his arm off.

And so Summer knew. She knew it all. But she liked me anyway. And as she came along with me to block Cole, I knew she had been there with me all along.

We turned twelve.

TWENTY-THREE

She slipped back into home so soundlessly. When I heard the running water and tinkling dishes in the morning, what I found in our kitchen did not shock me. She stood, as lanky and slight as she was the first time, cleaning up the mess I couldn't believe I had let myself get used to. We were raised better.

Autumn, please call me back—Noel Montgomery—as soon as possible.

I FLIPPED THROUGH JOURNALS FOR blank pages, to write love letters to her. There was much worth keeping from it all, so much more than rocking chairs and hats on tables . . .

The prettiness of our colorful bike tassels fluttering like wings in the wind.

The slapstick clown and pantomimist who performed for kids at the county fair.

The crackle of popcorn kernels exploding in the cast iron skillet.

The delicious, but stolen, wafers left over from Communion we weren't qualified to have, found on the altar of the Catholic school chapel where we waited on our late mom.

Shortbread cookies Grandma bought in bulk when Girl Scout troops came round.

The first sloppy tries at lip gloss and sparkly eye shadow and glitter nails.

The thrill of boy toys, like swords and balls and train sets.

And still the calm predictability of collector dolls in taffeta, with pearls in their ears.

Autumn, one of your neighbors buzzed me in but you didn't answer. They said you sound home, so that's good to know. But I'd also love to hear how you are doing.

BY MID-SEPTEMBER, JAYLYN STEWART WAS a freed #BlackLivesMatter hashtag on a media tour to emphasize he never killed anybody in his life. And, that he found God.

Clients called. I didn't answer or respond. So their double-talk began with customary salutations about Mondays and Fridays. Then, it veered into veiled warnings about nonpayable invoices. They finally cracked to blatant complaint and contract suspensions in the language of consulted-on, paraphrased legalese.

Norma Roth was different. She was set for a slow season after her spike of summer hires returned to college or grad school. She called me not to do more work for her, but to refer some girls her way for temp work. Our cabinets grew more and more spare. Summer had to grocery shop. I was out of money, after all. We were down to oatmeal, couscous, quinoa, frozen California blend, and stockpiled tomato paste for vitamin C cravings.

The tea party was nice. Even Asha said so. We set it up nicely for her.

"I've been calling you," she said, when her knocks escalated. "What's up?"

"Oh, nothing, I'm just having tea," I told her.

"Loose, I hope," Asha said. "I told you that bleach in bags causes cancer."

"And I heard you," I said. "It's been really busy."

Asha left and returned with a blessed meal: curry chicken, cornbread, baked sweet potatoes, and collards sautéed with olive oil and soy bacon bits instead of pork.

Summer was exhausted, figuring out what we were supposed to do now. I pointed to Summer's closed bedroom door, as I did get rather lively with Asha.

"I have a guest in town, from back home," I smiled. "Sorry, but she's kept me really busy. Sleeping now, but maybe we could all go out later."

"Why didn't you tell me you had a guest?" Asha said. "I would've brought more. Pack a portion. I don't want to be rude."

"No, I'm glad you came. I would have introduced you, but . . ."

We set her pots, my plates and teacups on Grandma's maroon blanket, in the corner near Mama's unhung and unsold paintings, drawings, and collages. Asha complimented my mother's genius. She poured more tea. She did not drink immediately. She wanted to read the leaves. The food reminded my belly what normal should feel like. As I ate seconds, I heaped the remainder of the cooking into Tupperware. Asha gave me a renewed cup.

"Drink until it's just a little left."

I was surprised the water felt tepid, not hot. Asha was surprised I drank so fast. She found me amusing, I could tell. She became serious and stared through the dark liquid.

"So, they've separated well. Haphazardly, but still unpacked. You are working out issues in your soul that clogged you up. And, I'm obligated to say this: Money's coming."

I was grateful, and I committed to making a party date before my guest left town.

•

Autumn, Montgomery here again. I saw your lights on last night,
but you didn't answer your bell . . . Your neighbor said you have a
visitor? I'm glad you have care there.

THE BUBBLE BATH WAS ALL gone. Body wash didn't lather as
well. She didn't mind. There was enough for the both of us. We
touched our knees in the water. We played cruise ships with the
bottles floating to the top. We went all around the world, to all the
places we promised each other we would go together. We splashed
and splashed, and ran hot water when the bath grew cold. We let
the water rise too high. So high it spilled over the ledge when we
scooted to shut the faucet off. And we laughed, because we would
be in trouble now. But not really. Grandma's spankings never hurt.

Hi Autumn. Noel Montgomery here. Listen, I'm sorry if I upset
you with our last conversation. That wasn't my intent. I thought it
would help to hear what I thought. Maybe I was wrong. I'd really
like for you to call me so we can discuss this further. I can help . . .

IT WAS OUR BIRTHDAY. CATHY mailed a card. Asha hung one
from my doorknob, taped on a sack of handmade shea butter mixed
with almond oil to sweeten the smell. Raymond had called, but not
about that; he did not know our birthday. Chase stood his ground,
a move of such angering finality I fantasized storming into SWAG's
offices. Summer could do the injuring. I could watch. We had nothing left in the apartment to make a cake. But, I knew where dessert
might be left over. I would be offered more than I could stand. And
it would be so good. So very good. But, then I would have to go out,
and leave her behind. And then she could not understand I would
return.

    I stayed.

•

Autumn, I can walk away if I have to. I still have concerns. But, it's your choice and I hope you are well. You can always stop in or call. Anytime.

WITH HER, THE APARTMENT EXPANDED to grandness. It was ornate, affluent, and pristine. The view was higher. There was a chill, but the seasons were changing.

In the night, I opened my eyes and she was there. In a new way now. She was out of my mind. That's where she had been. I only knew that because now she was form and shape without color or detail, like a woman dipped in dirt our mother ate as we stole the iron in her blood for ourselves. The shape of her face told me she smiled. And she came to my own tiny bed where I was lying, and this was strange, not the way things should be.

But she came closer and closer, to sit next to me and rub me with hands rough like dried mud. And her shoulders broadened, her legs lengthened, and her arms stretched. No caress. A hard press. It was a smashing, her heaviness. I couldn't move, or breathe, or speak. I could feel myself push up against her, but nothing changed.

Then she was gone. Just like that. I could breathe again. I knew it was not her.

I was scared. I needed my lights, but the lamp and switch had erased somehow. So did all the windows I could jump out of. I forgot about the lights because I knew the way. And it wasn't even the dead of winter. This time, I would leave no footprints in the snow. I would be She-Ra, and fly away. I was relieved I could move again. I leaped out of bed. There was only the door now. I came through it, wanting to see the peace sign on a sheet.

But she was there, blocking the rooftop door. She was all figure and mud and no face and something like two tiny horns on her head now. And she walked forward and I backed up. She moved faster than I did. She did not care if I fell back in the long hallway. I turned and ran back to my tiny bed. By the time I pulled the covers over my head, all the room's contents had erased.

She twisted around the doorjamb and ran to the bed again, next to me and then over me. And this time when she pressed her dry, dirty body onto mine, I carried no breath to make the sound of "Help." I tried, and felt it was in there. But it wouldn't push up. I kept pushing for something deep inside me to make the word. But there was nothing inside of me, not even the energy to mouth a syllable or whisper.

The whole world was hard mud with no oxygen, and I was going to die now.

"Hello? Hello? Yes, this is the Montgomery residence . . ."

Fall

Twenty-Four

He could not unearth a history of mail delivered in her own name to her own address. He could not see one picture of Summer together with me, or alone and distinct, in her own apartment. He glanced at a life insurance policy from her mother and saw she was no beneficiary. Her own sister put off pressure for weeks, popped up zealous and then forgot to show back up again. Her own neighbor for years did not know her well. Her own boyfriend moved on, rather quickly, to her twin. Her own stepfather, a man her sister referenced often, reportedly resigned from a local NAACP due to sexual harassment claims according to old articles dated just before her puberty years. And this was all the detective in him saw through before he sank into the private diaries I allowed him to investigate. For clues.

Noel Montgomery, wearing glasses, peered at me. He sat in front of a window overlooking the Graham Court's yard. It turned out, he had a home office. His interest in art in my place had been authentic: a Black art tapestry made up the wall in front of another glowing aquarium. I lay on a beige couch, flanked by dark end tables, joined by all the tricks of his trade: a Zen noisemaker and stopwatch, a fire extinguisher and first aid kit, pillows and a plaid throw, and a forearm's-length crucifix in the center of the one blank wall. Behind the office door his wife pat down their long hall onto the faint orchestral of a late-night snack, perhaps a sandwich and tea or leftovers of the dinner she had made for her husband. Perhaps she was preparing for the same medley of people who strolled through on Easter, like I did. *Clients*, with such broken lives or families we'd had nowhere else to celebrate.

"I wasn't trying to deceive you," I assured him.

"Well, thank you. What weren't you trying to deceive me about?" he asked.

He looked more human when he was baggy-eyed and unshaved.

"I knew she wasn't missing," I told him. "I just didn't want anyone to think I'd have a sister out here prostituting herself through life. Or on drugs. That's what the world usually says when women disappear, and there's no body or blood."

"Yes, stigmas get in the way of the truth," Montgomery said. "It can feel bleak to feel no one cares about you, as a woman. It can exacerbate everything else you must cope with. Like grief, loneliness. Autumn, how does it feel to be in contact with Summer?"

I admired him for his efforts to shunt me into some truths I knew, now, finally.

"Well," I sighed, "it feels traumatic and relieving and sad and exhilarating all at once. I feel emptied and hollowed to think of myself alone in my apartment, no one there anymore, with only a false figment to keep me company. It feels good to have her near me. And scary to know how she got there. I have never had such a night terror before."

"I'm glad you called me. You aren't thinking of hurting yourself, are you?"

"You mean, jumping off my roof?"

Montgomery smiled. He was more courageous than I was to

ignore the reason behind our bizarre meeting: a lonesome woman's urgent needs for care, a social services solution to allowing real health insurance to slip out of a poverty-line budget.

"You didn't jump. You climbed down, on your own. First responders know how to read people, quickly. They have to. Coming after you could've made it worse."

Anyone standing on a rooftop in winter is out of something or on something. I was both. That night last December, the caul of another identity dressed my skin. Summer was who I wanted with me when I did not want to be alone. She was an ally, a formidable doppelganger against disrespect, offense, rage, and violation. Then, she became an excuse.

"I'm still Autumn Spencer, even with Summer. I haven't changed. You can be straight with me."

"I'll talk to Autumn just the same. It's more important that you talk with Summer. This is a part of you. It can't be separate from you. We have to get you whole again."

His phone rang, twice. I tensed. Another nutjob on my tail, waiting for me to pass the baton. His last name was the only correct thing I had crystallized of him. Montgomery (I didn't know what to call him now) appeared frailer, less like a detective. He was also left-handed. He looked familiar but only vaguely, like a visiting relative resembling photos from the past.

His advice sounded simple, but made no sense: "Now that you're aware, you're going to have to come to terms with this gift you have to place things elsewhere in your mind and integrate yourself with Summer, accept all you handed to her to carry for you."

"How is it a gift that I've messed up my life slipping between two lives?" I asked.

"I've heard of much more serious manifestations of dissociative identity disorder. Overdosing. Alcoholism. Violent crime. Unacceptable and damaging acts committed as an alternate personality.

And the real, dominant one suffers from that. You have bad habits to break, moods to control, binging to stop, trances to rein. This outcome is fortunate."

"Fortunate?"

"Yes. You gave yourself a creative funnel, what you call your artist, your twin."

"Wasted money," I laughed. "Stuff. I guess I should check with Parsons to see if all that money I gave them for non-credit courses added up to that certificate after all."

"You should. Remember, in many ways, you were doing good things with it or not even thinking about this other person. And it all adds up to you. It's no subtraction."

"Tell that to my bank account. Does Summer have a social security number?"

"She's your twin. You two shared everything, right? You'll have to learn to get along with her. A good start might be to put some of those bills in her face."

I was not going to try to decode it all in one night.

"I think I know what happened on the roof," I said. "Care for more of my blues?"

"Certainly. I've understood you were a victim of child sex assault. The dissociative outcome is prevalent for those survivors. I still do not understand how it led to that night."

Someone called. A man who liked me. He wanted me to come out. Bar 13 was in the Meatpacking District, not entirely converted. Back in the day, it was the go-to spot after Parsons, Mannes, and other New School security locked the campus doors. The potent mishmash of past slaughtering and traffic exhaust nauseated me before I went inside the smoke-filled club. After that, it was all would-be suitors' bad breath and strong spilled drinks. I could not find the group of so-called friends I thought waited for me. They moved on to another destination, without even telling me. I texted the person who invited me. I was inconspicuous and alone in the phantasmagoria where men of all colors inched up to me little by little, one by one. Nobody texted me back. I was enraged. Not over the total strangers I admit I did not care much about. I was enraged at abandonment, its stinginess and arrogance. There was nothing, nothing I could do to vanquish my mother's abandonment.

"I felt so stupid, and powerless," I cried. "Alone. I planned to go have fun, but I just spent my money on watered-down drinks. It wasn't my scene anymore. I was lonely. I had a man with me, like a real good boyfriend finally. But now I know I barely saw him there."

Chase.

His employer, SWAG Marketing, was my sweet find when it first started up. I was the "Temporary Cutting-Edge Content Creator with Keen Instincts for Multicultural Markets" they were looking for. In their suite of a coworking space, I first encountered a man with a nice accent. Mama was not sick then, back in 2013. She was just "not feeling well." Chase did not wander to the couches, yoga mats, and Ping-Pong tables. He stayed behind closed doors. He was uncommunicative beyond pleasantry and client updates delivered like speeches. He was often the most serious face, and the only Black one besides mine. His wardrobe impressed me. His focus inspired me. His effortful greetings warmed me. His belief in his career, as a shield against discrimination and degradation, taught me.

My assignment ended after two months. I still thought of Chase. He could be a nice inroad to freelance work for executives who might remember me. My voicemail to him led to our emails. Our emails led to his invitation to a penthouse networking party in Midtown. That invitation led to a carefully worded friendship. He had an older woman girlfriend, also Grenadian, way out in

Sheepshead Bay. He said she was married, all along, and using him. I suppose I was the rebound. We kept finding reasons: a new restaurant, a movie, just talking on the stoop. We first got carried away as he helped me to bag books to sell at the Strand. Just one season after that, Mama was sick. I recalled he once told me he felt like he took advantage of me, and did not want to. So, for a time, we became "just friends." Support, contact, and care in a city where associations expired fast.

Until Grenada. A business trip, for both of us. To help me on my portfolio, he said. After the trip, coinciding with Mama's passing, I could not square feeling good about anything, not even a good thing. I smeared Chase in emotional crimes he never committed.

Sex had always been something the man initiated, my body a lush retort to the things done to it, on authority of touch and maybe a little skill. It was a man's desire, not mine. Chase changed this. As much as I enjoyed him, the pleasure conflicted me. I never let myself go. Whenever I did, it felt shameful, like an affair that could not be a romance.

"I believe I wanted to push Chase away, and find reasons for what I felt with him to be wrong, like we were cheating and not just being," I continued. "I know I hurt him."

"Dissociative identity disorder causes many complications for the sufferer's support system," Montgomery said. "The amnesia, mood swings, and impulses are challenging. Even if they are understood. In this case, they weren't. He couldn't have saved you here."

"He helped," I insisted. "That night wouldn't have happened if I was with him. I don't know why I needed all the other people. I met someone, a man, in Brooklyn."

"I'm not sure you want to get into any new relationships right now—"

"No," I assured him. "He was just a guy on the street."

"He hurt you?" Montgomery asked.

"Oh, no," I laughed. "He helped me. I stayed with him. In the way back of my mind, I knew him. I knew the neighborhood, the stores, his apartment. It felt like I'd seen it all in a movie theater, not real life. He called me a friend. He said people missed me."

"We need to explore how many of these altered states, or fragments, you have," Montgomery said. "Your concentration on Summer alone for all this time leads me to believe you may not have many. If others emerge, we will work on them then."

Montgomery settled into the deep armchair. It was a brawny hold where he listened to ugly confessions and truths were handed over to him for safekeeping and padlocking, the keys thrown away in confidentiality and trust, as if he were a priest. Tonight, a note-pad and pen rested beside him, useless and irrelevant.

"On the roof, I heard the voice," I continued. "That's all I heard. It was so quiet. Harlem is, really, a quiet place at night. A bus or two in the distance. That's all. But I knew the voice so well. I heard it all the time, at home. *Autumn, Autumn, come down . . . come right now. Get down from there.* That's all I heard. I thought it was my mother."

"It was your neighbor downstairs," Montgomery said.

"I never thanked Belinda. I avoided her. Then she left."

"It's not too late to thank her now," Montgomery told me. "Autumn, your reality is harsh. You *are*, well, alone. Not too many people exist with no nuclear family, at your age. You are . . . ?"

"Thirty-five, today," I sparkled. "Well, yesterday. But I guess it's still my birthday."

"Oh," and he blushed. "Happy birthday, Autumn."

"Thank you. I had a table reserved at Red Rooster tonight, for me and Chase. We didn't go. We're broken up."

"Well, that's no good."

"It is what it is."

"You never know what the future holds. For now, I want you to understand these realizations you're coming to deserve all your attention and care. I want you to tell me if you ever told anyone these things. I'm unsure of Illinois law, but there could be a chance for charges still. But that's something you'd have to want, no one else."

"Mama started to see things." I couldn't stop the memories now, a Vesuvian rush of misunderstood moments and hurtful enigmas piled up over the last few years.

"I would look all around, even run my fingers along the walls and get the broom when she told me 'Kill that spider,' or 'Get that bat outta here.' She said 'Thanks, Mama' when I brought her a popsicle one time, because she would not drink enough water. Penny changed her bedding and bedpans and went home for the night. I insisted she take a break. Mama just took naps, three or four hours here and there. Then wake up and stare, wake up and stare. I sat by the bed and started telling her. All about him. Mr. Murphy, not Cole. That he didn't love her. He didn't love me. He didn't love us. He raped me. She listened. She watched my lips move on every single word. And she said, 'I need to sleep. Just lemme sleep.' She didn't act shocked. She didn't say sorry. She just fell asleep. And for a second I wanted her to die. Was that wrong?"

Montgomery surprised me.

"It's a tough call. As a parent myself, you have a tendency to be in tune. I don't know if your mother sensed problems. Maybe she felt the better life he gave you all then compensated for any suspicions she had, or whatever she understood you told her later."

"So, she let me get hurt for show? Appearances? Things?"

"I wouldn't think she would knowingly hurt you."

"She hurt me. She brought him. I'm her daughter. I *was* her daughter."

"You *are* her daughter," he said. "I'm relieved you are caring more about the one she had, and not the one she didn't. That's where your work begins now."

IT WAS DAWN WHEN I finished what I could now share about me and Summer. A light appeared under the door. Mrs. Montgomery knocked, then spoke: "Celeste found her keys. They were with security. Marcus just dropped her off."

"Splendid," Montgomery said. "I really didn't feel like driving to Brooklyn tonight."

She said to him: "You're saved." And to me: "Good night, doll. Get home safe."

We walked to the courtyard exit. I was leaving the square panopticon to go home to watch myself now.

"I'll hold off now on psychiatric referral, but if you disappear again . . ."

"I won't," I assured him. "I promise. Not anymore. I believe you now."

"Okay," he sighed. "But remember, go outside every day. Don't stay up all night. Limit the news, the internet. Eat three times a day. And, call my cell if you ever feel unsafe or disoriented or lost. We have an appointment this Friday. I'll confirm."

Silent, we awaited a cabbie on the block. Then I remembered my manners.

"How much do I owe you?"

Nearly my last $100 wadded in my purse, in cash.

"No charge," he said.

I swirled my eyes, proud and scrupulous.

"I'm covered," he told me. "You can thank We Go On. They fund me. I'm a survivor too."

TWENTY-FIVE

ostly for Montgomery, I filled out an online form to join the next Survivors Meeting at We Go On. He became aware of the advocacy group after his son, Noel Jr., slid into opioid addiction from painkillers for a knee he injured in a Syracuse basketball game. Soon, his character changed. Then he dropped out and went missing for weeks. A housekeeper found his body in a by-the-hour motel room on Lenox. The bottles and evidence of alcohol, crack, marijuana, Vicodin, and hydrocodone surrounded him. Montgomery and his wife became group members around the time their son would have graduated college, debt-free after the basketball scholarship. Then, they graduated to volunteers. His pro bono work was in addition to private practice.

I could not bear the grim meeting to be the total point of my day. So I initiated a call to Raymond, and agreement to rendezvous, my olive branch to atone for my nonresponse to his sincere messages: thinking of me, had a good time, hope I'm well, don't disappear again. I would meet him at a real restaurant now.

We Go On was a three-story stone house steadied between constricted five-story walk-ups on Sixty-Third Street. Its website showed me it had offices and special-events rooms people must have donated much for. Its location and ambience were a departure from social services organizations and clinics I skipped past uptown, in buildings ashen and dusty even as the janitors cleaned often. A buzzer system greeted me in a shiny foyer. I announced myself to a secretary I could see behind a large oak desk. The vintage décor inside included frilly dressed dolls with pearly faces on a shelf, tall vases with bamboo shoots, and cubes of short-stem fresh bouquets. Requisite inspiration highlighted the walls: images of ocean waves, flower fields, and swirling blue spheres as the settings for printed platitudes on hope, dreams, and tomorrow. The telephone was set to an annoyingly hushed ring; Becky put her finger up to me and answered it, for ensuing chitchat about a copy machine emergency. She hung up and apologized.

"Hello, I'm Autumn, Autumn Spencer," I told the young girl. She wore a fast-food style nametag that read BECKY, INTERN.

Lovely. My crazy qualified me as case-study teaching fodder for future generations.

Becky went to a computer to pull up a FileMaker Pro screen. Apparently all my surface details poured forth there: my name, address, age, marital status, educational background, social worker or psychiatrist, emergency contact, closest hospital, known medical conditions, and notes on my "event"—a section I had left blank.

"Yes, we have you in for today," Becky said. "You're early."

"For a change," I smiled.

She led me back to a lounge reminiscent of higher-end telemarketing and sales companies where I had temped.

"See you soon!" she beamed.

She'd given me a glossy red folder. One fast open to glimpse the words *support*, *risk factors*, and *engagement* was enough. A peel-and-stick-on name tag paper-clipped to the folder's pocket. I avoided it. Crisp, recent magazines splayed on a table. A tea collection folded out on the counter next to a Keurig. Snack bags leaned against one another in a wicker basket. I selected a pack of fruit snacks. I popped a capsule of green tea into the top of the Keurig. I went to one of two armchairs and picked up a *New York Magazine* on the table in between them. Luckily, I had my hot tea by the time a few people trickled into the lounge. I did not join them. They seemed intimates already, touchy and chummy. I soaked into the magazine.

I was momentarily startled by an advertisement inside. It was for a line of luxury men's suits, hats, and accoutrements out of Greenwich, Connecticut. Gabriel Johns must have licensed his name and image to the brand. He smiled back at me: a distinguished older gentleman smoking a cigar on his nutmeg tree estate, with enticing copy and quotes to make him appear a humble everyman who could still afford all this. I wanted to pull out my phone to call Chase, to congratulate him. But I would not know what to say if he asked me where I was and what I was doing.

Instead, I looked up to see the group expanded to men and women who appeared dressed for work on Wall Street with a few prepped for nights on skid row. They moved in unison and automation, writing and sticking on name tags, patting each other on the back, speaking close to each other's faces. My expectation of emo kids and goth adults was shamefully overturned. A silver-haired Black woman was part of the group, comported like a friend of Rosa Parks, down to a polka-dot handkerchief in the pocket of her red suit, grounded on sturdy pumps. She looked my way. Steadying herself at the head of the table, she spoke with a wet-haired White woman who seemed to provide an update on her housing situation. Wet Hair stuffed snack bags into her loose bag sashed over her body.

At six on the dot a brunette man came into the room, clapped, and started hellos to everyone there—starting with me. His name tag read FRANK, VOLUNTEER. The rest rushed last-minute coffee and tea before seats at the table began to fill. The musical chairs left me right by Frank. I wanted to sit at the far end, in an empty chair. But Wet Hair's saggy bag occupied that seat, so she could keep rummaging through it for gum, chips, a nail file, mirror, Chap-Stick, and other things.

"Yes, I have gotten a haircut, finally," Frank said when all places were taken. "Thank you everyone for noticing. It was time. The hairline was going to recede even if it grew to my waist, so I graduated myself to official middle-aged man last week."

"You look so much more handsome that way," Rosa Parks's friend said. "Like a real gentleman and nice young man now."

"Young?" Frank asked. "And the member of the year award goes to . . . Barbara!"

"Who's your barber?" a boy with painted black nails and his own shag asked.

"Nowhere special," Frank said. "I went to the Aveda school. Right on Spring."

He drummed at the table, pursed his lips for what seemed an announcement of merit and high reward: the next Miss America, Best Picture, a Pulitzer. And the winner is . . .

"So, let's get started, guys."

I had hoped to avoid that moment when you have to stand like a new visitor in a church you only plan to visit once. Frank began the roundtable of introductions.

"We have a new person here today. I already know her name, but you guys don't. And she does not know yours."

I would not be spared.

"So, introductions as usual. My name is Frank Castling, and I am a survivor of suicide. As in suicide attempt. I don't know anyone who's actually taken their own life. But after a lifetime of bullying, and suffering in the closet in college and my twenties, I wanted to overdose on pills. I survived, finally came out as a gay man, and advocate today for both gay rights and the millions of people in this nation affected by suicide. Luis, please."

Luis was a construction worker with a wife, three children, and a family he left in Guatemala, and a history of alcoholism he goes to a group for too, and a brother he once paid $3,000 for, to a voice on the phone promising his Rio Grande crossing, but the brother has not called to say he is in America and it's been five years. Carla, a redhead costumed for a Walmart family commercial, was a rape survivor who failed to get a conviction and wanted to die when new DNA techniques verified her attacker, but he could not be tried twice. Anthony was a soft-spoken, cherub-faced man who grew up with an abusive father whom he blames for his ongoing mental problems and the threats he made in college to shoot himself, which his mother talked him out of before she divorced his father they no longer talk to. Daniel was shocked when his nephew killed his brother, and prefers to share nothing more. I learned Barbara locked herself in her garage full of carbon monoxide before her neighbor came to see why her dog was barking so loud. Her catalyst was her daughter's murder during a home invasion, while Barbara and her husband were at a holiday function. She's still married to her daughter's father. The dog just turned thirteen.

Wet Hair's name was Carolyn, and she was a heroin addict whose two precious babies were taken away, and her last suicide attempt was in April when managers of her group home called the hospital to come get her for not taking her meds and threatening to slit her throat with a kitchen knife; but she was taking her medications every day, and the social worker told her she could see her kids now in supervised visitation with protective services. She was trying to find a job and had a few interviews, and the supervisor of McDonald's called her back to meet with his manager, but she was sick that day and then somebody stole her interview clothes when they were drying at the laundromat, and it would be better if she could find a job close to her new place in the Bronx, but there are no businesses there but family-owned stuff and liquor stores and bodegas with roaches and old milk, and a caseworker gave her fare for the train here but . . .

"And now, Missus Autumn Spencer, tell us about yourself," Frank managed.

The template seemed so personal. I stayed silent.

"Whatever you want to share," Frank nodded.

"Well," I thought on each word, "my name is Autumn Spencer. I'm an only child. I moved here from the Midwest. I have no parents. I live in Harlem. I work for myself. Friends there thought I should give this a try. And, well, it's been quite a challenging year."

Frank moved on to the discussion topic of the day: service to those in our lives who need us, want us, and depend on us. For this, we were to make a list of five people we think look forward to seeing us and need us, and something about how we service them as a loved one. The group handled it like a pop quiz, with procrastinating questions.

"What, these are people I live with?"

"Do they gotta be family?"

"What if you have more than five?"

"Wait. What do you mean by 'in service to'?"

"I only got three. Is that okay?"

Frank managed each question with a thorough answer while he never took his own pen off paper, writing with a promise to us he would be the first to go. I made the best of it.

Asha: She knows I will always answer my door, I don't charge her for mooching, I pay her when I sense she needs me to, and we always have fun no matter what.

Cathy: She looks for my calls and emails, her family likes to see me come around, and her children will think I am their "Aunt" if she has anything to do with it.

Aunt Mae: She calls me after a few months if she has not heard from me, and I can always stay with her if I ever move back to Hedgewood. She wants me to live with her.

Cousin Terry: She looks forward to the gifts I send her children, she emails me her problems because she says I have smart answers, and my mom was her favorite aunt.

?

The fifth space was one where I silently debated the fuzzy lines of want, need, and love—over relationships of convenience or shared circumstances. I mentally sorted revolving faces and names who would be in my life if the ties of time and space that bound us collapsed all of a sudden.

Fran: She appreciates I am a good tenant, I cause no problems, I pay rent, and I have been a nice person to talk to over the years.

All of us but Wet Hair managed to complete the assignment. Her questions continued long after she insisted, "Come to me last . . . I'm still thinking about it."

For everyone else in the group, the usual associations came up: Mom, Dad, husband, wife, son, daughter, grandchildren, brother, sister, pastor, even boss—one who actually appreciated his employees to be on time and stay past closing. These were the voids and absentees and deletions of my unorthodox existence.

Finally, with Frank's prompting, Wet Hair stretched her list past just her two kids.

"I can go ahead and put down everybody's name in here," she told us. "And, I can say I service you because I come to group, even when it's raining cats and dogs like it was last month, and I ain't got no umbrella. And we talk about our lives and our problems. Well, it's not always problems. Sometimes it's just life. So that's . . . Frank, Barbara, Carla, Luis, Daniel, and Anthony. And the staff. Becky, Diane, and the one guy's name I always forget. He's here in the daytime mostly. Everybody except for the new lady . . . what is it?"

"Autumn."

"Yeah. It's not I don't think you're a good person. It's only we just met and all."

"I understand," I smiled.

"Thank you, Carolyn," Frank said, and all others followed him. "So these services we perform to ease burdens and contribute to others' lives increase our social footprint for the entire world. Seriously, the whole entire world. These footprints walk on well past us."

By the time we all shared our lists and comments, it was past eight o'clock. Raymond had called my silenced cell phone twice, and I was famished for much more than fruit snacks and tea. The table lingered in small talk I was not prompted to join in on, since "we just met and all." Yet, the barriers to smiling at me had been crossed. I returned the gestures.

Frank caught me before I made it to the exit: "I'm so happy you joined us."

"Thank you. I'm happy I joined too," I said. I wished I had the "good hair," straight enough to fuss behind my ears to signal it as impolite to pressure me to more nervousness.

"How'd you hear about us?"

"A friend," I told him.

"Great friend," Frank said. "Well, we're here every two weeks for this particular night group. Attendance comes and goes, but members stay consistent long-term. We have a lot of stuff between meetings too. Outings and trips to free stuff around the city. Are you subscribed to our newsletter?"

"My freelancing has me running newsletters for a few business, so I know they can be especially valuable for engagement," I said. "I'll think about signing up. Good night."

He waved at me and then turned back to the room to clap his hands, "Okay, folks. Security's peeking in, giving me the evil eye. Let's let 'em lock up and get home!"

I had urge to tinkle, one I withheld out of my duty to hear all. But I decided to bank on a McDonald's or Starbucks rather than risk a conversation trap in the bathroom. This sacrifice against my bursting bladder was futile, however. Barbara came up behind me as I stood a little down the street on Sixty-Third looking from side to side to get my bearings.

Twenty-Six

I looked at the pain staining another woman's eyes and forgot about my own. I was astonished to feel lucky.

Barbara's first suggestion was "a drink somewhere," what I was supposed to do with Raymond. I did send him a text while I squat over a sprinkled-on toilet: "Hope you haven't left yet . . . I'm running late." He didn't text back. I guess he gave up on me. So be it. I didn't yet trust my ability to restrain myself to just one or two glasses of wine anyway. I weaseled in a coffee idea to substitute. Barbara and I quickly found a slow, uncrowded Starbucks.

"I became president and founder of my own nonprofit, to keep folks in recovery from relapsing," she explained. "That's why I like Carolyn so much. She's got heart. Lot of folks don't get as far as she has. I've seen it myself."

She paused to sip tea and nibble a cheese Danish.

"I had a network of small art studios, restaurants, hair salons, vintage boutiques, and even a record store. All on board with me, for no kickback. So long as recoverers who signed up did a monthly drop and met with a social worker, they could work."

The café's loud music turned to Johnny Cash, "I Won't Back Down." She snapped her fingers, mouthed a verse. Then she quickly folded into the stiff posture I first saw her in.

"I didn't like the location. Worst part of Corona. Bad influences. However it's often effective to fund programs in buildings in the projects. It's the best guarantee people who need it will show up. So I made a difference in many hard lives. But I'd give it all back, though, the awards and big magazine mentions. The house. If I could get my daughter back. All those accomplishments backfired when I lost her. They never caught her killer."

I'd seen talk show guests like her: cast in stone, unruffled, and open to any question. For as much as her mini-autobiography forced another latte to give me something to do while she talked, I admired Barbara. Her stoicism and candor were light-years ahead of mine. But then again, she'd had more time.

"What was your daughter's name?" I asked. I could feel her brighten the air around us to think it.

"Simple. Anne. I know it's old-fashioned now. It was my grandmother's."

"With a name like Autumn, I can't be too judgmental."

This was a point I would have said I had a twin sister named Summer, the porno name of the pair. Yet I stopped this as it furled to my tongue. I sensed it would all be a lie.

"I can't know how you feel," I offered. "My only daughter is a sponsored one. Fatu. Africa."

"That's very good of you."

She had wiser counsel, I'm sure, than little me. I flatlined in her mind as just Autumn Spencer, from Illinois, now in Harlem, without my own mother—whom I let her know passed away from cancer. Casual passersby and nearby customers presumed us to be mother and daughter, perhaps.

"How long have you been going to We Go On?" I asked her.

"About three years now. I knew about it, from my own work in the community. Never thought I'd be a client."

"So, that means they've helped if you've been there that long, then."

"Oh, sure," she insisted. "Of course. It's that shared common thing, more than money or race or where I come from. Nobody else will talk about it with me. Least not for too long. They might know how it is to be low, because nobody gets outta here in one piece, but not so low you wanna die."

We'd both had similar heroines—neighbors, in a city scorned the world over for having the meanest streets on Earth. Chances are, had she or I been submerged in the wider geographies of a place like Hedgewood, where the only din of open-window weather is cats in heat, we would not be sitting together now. We would have succeeded in our final goal. Perhaps, because I was Black, she sensed obligation to reel me into more than a group setting. It's something I would have done to the only dark face in a line, disaster, or conference room. Did it make me racist that I'd throw the oxygen mask to a young sister across the aisle before I passed it to the senior White woman in the middle seat next to me? I had hope that this comedic, haphazard tribalism would set aside when there was no time for us to see identities at first.

"I had a similar experience as you," I shared. "I know you turned the key in your ignition, sat, waited. Would you've come out on your own?"

She didn't hesitate: "Nope. Not at all. You ain't the first to ask me that."

I told her the full of it.

"Well, for me, it was going to the roof of my building. Middle of the night. Coke. Booze. I called myself jumping. Nothing happened. Nothing more than a neighbor saw me and called authorities. I wound up in a hospital, just out of my mind. The worst part is I froze my bare feet and ass off. I crawled down a fire truck ladder

in a nightgown, no panties on, the wind blowing all my business
out to Harlem. And the same roof door I went out was still open all
along. Why didn't I just turn around and walk down?"

"We people do some dramatic things," Barbara said.

"Yeah," I laughed. "We sure do."

SIDEWALK FLOWERS I PURCHASED CONGRATULATED me on
attending the meeting, shunning alcohol, and catching my Summer tendency in action. Shop window lights seemed turned up.
Strands of hair in people's heads distinguished themselves. Sign
lettering was sharp. Every single car, truck, or cab on cramped
streets stood out in its own right and not as part of one choked
mass. I concentrated on oblivion to men's oohs and aahs, when
their instant smiles let me know I turned them on. I brushed off
their shifted tones—more high-pitched and straining for charm—
as they handed me my bags, train pass, or street food.

Asha's door had been silent when I passed it on my last few
outings. I could have imagined a man snake into her sidewalk-level
window. I preferred more than corroded thoughts now. Maybe she
was out canvassing for clients or herbs in Chinatown, still hustling
even this late. I wished her somewhere arm in arm, hip to hip, or
sage pose to dog pose.

As always, I heard the sport of family and nesting on the second floor. On impulse, I knocked. I knocked again, louder. Then I
clanged the bell.

The nerdy man gripped a cordless phone to his cheek when he
opened the door. I was grateful. My mission was not to linger, only
to present and announce the new, quieter person I would become
from now on. A second impression.

"Hi." He looked much older than his wife, or maybe he didn't
cover his gray.

"I'm your neighbor, upstairs?"

"Yeah, sure," he grinned. "How're you? Nice flowers."

"Thank you. Oh, and good." I felt it was true. "I came by for your wife. She here?"

"Not at the moment. She's, uh, at some event . . ."

"Dad! The cabinet door fell off again!"

"Just a minute, Sean!"

"I wanted to tell her thank you for stopping in to check on me a while back," I said. "There's just something about going through old things, not wanting to do it, but having to. Well, let's just say it took me until this afternoon to put the mess back together."

I leaned on my right side with my arms folded as I explained.

"No worries," he said. "You don't even want to see our place right now. I'd invite you in, but you'd think we were the Addams Family."

I put up my hands: "No, no. It takes time. I'll let you get back to your call."

"Stop by anytime," he waved. "One of us is usually here."

This mission of apologies, for Autumn and not Summer, would have to be done in tandem with clearing the aftermath of the weeks before. My apartment was still flipped inside out, its disarray and uncleanliness bubbled up like a cut freshly splashed with peroxide.

I met the bright star's glare on the sheet over the padlocked rooftop's entrance. It was at once an unmanned garrison erected by compassionate homeowners thrust into the new position my occupancy demanded, and a shrewd measure against a tenant family's lawsuit. Fran had renewed my lease in the winter, without hesitance. Their tolerance of my late payments, their wider smiles, the cleaner hallway, and the extended conversation of the last nine months was their version of caretaking for a girl whose only family seemed to be a mother they saw once or twice before she passed away. Their *service*, as Frank told me.

TWENTY-SEVEN

It took a few years for Cole Murphy to bring less gifts and more of his paperwork to our house, for us to alphabetize, double check, and put in folders. Sometimes, if Mama was more interested in a TV show or phone call, he called her "woman" in a not-nice way. She would go out for cigarettes sooner than her usual stop in the mornings, at the first gas station in town. Grandma stayed out of the times Mr. Murphy said "Grace" like it was anything but.

Cole Murphy claimed things I didn't know were not true: "You know" and "She knows, too." I knew his spiky chin irritated my neck. I knew I did not like the smell of his lips on my skin. I used the seat of my father's motorcycle to ease the ongoing pull starting underneath my navel and moving down to where I met the seat, alone and thinking of the boys my age instead of an old man; Mr. Murphy interrupted this. He offered to clean out that shed after its worn-out years, as Mama's little artist place turned to history's dumpster.

Unsoaked brushes hard as peanut brittle. Paint containers stuck together. Glues spilled in lumpy mounds. The kiln would not power anymore. The pottery wheel was rusted. Its grind was sharp. The roof leaked.

"I can fix it up for Autumn, Grace. Put a nice big desk in there for her, and some bookshelves . . ."

I said I did not care. But this is what twelve-year-olds say about everything. Mama told him of her husband's motorcycle: "Don't touch that bike."

Over the summer I turned thirteen, a little more of the shed's mess organized inside or wound up at the curb for garbage day. Mama called my disinterest in her boyfriend's efforts "unappreciative." Grandma insisted he was wasting his time: "Put yourself a pool table and darts out there for your man friends." He did not have too many. My silence over his version of a boy's tree house ended his nonstop talk of it. He even got on his knees to plant the hardy annuals around the shed's perimeter: petunias, marigolds, geraniums.

Over the same summer, I wrote a letter to the *Hedgewood Sentinel*. A response to their daily classified ad for carriers. A young man in glasses named Jason answered my letter. He drove to Trummel Lane in a rusting red truck. He brought a map, paperwork, a satchel, perforated collection tablet, and stapled guidebook. Mama, Grandma, and Mr. Murphy watched him orientate me. Portly and bald, he sweat so badly Grandma took to wiping his glasses and neck with a napkin as he explained financials. Mr. Murphy grilled him on it all. My independent contractor status. My biweekly paycheck from the *Sentinel*. My gross payments. My eventual net profits. My penalties for nonpayment for pre-purchased newspapers I was to own and be fully responsible for. I was an entrepreneur, already, according to Jason. I was proud.

Mr. Murphy said I could use his renovated shed for my "business office" and library in one. I would not. I stopped going in. On Sundays, the newspapers came at dawn instead of the afternoon. The edition tripled in weight and size, for a grueling carry. I had to make two trips back home to pass them all. But the more I told

Mr. Murphy no—to his offers for takeout or a new outfit or field trip money—the more I could meet him at the eye. I could back away when he came behind me or on top of me.

It was really just one time that Cole Murphy sat me in the rocking chair.

I planned a new Sunday morning strategy: to stay awake until 4 a.m., when the *Sentinel*'s delivery truck threw tightly wound newspaper bundles on my yard. Then I could pass, skip church, and sleep in. One midnight, I needed a new cup of coffee. At thirteen, I could not stand the taste then. So I wanted ice cream in the cup like a hot root beer float.

Maybe he heard the television on, or the wood dining room doors open and shut. I was mixing coffee and ice cream together in one gooey swirl when his gremlin feet slapped the kitchen floor. The only other noises were the hum of the oven light, and a ticking wall clock shaped like a breadbasket.

"It's almost one o'clock in the morning, young lady," was his opening.

"I know what time it is," and I was mad. He was ruining my plan. I threw the mug of butter pecan ice cream and coffee down at his feet.

"You need to clean that up."

"You need to go home."

"This is my home."

"It is not. It's our home."

The standoff was brief, the solution ill-timed. I was not big enough, or ready, yet. He lashed out to grip my right arm. His rough nickel-size fingertips fastened my elbow. He pulled me back and forth as I kept my feet square in one slippery linoleum tile. So he moved his big fingers to my waist, and pinched at my gut. He slid me through the kitchen door into the dining room. The closest thing to throw me down on was the rocking chair. It cracked under my weight. I wanted my church shoes on, so my feet could bang on the hard floor and Grandma could come down to yell at me about waking the devil, to catch the one already up. His grip was hard, his spittle was hot, his face was knobby and mean.

"Cut that noise out," were his words. "Right now. You want your Mama to know about this?"

He pressed me down with one hand and took the other to the string of his night pants, to fiddle with the knot. The rocking chair tipped back so far I almost fell over in it. He clinched the back of it so it would not crash into the china cabinet and break the glass with my head, right in front of the pretty brown doll, still there from the first birthday he gifted me on.

We stopped moving, for a while.

"I'll tell," I hissed. I twisted my face from side to side as he brought the fat weight up from thin checkered pants he eventually gave up on unlacing and just tore.

"*I'm telling . . . I'm telling.*"

Mr. Murphy stopped it all after he saw hatred pucker through splashes to my face.

THE ROCKING CHAIR BECAME A relic of our past life as the first three in the house on Trummel Lane, now boiling down to a grayed twosome. Mama and Mr. Murphy became more left unsaid, outings less frequent, and affection down to helping with zippers and neckties. My room stayed in place as I wanted it, but I could not forget its switched usage: less a girl's palace and more a salvation from straitjackets, strange doctors, and medication.

Mama blamed it on something else. My smart mouth, disinterest in church, fanaticism over school, my temper, funny moods, and bad attitude were all her fault for not taking me to my father's family enough. We had a tense negotiation for me to stay in Illinois rather than go—at eighteen—to the East Coast all by myself and so far away from them. So then her cover to remain blind to her man messing with me was "that White folks' school." She claimed if she was firm that I stick around my own people, I would not be so "strange." Mama said if she had not bought the house on Trummel Lane, she could have saved the life insurance to send me to a Black college.

I would be "happy."

I was happy. I made myself so, as a harlequin with confidence and work ethic.

I walked on with a cracked skeleton of happy beneath my perplexed secrets and simmering rage. I basted in a forever-poisoned girlhood. I detested Trummel Lane, small-town bars, and fast-food summer jobs under supervisors who were shocked when I said I would not return to be a manager. I moved into a suite of four women, in an old hotel on Lake Michigan converted to a dormitory. I was no stranger to living with alien life forces, so it went well. The skeleton grew flesh and color again. Its blood rushed back. I talked of books and images and politics and my own perspective. I continued to write the longest papers and finish the books first. I came in with no plans or ideas for my future, no prepared props to self-aggrandize along with the others. But eventually I saw a statistic. Most schools had a four-to-one ratio of English to art teachers. So it seemed safest to fall back on what I knew I could manipulate quickly and cheaply. Words needed just a keyboard or pen, not supplies and space I'd have to buy.

By senior year, I stopped coming to Hedgewood. Grandma, put into words like "slow" and "silly" and "tired," became a subject of my and Mama's every phone conversation to recap our days, weeks, and then whole months we did not talk. Mama drove up to all my little events at the school, but did not stay long. She went back to my dorm room, pale children and weed smoke and sex acts carrying on around us. She thought the wan, blond mothers of my short-term friends threatened to turn her against me with every low-key Carly Simon and Carole King song I wanted to let play on our car radio. She drove up to take me to dinner once and I called her music "sad Black woman songs." We argued, and I avoided seeing her until my college graduation day. Relatives accustomed to Autumn being "away."

Grandma's domain became the Hoveround Mr. Murphy paid for. She went down to mashing food flat and laughing at unfunny things. She asked "Who?" and "What?" and "Where?" to any statement, even when no questions were involved and we repeated for her. And I could not form a straight narrative. My confession to her trickled out in fragment sentences before I retreated to my old bedroom on nights Mr. Murphy knew I was back, so he scared away to his own home on opposite outskirts.

Strange with me.

Funny acting.

Kind of touched me, once.

Well, maybe it was more than once.

Isn't good to Mama.

Wasn't good to me.

Did things.

Showed me his . . .

On the last morning I saw her alive, she chuckled my redemption over a bowl of grits: "I never did like that motherfucker."

We buried Grandma on her life insurance policy Mr. Murphy paid the premiums for. Mama named Mr. Murphy a pallbearer, an "honorary" son. I stayed home during her funeral. Across the foot of Mama's bed I found the maroon blanket Grandma crocheted for us the year it all started. I took it away with me.

"CARING FOR A PARENT IS hard in the best relationships," Noel sympathized. "Your mother's illness did bring you two closer, but unresolved conflict was your burden to live with. Maybe Summer's feeding ground. Have you thought to write Mr. Murphy a letter?"

"What would I say?" I asked, my voice sharp and strained.

Officers Jackson and Torres were still there, smiling at me at the front desk, in total acceptance or peace or awareness that I never had a real missing person case and I was the last to know. I paid attention to other clients who came before and after me now, in wait for "Detective" Noel Montgomery. Unshaved men, hobbled women, kids whose hard lives showed in the weight of their eyelids. Some had keloidal wounds and unkind smells. I simply braved the posture to always appear as the "Strong Black Woman," put back together with practiced habits, but just as broken as the rest.

"You can tell him how you feel, and you did not like being assaulted," he said.

"I could not begin to express it. And I don't think he can read anymore. Or, maybe he can do that. I'm sure he can do that. We can always do that, can't we?"

"I sure hope so," Noel said. "It depends on what his specific conditions are."

"Well, I'm sure no sunny volunteer would finish reading any letter I had to write to him. It would be no love letter, that's for sure."

"Confronting your attacker might be—"

"There's no need to confront!" I yelled. "It does no good, now. He ruined my childhood, messed it all up. And it messed up my adulthood too. I've gone broke. I messed up my relationship."

"Autumn, anyone can expect some serious life changes after a parent passes on."

"Yeah, but not like these."

"I've wondered if I should have handled your case differently," Noel said. "There are guidelines, but no playbook. I'm not perfect.

It seemed like being Summer's hero was the only way you wanted to open up about why you thought to end your life. I felt it was best to help both of you in the process. When I saw it was only one of you, I was at a loss on what to do."

"None of this is your fault," I told him.

"Not necessarily my fault. Just my professional bad call."

"You just met me. Anybody who messed me up did it well before then, or you wouldn't have met me at all."

"Well, thank you. That's good to hear."

Noel Montgomery knew when to pause so I could think, when to sip water or turn over the hourglass once our time long expired, a kindness I could never repay.

TWENTY-EIGHT

My lighting was streaks of noonday. My subject was myself. I lie on my bed with my camera to rove over every stretch mark, ripple, patch, mole, scar, and hair on my body. I concentrated mostly on my face, as the real me and not a motif, facing the world in my hurt characters. Though I smiled just to see what my smile looked like when I was alone, and it was only for me. I reviewed the shots and the face they arrested. I was more manly and chiseled than I ordinarily saw myself as, baby face no longer, real woman poised to take its place. The silver was not as threatening as it appeared in other women's newly graying hair. Depending on the angle or side, favor ran the spectrum of both sides of my family. Aunts and cousins I had not seen in years greeted me in my poses.

I rose from bed and pointed my Canon EOS camera at my nude figure reflected in the bathroom mirror, *The Persistence of Memory* behind me, in both indictment and diagnosis. My color was uneven throughout the length of me. Gradual shading changes left my thighs a chestnut color while my chest was sunny brown. My breasts were dainty, in proportion. I snapped this woman over and over, seeing her as fuller and more mature.

As Autumn alone, I used the digital camera when I needed to

add original images to websites and blogs. It found its way to Summer's hands when I had flights of fancy that I was, like my mother, an artist just waiting to be discovered, if only I had the time and connections to make it work. I collected my tries in the notebooks, binders, and journals I stacked in between my "sister's" expensive, weighty photobiographies and art books. So much money spent, wantonly, over the years, I discarded these things, like Christmas toys missing batteries in the boxes; I did not have what it took to power the work beyond inspiration and self-medication. Summer's habits enlivened me where Autumn died. I had no plans to correct the unfulfilled wish. Now, everything was so airbrushed, computer-generated, retouched, and devoid of sense that I felt great compassion for the people not knowing how to act or treat each other. So, in actuality, I fit in all along. Nobody was used to looking at real people anymore.

I dressed in simple jeans and a peach T-shirt and sandals, with my cream Angela Cummings silk and latex scarf I found balled up in a Ked. I was necessarily reserved when I picked up my last art supplies at the dollar store: a three-hole binder and protective sheet covers, lined paper bound inside. There, I would roll the stone from her tomb in my mind and free-associate her in her own right. Atop my piece, I Sharpied my title in cursive.

Speaking of Summer.

THE NEW RULE WAS SUPPOSED to be "No wine" but it became "No wine alone." I also lightened up with boxed wine, cut with plenty of ice cubes in the tumblers. The bodega sold it now. Its ready and willing spout rested on the floor between me and Asha. This time, I had no guest to introduce to her. We had our butts against the wall and our legs in the air, our feet flexed. She called this "leg draining," or Viparita Karani in Sanskrit, or "Just 'legs on the wall pose' if you can't pronounce all that."

The decision was made for us. We needed "real jobs." No Asha, no incense smoke, no chanting, and no music in weeks were not signs of fun times as I'd wished. Sugar Hill Holistic Care by Asha Goddess had a CLOSED sign. Like me, she was flat broke.

A chance meeting with a dancer led her to bartending in a Queens strip joint, and Asha rarely drank. She lasted a few weeks. It wasn't the work. It was the early-morning commute nearly the length of the A train. By her off time she was clamoring for a seat among the homeless who rode overnight for the longest uninterrupted sleep in the city.

"Lemme guess, the health insurance was hand sanitizer at the bar?" I asked.

"Not even. Too many germs floating around in there, and the big tippers got the most."

"Maybe we should go sign up to dance. It'd get me back in the gym."

We finished our Vinyasa break to return to screwing in mounts for Mama's precious works I'd neglected in corners and piles. Asha directed me so I hung nothing crooked. I made room first for the personal, inspirations of our old house and attempts at family faces. Also, the abstracts, for I knew they illuminated the spectrum of her moods and senses along the journey to her final rest. The first bright idea to strike without Summer's intervention was their mass donation: to Asha, our building, the We Go On office, and even Montgomery might like to have my mother's creations she was too insecure to peddle.

The next bright idea to strike me all by myself, without Summer's help, was to reroute my email back to my longstanding college alumni account. I could look more serious in hiring manager's inboxes, plus cut down digital spam. Then, I put a bold yellow sign on the bathroom mirror with a smiley face on it. I wrote the letters *A-P-P-L-Y* to make up the smile. I'd always thought I would be too successful to remember those words in my midthirties. But Summer swallowed a lot of time. Autumn was basically starting over.

Just in case, and with Chase an ex-factor, I gave Asha a copy of my door key. She used it quickly, to come use my internet. It was a small price to pay for suicide watch.

"I've been thinking about approaching one of my clients for a damned job," I told her. "She owns a temp agency. She's really cool. Maybe I could ask about you."

"Hah!" Asha laughed. "You know temp rhymes with pimp. And panty hose gives women yeast infections, honey."

"Asha, the working world has gone business casual these days. Obviously, it's too cold for flip-flops and flower child sundresses, but . . ."

I cut off cable before the internet, or lights for that matter. Asha fiddled for a clear radio station rather than roam freely through cable music I no longer had. She stopped on smooth rock. She stood in her simple cream slip dress. I wondered what Summers she talked herself into and carried along, who turned the lithe figure and flawless skin that could have modeled or done anything into a broke sister on borrowed time, in the too-expensive brownstone apartment she lucked on because an older woman passed away in it.

"Well, yeah," Asha said when she lay back down. She was half drunk herself. "I'm not exactly the standard cookie out here. But, I guess it's about that time I join the herd. My mama's good-looking. It's where I got it from. But no rich daddy's taking care of me anytime soon. Or rich man, either. This constant grind to get paper wears me out."

She never mentioned it to me. I had to know why.

"How come all this time, you know, since this winter, you never said anything about what happened? And stayed my friend?"

"You mean about you out on the roof all by yourself, in the dead of winter?"

"What else?"

"Oh, girl, hey. Who am I to judge? I got baggage I never told you about."

"You've given hints," I said.

"Give yourself a few years and that's all you'll give too," she laughed. "I knew you were fragile. Took me a while to hear a fire truck and see flashing lights on the block and not think it had something to do with you. But, I was here while your mom died. I saw you go through it, alone. If my own family wasn't so ratchet I'd say I couldn't understand why no one came to be with you, not even your sister you seemed to be close with once. I'm glad I was here and I spent time with her."

"Thanks for that, Asha." I felt ashamed of the mistruths I must have fed to so many, and Asha was one of the few who deserved the truth now that I had it. I would give it to her, one day, in time.

She gulped down the tumbler of pretty pink alcohol to go refill her glass. "But, see, that's why I help you take care of yourself. I'm going till a hundred, I tell you. Vegetables. Green tea. Every day like them Asians. You see how they look. Am I lying? Lots of onion and garlic. Italians just the same. Look how old the Godfather was. But, yeah, not enough folks wanna buy into the ideas. I guess temping is cool. It wouldn't be forever. I can save for the business. These colonics are running for $400 a pop. Or poop. Maybe I can temp long enough to save up for the hydrotherapy unit and speculums."

"I love you, Asha," I laughed, grateful for earthy amateur nursing just steps away. "Do you know where Belinda and her kids went to?"

"No, matter fact, I don't. You'd think after all these years living with people we would have been friends, not just neighbors."

"Well, she was in a rush," I slurred. "Did you ever see them around?"

"Nobody sees garden apartments but garden apartment windows see all," she said. "Belinda took chances her key would work, better than dragging her brood to a mission, or riding the train overnight. I caught her or her oldest boy all the time. She was mortified. I said I would never tell anybody, and that's that."

So far, all possible delusions I suspected remained confirmed as real-life truth, illusions at worst. I'd actually heard Belinda, her children, and even seen her oldest son often. I did not hallucinate them. Only the movie my memories made wrote in new parts. To integrate myself, or selves as I was told, I needed more than Montgomery's limited insight to know just how far this thing went. My sly mini-interviews led to disclosures that no one ever framed my disorder as more than erratic behavior, confusion, and grief.

"And, what'd she ever say about me? About *that*?"

It was better to hear when I was tipsy. I would forget it by the morning.

"Not too much," Asha said. "She was always carrying too much to chat too long, or trying to hide the kids. But, come to think of it, she said, 'I'm really glad these folks raised the rent on us and I had to do doubles to try to pay it. Late hours saved a life.'"

TWENTY-NINE

Filing applications, paycheck stubs, W-2s, time cards, and whatever else in Norma Roth's office for $60 a half day was no downgrade whatsoever. My body upgraded to a set bedtime and waking hour, my therapist's preference. And I could manage the tasks Norma still paid as freelance within work hours she paid me for as well, with her right there for me to check in and consult with. The necessity of a fall wardrobe, too dark and layered to be thrown together in a rushed hoot, finally pushed me to restructure my closets to an adequate color-coordinated, compartmentalized level my nice things deserved. How had I ever managed to get dressed before? I even fit in another time with Cathy down in Union Square, sans the children. Just regular girlfriend time.

In gratitude for Norma's immediate "Why sure!" offer to employ me, plus pitch Asha out to phone work, I kept the pot of coffee refreshed for new applicants and staff. Most times I was unchallenged, patting at my old sweater sets and itchy earth-toned pants. So I watered philodendrons, Lysoled phones or desks, and alphabetized the small lobby's magazines. This spurred Norma to accuse me of hyperthyroid disease.

"Sit down, darling," she said. "You haven't had your babies yet.

You need to rest your uterus as often as possible once you're in advanced maternal age."

Norma, my resting uterus, and I shared an extended Tupperware-packed lunch, and cups of free coffee that saved me $30 a week.

"With how long the company's been active, and how many people you've employed, you could really branch out into speaking and consulting in HR," I told her. "There's a lot of money in it. No startup costs on the web. People build brands overnight."

"I can take your word for it, doll, if you say neutrals are where the web is going these days," Norma told me in her cluttered, open-door office. "But I wonder if you think anybody would listen to me for too long and not get offended. I like making money, anonymously."

"It's just a thought, Norma," I laughed. "A couple thousand per gig or corporate training session adds up fast."

She finished off her daily salad, picked up a butter sliver to smear on her bread, thought about it, and then threw the entire small loaf into the garbage with her plate. Her can was full of papers, tissues, apple cores, hard-boiled eggshells, Diet Coke cans, and water bottles. I rose to tie the bag together.

"That sounds quite nice," she said.

"We'd just have to pep up your section of the site, and give you a separate blog to grow you an audience."

"I couldn't think of anything to say more than once a year . . ."

"Oh, I'd write it," I laughed. "Corporate trends in HR, dos and don'ts for jobseekers, tips for bosses and supervisors, company culture suggestions."

"You're speaking a foreign language," she said. "I just show up to work every day, and treat people nice in between. So long as they do the same for me."

"I think you have much you could tell others," I repeated.

"Well, I'll certainly think about it," she said.

Her phone rang, she sighed, rolled her eyes, and picked it up.

I headed back to the peaceful vortex of A to Z and 1 to 100 and "Roth Staffing . . . how may I help you?" when the receptionist was out smoking or on extended break.

I got used to the thump of my loafers and chunky heels on tile. I picked out the framed photos I would set on my desk where Chase's would have been just months before. One was me with Mama and Grandma, in front of a nice cake on my tenth birthday, when I accepted a tall doll on a round base. I was happy to explain it to anyone who asked.

ON HUMP DAY RAYMOND HELD my hand as we wandered through the fifth floor of the MoMA. It was the first time we had seen each other since the summer. We had met in an art class; I saw it fitting we should go to the art museum. My ulterior motive was to see *The Persistence of Memory*, live in its flesh, far beyond the mere print in my apartment I debated introducing Raymond to later that night. His enthusiasm was still there. Over a shared caprese salad and glasses of white wine in the museum's café, I turned down his invitation back to Bushwick. I was just not up to traveling too far from my own borough, or burrow, until more of my life made sense—past and present. At my place, he would not need much beyond a razor, borrowed from me or picked up at the bodega.

He was so good-looking I couldn't help but debate it. For now, his company alone reassured my ego. I elevated our one-night stand from an accident of greasy Chinese food and pizza to some semblance of propriety. In the two months since I ghosted, he'd found a full-time job in a music store. He paid for our museum tickets and roses. We took a selfie in front of the painting. He teased me to make it my new screen background. I obliged.

"I see you like the Romance men," he said to me in front of the work, its somber dull blue and bronze hues my stark reminders summer came and went.

"Yeah," I told him. "I have a small print of this. It always seemed to speak to me."

"You have a Frenchman too?" he teased.

"No, I don't work like that," I laughed.

"Just Italian?" he asked.

"I'm working on the entire globe," I told him. "Africa and India are next. Or, according to my friend Cathy, I gotta go Caribbean like her. They're all over Brooklyn."

We skipped through other floors and galleries like two people should at first: on lighter feet and subjects. He still thought my sister was missing. I went ahead and let him think it. To explain now would burst forth other explanations I did not owe. If he continued to be there, I would come clean. He wrangled me into a kiss, near the blank-faced and drained older female museum guard who interrupted us. "Don't get close to the painting."

"Let's go see Carrie Mae Weems before we go," I told him. Our locked pinky fingers led him behind me.

His confrontation with Weems was as startling as I had intended it to be. I was, after all, a Black woman—no matter whom I shared my bed with. Her harsh red-filtered nineteenth-century daguerreotype portraits of half-naked slave men and women, with textual reminders for her audience to consider them as scientific guinea pigs and anthropology specimens, clarified me in his White man mind—beyond a juicy brown loveliness to pour into, when and if he could catch me. A Negress devoid of pop culture abstraction, stereotypical contouring, or identity cropping. His beholder's share was an angle on Autumn Spencer I would find too awkward to blatantly discuss. He took it well.

"I always wonder how your people survived those things," he said.

"*These* things," I said. "It goes on, still. Just in new forms. I've been lucky, I guess. But if we go to Barneys together, security will think I'm the one most likely to steal a bag."

"I never steal a thing in my life. People just like to give me things. Especially women."

After the MoMA, his budget was down to a careful choice from both our standpoints: his was plenty of wine for later with Halal street food or a modest sit-down dinner, and mine was another stint as a hussy or a courted lady at dinner. I chose dinner.

In a midpriced wine bar with enough bread to stuff us down to a few small plates as meals, I told him the truths I journaled every day now: I miss my Midwest version of "the country," I'd love to have in-laws because I am without parents or siblings, I want to reconnect with my father's family. I found Raymond, too, missed his family, in a village called Positano, on hills by the sea. He missed goat's milk and real cheese. And he had a daughter back in his native land. Ghita was going into her teens now. He spoke to Ghita every few weeks, mailed her American clothes and snacks, and visited once a year.

"Sounds like a good relationship," I told him when I had had enough of gazing admiringly at all his Facebook photo albums. "We have more in common than I thought. I have a daughter far away too."

He peered at me. It was so much more different for a man than a woman. Certainly he calculated my higher price in seconds.

"Don't panic. She's in Africa. Fatu. About ten now. I sponsor her for a charity."

I put more olive paste and Brie on bread to pop into his mouth. He held up a spoonful of lemon mousse for me. It was almost ten o'clock, but he ordered a coffee.

"You're trying to have me on the train late," I laughed.

"I'll put you in a cab. Or, I come up with you, if *your boyfriend* doesn't mind."

My attachment to Raymond was not just a lovemaking naturally smooth and without intention or force on my part, without motive or gratitude or undue shame. He was the most current projector into who Summer really was, a woman outside of my elements and obligations. Her own sparkle and muse, however poorly discerning at times. He showed me how she resolved going along, rather than leading the way as I thought she always did. He was kind to me. I could not mislead him.

"Well, there's no 'boyfriend' anymore," I explained.

His face showed me he thought the song could be about him.

I explained more: "There's no 'he' because I want some 'me' time right now. It's been a pretty tough year. But, having a friend like you is more a solution than a problem."

"We can't be friends if I can't find you," he said. "You disappear more than any woman I ever know."

"Well, there's an explanation for it. Maybe I'll tell you one day."

Raymond and I parted with a stronger tie to each other. I couldn't see being out of contact with him again for nearly two months. He was a decent man. At this more adult level of things, the necessity to take stock led me home all by myself. Raymond paid our bill. We waited for his M and my D at Rockefeller Center. We decided our next date could be the New York City Marathon the first week of November; he had a friend in the race.

Riding uptown, I napped and dreamt of what could be my first trip to Italy—landing in Rome, renting a car to drive through hills by the sea with a stop at a hidden inn along the way, and meeting a real family complete with a teenaged stepdaughter: mothered by another woman but abruptly best-friended by me. It was just a thought.

Upon entering my apartment it felt like I alone lived there, and this was fine. Again. As it had been the day before. Neutral and clean. I did not pause at doorways, or push consciously to avoid this way or that. Something about going out to work—the set point, the automatic path, the same way, the same time, the same day—mechanized me into passion to wallow in the simplicity of being here. The beating hearts and silent mouths around the office had shown me the accomplishment of the routine, trite and mundane: colds attended to promptly and thoroughly, a disciplined circadian rhythm leaning into lunchtime, nails filed and eyebrows waxed before a social disaster of running into a long lost face.

I had always thought that cycled person was not me. I loathed it when I had it. I felt suffocated. But it was not the real job around me. It was the load of space to clear out of the inside.

And when Summer disappeared again, I did not have to report her missing.

Thirty

In putting away more of Mama's old supplies and things, my neighbors' part of cellar storage foreshadowed what my home turf might look like for the fast-approaching holidays: It would be lit up from stoop to roof with dots of Christmas lights, blow-up candy canes in the gangway and cement garden, wreaths and mistletoe on the doors, and maybe two life-size reindeers complete with sleigh. Gold and silver balls, glittery hanging angels, and felt gingerbread men lay atop other standard tree decorations in a milk crate like a seven-layer salad. I groaned loud enough to be heard on the second floor.

But here and now for Halloween, the new neighbors did not necessarily ask me if I minded a haunted house for a while. They warned me.

"We really get into the holidays," Maria said on the afternoon I passed her and Sean sweeping dried leaves and windswept litter. Then they set out bright carved pumpkins and dried squashes on each side of our stoop steps.

Fran must have withheld their upstairs neighbor's recent history and the mansion's old maid's death in her apartment there; by early October, Styrofoam tombstones appeared planted inside the gate. Strings of foam cobwebs, and interspersed plastic bones and skulls, connected the believable headstones. Either Maria or Charles finagled keys to the roof door's padlock, as ivory sheets made into ghosts flew over the cornice, roped to some anchor at the very top. A life-size skeleton in a top hat and bow tie hung outside the first entry door. Thankfully, the trio confined the neon-lit witch faces and carnival masks to their street-facing windows. It was, of course, the new White people in the neighborhood who dared draw so much attention to the address.

More and more, the same boys with mouths so filthy Asha and I wanted to throw cold ice or a kettle of hot water on them stopped to point it out: "Dang, y'all, shit sick, yo . . ." The parents who normally pulled toddlers down the street were forced to stop. Some little kids even wriggled through to play in the "cemetery." For the first time since I had lived there, two winos decided to drink from paper bags and take a rest on the stoop. Asha told me about it. She felt it prudent, alone at two o'clock in the morning, to mind her business and let them drink. Maria struggled in with overstuffed Costco bags smelling of chocolate, and asked: "So, you guys get lots of trick-or-treaters around here?"

Clearly, they missed Connecticut.

Holidays were for people who shared day-to-day life. Each opportunity for Halloween left me feeling like I belonged nowhere. Everyone I knew had a solar system, nest, pack, and habitat, an impenetrable sanctity. I once had it, on Trummel Lane, before Mama met Mr. Murphy. This intimate level of knowing others flicked through parts of my life, when I had had roommates and bunkmates. Now, I could see all the fuss.

"We're taking Sean to the Harvest Festival on the Upper East Side. As if we don't have enough pumpkins anyway. But these ones are less for carving and more for seeds, and the meat. Maria gets started early on Thanksgiving pies," Charles let me know.

Me: "Sounds like a lot of fun. But y'all do your thing. I hope I get to sample a bit at the holidays."

"Saint John the Divine gives such a wonderful event. Very *safe*. It's ticketed only. An old-fashioned movie, with the organist. We always have hot soup and cider at the home before. The sisters would just love to see you, Autumn. We miss you," Penny told me.

Me: "Thank you Penny. I miss you all too. You know, I'm working now. It's just part time, but it's regular money. I'll let you know how I feel. Tell everyone I said hello."

"I finally cut Oscar's hair! I'll email you a picture of his little fro. Too cute! So . . . Oscar's Jimi Hendrix and Sara's Janice Joplin. I got them tie-dyed scarves and pretend guitars. And kids really do trick-or-treat in Park Slope. The stores give out candy. Stay over if you want, if you can stand a Haitian man's snoring. What's your costume?" Cathy asked.

Me: "Dunno. A full-time, salaried nine to-fiver nobody's hired as such yet? But thanks a lot, Cathy. I'm just getting a lot of things back together now. I'll bring you guys' Christmas gifts in person this year, and stay over then."

"We're always looking for volunteers for the Police Athletic League community party, honest people for the toy and candy bag giveaways. About three hundred kids come through. Most of 'em unsupervised. You'd be a good chaperone for the little ones," Montgomery said.

Me: "Oh, I haven't volunteered in so long. It would be nice to do so. I'm sure the costumes are gonna be wild. The things kids in Harlem can come up with. If I feel up to it, I'll come. Add my name to the volunteer list, just in case."

"I used to give parties all the time. Caterers, bartender, hired help, the whole nine yards. This is my first stab back at it, scaled down though. I'm making my famous chili. One of my daughter's old school friends is the DJ. Don't you dare bring a thing. A costume's required though," Barbara offered.

Me: "Sounds like so much fun, Barbara! I haven't been to a good costume party in, well, too long. I just imagine the subway on Halloween is spookier than the city on any given day. I'd have to rent a Zipcar. If I can afford it, I'll drive out. But freeze me a bowl of chili no matter what. Don't forget."

The only holdout from these busy beehives of family, domesticity, and homesteads was Asha. She was already costumed: in button-down shirts, black pants, and closed-toed shoes for the phone sales Norma put her on. Apparently, her Georgia accent worked in her favor. She was quite pleased with Roth Staffing.

"I haven't seen a $500 check in one week since my ex forged 'em at the currency exchange his aunt worked for," she told me.

MY LONE CONTRIBUTION TO MY imposed haunted house came courtesy of Frank's messy "hands-on" We Go On session; four sessions had made me officially, argh, a member. We worked among cardboard cutouts of Dracula and Frankenstein alongside paper ghosts. Frank had picked our pumpkins from a patch in the Bronx.

"I want us all to think about our best mood and show us with your pumpkin," Frank instructed. "And there is never any such thing as a bad mood. Sometimes my best mood is a little pissed off, when I see things I don't like in the world, or people try to get over on me. So, there's no bad moods here. Okay guys, pick your knife and get to carving."

"And don't nobody slit your wrists," Carolyn reminded all. "Pumpkins only, okay?"

We all reassured her. Our brand of humor was shared and allowed in this room. Every two weeks we could let it rip. Carolyn stocked up on candy for the time being, and for later with handfuls in her bag. This week, her ramble involved a new home-care worker position in the Bronx with a senior man who thought she was his daughter—for real.

"I keep telling him my name is Carolyn," she told us. "He wants to keep on calling me Donna. And he wants to talk about 'your ma.' So, finally, after my third day, I said 'If you wanna call me Donna, go right ahead. I get paid the same no matter what you call me.' Thank God it's only four hours, three times a week."

"Four hours adds up," and I explained. They were happy to know I had a gig now.

By now, the usual group members were the only ones besides Noel Montgomery, and me, who knew of Summer Spencer. I needed the static confidence of everyone else in my life who never knew Autumn only pretended to be so ordered.

"I've lived with a real ghost," I said, my hand steady on the warped wood handle of a capable blade. "She was a twin sister I thought I had. Apparently I was the only one who knew her. She went through all the things I pretended I never did, and did all the things I thought about doing but wouldn't. Except for some. Like, trying to jump off our roof last year. Still not sure why I had to go to a rooftop for self-pity. I could have just stayed in bed for that. In any case, I didn't jump. And, what do you know? New neighbors move in and hang real ghosts from the roof. I hope that's no sign history's gonna repeat."

"It won't," Barbara said.

My pumpkin became a jack-o-lantern with baby teeth, a winking eye, and perfectly arched brows of course.

I ESCAPED THE ROTH STAFFING office to find our stoop already busy and crowded with ne'er-do-wells who roamed the block, policemen who patrolled it, and real trick-or-treaters braving crisp fall weather. With spooky music, hourly repeats of "Thriller" blasted from apartment surround sound amplified by Sharper Image, a new Halloween tradition arrived on our block with Charles and Maria's early afternoon start.

Asha had an ulterior motive to join the party: her recently printed flyers for Sugar Hill Holistic Care by Asha Goddess. After my abandonment of it, she had learned backroom web design well enough to professionalize a website on her own. We painted on clown noses and cheeks in lipstick. We found a use for long pink and blond wigs the strippers at Asha's old joint passed down to her. I uncovered the ties and suspenders from my serious-businesswoman-fashion phase.

Our new neighbors, in much more elaborate Addams Family costumes, were quite pleased to recruit us. I got to know them on the stoop with my back against a shrinking, frowning pumpkin going black inside. At the landing were apple cider jugs, bottles of imported beer, paper plates of their son's stove-roasted s'mores, and stove-top popcorn. I finally guessed the community attorney do-gooder Charles was the pothead. He was not really there, disappearing often to come back pink-eyed.

"So, are you ladies planning to stay here long?" Maria asked, as she stared at one trio of eager beavers, in makeshift ghost costumes and white face makeup. Their pretty young mother wanted pictures of them in our adjacent "cemetery."

"Be careful not to fall over the cracks in the garden," Maria smiled at them.

I tried to explain myself over a blaring of "Monster Mash."

"I could see myself staying in New York, with the right circumstances," I said.

The beer was Argentinian according to its label, soft and crisp like a cream soda. I gave myself license to one more, as I was not drinking alone.

"I'm buying property soon, but this ain't the place for me anymore," Asha said. "It's outrageous now."

"We're looking to buy," revealed Maria, not surprisingly. "We're renting our old house. It was so far. Believe me. Charles is so much nicer now that he gets up at seven."

The trio of picture takers moved on to another place halfway down the block on their route to find open doors in Harlem on Halloween.

"I had never considered living in the city," Maria continued, "but we really like Harlem. It's so convenient. "

"It is," I agreed. What else was I supposed to say? I pulled marshmallow out of my wig, noting a smudge of one of my favorite lipsticks, MAC Vixen, on the graham cracker of my s'more. It would be a long time before I could throw bills down for it again.

"I came to Harlem from Chicago," I recalled. "I thought it would be exciting to live where James Baldwin and Alicia Keyes and Maya Angelou lived. You can't go wrong with that."

"Oh, I did not know Maya Angelou lived here," Maria said. "And who else . . . ?"

Asha began to recite what would have been a thorough sermon on Harlem's heritage and its steady erasure as such and . . . More trick-or-treaters showed up.

"Hi, SpongeBob," I told one grinning boy. He walked with his father in MTA uniform, a Duane Reade plastic bag in his little sweet hands. I reached my hands into our candy pumpkin and filled his bag nearly halfway for it.

"You guys really did it up here," the deeply laugh-lined father said to us. "Haunted house in Harlem. Boy, oh boy."

"That's exactly what we were going for," Charles said. He had appeared at the doorway yet again, with Sean leaning against the jamb in curious uncertainty to his new foreign community, just like I had been on Trummel Lane around his age.

"Well, when it's not a haunted house, it's a pretty nice place to come take care of yourself," Asha said. She handed the gentleman a flyer. He looked at it with interest.

"What's Reiki?" he asked.

"Well, it's a process of touch to heighten your senses, relieve stress, and balance your bodily functions," Asha told him.

"And she's quite good at it, if I may say so myself," I added.

"I didn't know you did that kind of stuff," Maria said. She reached over Asha's lap and lifted the beer bottle paperweight off the pile of flyers to read one.

"I do. Just come right on down or let me know. An appointment would be better. I'm in and out. You'll feel like a new person. My rates are negotiable."

"I have a shoulder problem," Maria went on. "My mother was convalescent for the last years of her life. It was what held us up from taking the leap to move here."

One random day, I might tell her about my own mother and leaps.

"All the lifting and pushing and turning. I tell you. God, it just wore me down."

"I can't say I'll repair it," Asha told her, "but, I'll make you forget all about it."

"Deal," Maria said, and they shook hands.

AC/DC's "Highway to Hell" played behind us from inside our house of so many spirits—past, present, and future.

WE WERE FORTUNATE IT WAS the weekend. No one had to work. It justified how the adults of our brownstone teetered from the stoop to our doors in the wee hours, totaled, long after the kids for whom Halloween was intended had vacated the streets. I did not care to join all the brag fests and boasting online, multiplied times ten on any holiday. However, just knowing I could have a competitive night to post if I did care made me less cringy at those in the game. Yes, everyone's kid had the best costumes. Yes, all the couples dressed alike really pulled it off. Yes, all the best horror film diatribes made their case. I had my fill of distant relatives' and faded associations' curated best lives, and turned to a more productive internet addiction of battling my inbox. Job rejection emails mostly. However, a note from the office of Gabriel Johns curled into the stream.

Dear Mr. Armstrong and Miss Spencer,

I regret to bear bad news, but Mr. Johns has passed on. He took his last breaths Monday surrounded by his children, grandchildren, and workers. He is to be buried on the grounds soon. The family wishes for a private service.

I want to invite you both to the public memorial next month. The details are attached. It is an invitation extended in goodwill to so many people he considered friends, colleagues, and supporters around the world. As I understand you are in the States, no pressure to come. Mr. Johns was very pleased with the work you did on his legacy.

Best regards, Olivia

Underneath, another email in response, made visible in reply to the both of us. From Chase, the first taste I'd had of him in three months.

Dear Olivia,

This news breaks my heart. Mr. Johns was so kind to me and such an influence on me personally and my people. My heart goes out to you, and everyone there. I know he was not your boss but more your family. I will do my very best to make it to the memorial.

Yours truly, Chase

Chase still had his effect on me, after months of us not speaking or seeing each other. I knew our distance was not easy for him, but necessary. I no longer blamed him. When unfiltered by inner chaos, his effect on me was even more intense. I wept for both Chase and Gabriel, and ran my fingers along Chase's words on the screen, needing to touch him in some way as I always had from the moment I first saw him. I did not respond. I fell asleep thinking of Mr. Johns's advice, passed to those of us with more life left to live: *Everything so easy today. Instant rice? Why such a thing? Even love. In my day you had to really, really love . . .*

THE BUZZER STARTLED ME OUT of sleep. It took me some time to come to. A stumbler to a wrong address? An Asha Goddess suitor, or customer? But my buzzer blared once more. I wrapped myself in the maroon blanket at the foot of my bed. I walked to look out. I saw a bespectacled man in a familiar pea coat, standing back from the stoop landing just enough for me to see his face. I moved to the fire escape gate to open it, lift the window, and juggle myself out of it. He watched me.

It was Chase.

"Don't fall, beautiful," he shouted up.

"Well, stranger, I'm better balanced now," I told him.

I was content to think I was still dreaming. However my senses were clear in surprise, unbiased and pleasured.

I patted my hair into some propriety and yelled down, "What do you want?"

He looked at me to think of what I wanted him to say he wanted. He had trouble deciding on this. So, he just reached into his coat pocket to pull out slips of paper.

"I have balcony-level tickets from a client, to *The Color Purple* on Broadway," he yelled up.

I saw ads in the subway and around. I was happy for it, but out of its budget class.

"Oh," I said. Then, "I'm sorry about Mr. Johns. I don't think I can afford to go."

"Well, I have a bit of work subsidy for it," he said, softer now. "Maybe I can see . . ."

I really was awake, finally now. And not talking to myself in my sleep.

"That's okay," I interrupted. "I mailed Olivia a card."

"That was nice of you."

"Why are we shouting in the middle of the night?" I shouted.

Chase hunched his shoulders and put his tickets back into his pocket. Then, he disappeared under the door's awning to mash at my apartment buzzer once more. I slipped back inside, to answer him.

I stopped to check my face in the spare bathroom mirror. The assortments of my personality shone through in a biography of creativity and self-making, moved from phase to phase like a passenger passing through train cars as landscape rolls by. I was unfair to loneliness. It never belonged to me. I was never alone. But I can, for sure, pin that shortcoming on Summer.

EPILOGUE

I ran low on ink, stamps, textured paper, thick envelopes, and good cursive to personalize thank-you notes back to all of them: Belinda, the girlfriends, law officers, relatives, neighbors, clients, and community folks who emerged in my time of need as suddenly as a cold sore, in unpredictable sequence and bulk. Sorrow initially dilated my time and the number of people I had to fill it. Now the sorrow was turned against me and back into what it was all along: the emptying of time and number of people who lived life with me day to day. The only traces left of Summer and Mama were pictures on my walls. Together, we had all made my home a statement.

Why do we end up where we do, and how do we change the ending?

Summer was a dependence who grew, albeit out of acceptable proportion and constraint, like a love story: first sight, meeting, clincher, conversation, touch, get-together, lovemaking, and fight remembered in such exact detail even those not part of the story could retell it from the anecdotes they've heard. Yet the lovers never disclose the day, moment, or instant this other person suddenly broke into their minds and thoughts constantly as the time of day. They protect the fall, a break in their otherwise singular, intelligent outer view—now including and beholden to an absence they keep present. Maybe it is because they themselves do not know when the greediness of love, or need, snagged the membrane of their interior life.

So I did not put Summer away entirely.

She comes if I see a mother on the city bus who should have used birth control if she was going to cuss at the children like that. She comes if I see an injured cat on a city sidewalk and I just don't have the money to take it to the vet or home with me, but I will stop to feed it. She comes if somebody throws a perfectly good bag of food in a sealed trash bin, when they could have left it discreetly at a tree root for a homeless guy shadowboxing hunger at night. She comes if I see sad puppy dog eyes and distended bellies on commercials late at night. She comes if one Black man shoots another. She comes if another White man shoots up a crowd. She comes if another White cop shoots up a Black husband and father. Maybe she will never go.

Summer was the daughter my mother would never know, my twin self born of secrecy, pain, and distrust. I knew when she first appeared, in my youth, but I could only vaguely recall how she reappeared past that and finally decided to stay. Maybe it was the first time I imagined daddy longlegs when I picked up Mama's hair from the floor. Perhaps Summer tilted into full swing when I saw what looked like oil spill up from Mama's mouth, much scarier than anything that ever came out of her old man's pants. Maybe it was the day I realized I could not hold a conversation with the first voice who ever spoke to me, before I was born.

Maybe I'll never know when Summer came to me, in full. Her flaws I discredited were the anchors of Autumn Spencer, my spine of rebirth. A notable circumference of bystanders kept me from slipping to darker and deeper crevices sans my inner core, strength, and sanity. They were kind enough to do what I probably only survived because they did: treat me like it's no big thing, I am still normal, all is well, and we all—all—have our own shit.

ACKNOWLEDGMENTS

Great acknowledgment to New York family for all those good times that blossomed a new Harlem story: Aicha Balla, Pamela Appea, Adrienne Paul, Marsha Desormeaux, Ebony Ezike, Tara Betts, William Bryant Jenkins, Darius Hill, Clint Lewis, Elise Johnson, Ron Kavanaugh, Celesti Colds Fechter, Atim Oton and Calabar Imports, Bernice McFadden, Margaret and Quincy Troupe and Harlem Arts Salon, Harriette Cole, Clarence Reynolds, Jenny Milchman, Troy Johnson, Marcia Wilson, Lisa DuBois and Rokafella. Also, Chicago family for being there when I was back to write it: Tara again, Khalia Poole, Sandra Jackson-Opoku, Candace Wilson-Montgomery, Kemati Porter, Josephine Hereford, David Boykin, Lakeya Jefferson, Tiffany Gholar, Jacquie Stewart, Diane Gillette, Dan Porcanstino, Lori Miller Barrett, Anne Jenkins, Paul Gee, Laura Nelson, Tatiana Swancy, Marvanna Cash and Nundia Louis. And John Mazur, for every writer's best friends, in many computers and more cats: Ralph, Alice, Sybil, Sparky and Pepper. And West Coast spirits: Erica Botts, Judith Trytten and Maya Jensen.

Thank you for loving early portions that determined the whole: Christopher Schnieders of *Intellectual Refuge*, Quincy Troupe of *NYU Black Renaissance Noire*, Diane Gillette and Anne Jenkins of *Cat on a Leash Review*, and Roberta Miles and Jillian Erickson of Chicago's Loose Chicks women's reading series, where I read aloud from the novel for the first time.

Bounds of gratitude to an unquestioning champion of this story from the start, my editor Dan Smetanka, and the Counterpoint and Catapult teams for their effervescent and color-blind care for the work: Jenny Alton, Yukiko Tominaga, Megan Fishmann, Alisha Gorder, Katie Boland, Miyako Singer, Wah-Ming Chang, Mikayla Butchart, Nicole Caputo, Jaya Miceli, Jennifer Kovitz, and Dustin Kurtz.

Last and mostly, my exemplary agent Jennifer Lyons—for proving an old, oft-saying where I come from, about God: "*He may not come when you want Him to, but He's always on time.*"

© DeJohn Barnes

KALISHA BUCKHANON is the author of the novels *Solemn, Conception*, and *Upstate*, which was selected as an inaugural National Book Foundation Literature for Justice title. Her other honors include an American Library Association Alex Award, an Illinois Arts Council Artist Fellowship, Pushcart Prize and Hurston/Wright Awards nominations, and a Terry McMillan Young Author Award. She also appears on Investigation Discovery, BET, and TV One as a true crime expert in cases involving women. She lives in Chicago. Find out more at kalisha.com.